KEPT

A Comedy of Sex and Manners

Y. EUNY HONG

Simon & Schuster Paperbacks

New York   London   Toronto   Sydney

SIMON & SCHUSTER PAPERBACKS
1230 Avenue of the Americas
New York, NY 10020

This book is a work of fiction. Although the aristocratic families mentioned in this novel—the Esterhazys of Hungary, the Sobieskis of Poland, and the Chun-ju Lee Clan of Korea—are real, the characters who are identified as descendants of these families are entirely fictional and do not have any connection to these or any other families. Further, all names, characters, places, and incidents either are products of the author's imagination or are used fictitiously. Any resemblance to actual events or locales or persons, living or dead, is entirely coincidental. Or, as Evelyn Waugh wrote in a similar context, "I am not I, thou art not he or she; they are not they."

For information about special discounts for bulk purchases,
please contact Simon & Schuster Special Sales:
1-800-456-6798 or business@simonandschuster.com.

Book design by Ellen R. Sasahara

Manufactured in the United States of America

1 3 5 7 9 10 8 6 4 2

Library of Congress Cataloging-in-Publication Data
Hong, Y. Euny.
Kept : a comedy of sex and manners / Y. Euny Hong.
p. cm.
1. Prostitutes—New York (State)—New York—Fiction. 2. Korean Americans—New York (State)—New York—Fiction.
3. Aristocracy (Social class)— Fiction. I. Title.

PR9125.9.H66K47 2006
823'.92 22   2006045001

ISBN-13:   978-0-7432-8683-1
ISBN-10:   0-7432-8683-9
ISBN-13:   978-0-7432-8684-8 (pbk)
ISBN-10:   0-7432-8684-7 (pbk)

To my family and Mrs. Terebush

And as we bring our characters forward, I will ask leave . . . [to] talk about them: if they are good and kindly to love them and shake them by the hand; if they are silly, to laugh at them confidentially in the reader's sleeve; if they are wicked and heartless, to abuse them in the strongest terms which politeness admits of.

—WILLIAM MAKEPEACE THACKERAY, *Vanity Fair*

KEPT

1

NOT APPLICABLE

AMERICA still frightens me, even though I have lived here for more than half my life. Not several years ago, the two highest-grossing musical performers in this country belonged to the country-and-western genre: Garth Brooks and Reba McEntire. I don't even know who these people are, yet they sell more albums than all the remaining performers in the top seven combined, something like that. If these people wanted to, they could take over the entire United States and run people like me into the ocean.

I discovered this fascinating bit of music trivia from a radio show that was being piped through the examination room of a private Manhattan medical clinic, where I sat barefoot, awaiting a consultation with a doctor.

A nurse handed me a clipboard with a pen tied to it, explaining, "Since this is an elective procedure, and not medically necessary, we don't want to commit to scheduling surgery until we discuss your comfort level with the consequences. You might want to fill out this questionnaire. The doctor will be with you shortly to chat."

The questionnaire began:

1. Does your family have a history of hereditary illness (please include alcoholism, depression, etc.)? If so, please specify.
___YES___NO

My father is a kleptomaniac; ought I to mention that? Once, from a restaurant, he stole a ceramic chopstick stand in the shape of a tiny whale. I don't know whether this is a hereditary trait, but, according to my father, it is an aristocratic vice. It's impossible to rebel against being an aristocrat. For, as I was constantly reminded, everything that an aristocrat does is axiomatically aristocratic, just as anything that a cat does is, by definition, catlike behavior. How can you escape from a tautology? People like us, I was told, face no real danger of being corrupted by our own actions.

I can trace my Korean ancestry back twenty-eight generations on my father's side and twenty-six on my mother's side, both lines having commenced with Chinese royalty who chose to marry and settle in Korea. There are those who would call me a classist, but that term is misleading. It implies that I am in favor of maintaining a class system as such, when the truth is I don't really give a toss about maintaining any class except my own.

It might appear that I was spoiled as a child. But how could I have been, when my family no longer has money—well, we have a little, but not gobs of it. I must say, however, that the way we lost our wealth is rather romantic. On my mother's side, the family lands were seized and redistributed to the peasants by President Park in the 1960s. On my father's side, come to think of it, I believe they just pissed their money away. That's not so interesting, I suppose.

To paraphrase Tolstoy—a count, and therefore One of Us—lower-class families are lower, each in their own way, but all aristocratic families are the same.

When I was little, my father forbade me to become a professional pianist. "You can't be a genius with your mother and me as your parents," he said. It was simultaneously self-censure and self-praise. To be blue-blooded is to be decidedly antipathetic toward genius. Genius, after all, is a freakish, wayward gene, like the gene for six fingers or a third eye, and there's no way such a gene could have crept into our bloodline.

I returned to the questionnaire.

2. Are your parents still living? If so, how would you rate their health?

____YES____NO

(Good, Fair, Poor)?

There wasn't a box to tick that said, "Are your parents in good health, but unequipped for the battle of life?"

When my parents first met in the early 1960s, at a picnic sponsored by their university in Korea, the first thing that my father noticed about my mother was her pale, ghoulish complexion. For it is a fact universally acknowledged that aristocrats desire anything that smacks a little of death.

My mother is a literal blue blood; her skin gives off a bluish tint, as if she just stepped out of an ice bath. Upon closer inspection, her strange hue reveals itself to be caused by the fact that her entire vein structure is visible through her skin. Moreover, she bruises very easily, and she is always covered with blue welts that have seemingly been inflicted just from contact with the air.

Happily, I take after her in this one regard.

My father, on the other hand, is ruddy and sanguine, and has curiously wide feet, which is not a trait that Korean aristocrats are supposed to possess. I doubt that's what the questionnaire intended for me to address, though.

On my father's side, I am descended from the so-called learned aristocracy, preened from birth to serve as royal advisers on affairs of state. In practice, however, these advisers spent their time raiding the king's coffers and sending nasty calligraphy to one another, and when the king sought their advice, they'd go "hmmm" for a bit and scratch their beards and come up with some specious analysis. That's more or less what my family continues to do today. My grandfather was a presidential cabinet minister. As for my father, I'm not entirely sure what he does and it's sort of understood that I'm not supposed to inquire too closely. My best guess is that he works for an organization that lends money to developing countries, though he emphatically insists it is not a bank.

He abuses his employees all the time, often making them weep loudly and soulfully, and yet they still pool together to send us fifty pounds of frozen lamb every New Year. That kind of thing happens in a class-based society.

3. If you were to lose your current spouse/partner, by choice or by your spouse's/partner's demise, might that cause you to regret your decision to undergo this procedure?
___YES ___NO ___NOT APPLICABLE

The weaker members of our family do tend to choose fragile spouses, as if by some self-destructive drive to avoid passing on our seed.

My cousin Min-Joon took the Korean foreign-service exam shortly after college, and failed. Twice. He then seized upon the notion of going to America and starting over as a dentist, despite the protests of his wife, his in-laws, and his own father against his joining the trade class. Min-Joon went to Chicago for dental school, then failed. Disgusted with her husband's failure, and depressed by their constant poverty, Min-Joon's wife took her revenge. One day, she strapped their two-year-old daughter into the car, drove it to a nearby park, poured gasoline over herself, and burned herself and the child to a crisp.

Today, my cousin is remarried and has no profession, and is living in Korea with his parents on a hefty allowance from his father. Of course I realize there's no causal connection between his wanting to be a dentist and his wife's setting herself on fire, but it just goes to show you that our sort doesn't fail quietly; we fail spectacularly, with firecrackers and Maypoles. It's best to be realistic about these things from the outset, and resist the bewitching dream of trying something new. We're simply not equipped for that sort of thing.

Individually, members of the Lee clan may look like careworn has-beens. But collectively (if one includes both dead and living members), we are all that gods are. We created the world, then sat back and rocked with laughter as we watched it attempt to run by itself.

But then something strange happened: the world *did* run by itself.

Which is perhaps why my whole family should have chosen this woman's manner of exit. That's what the gods do when they are in their twilight. They retire to Valhalla and set it on fire.

4. If your financial profile or lifestyle were to improve dramatically in the near future, might that cause you to regret your decision to undergo this procedure?
___YES ___NO ___DON'T KNOW

This is a very American question, as it assumes that a fortune, once made, leads to an ever-upward trajectory. It's not like that for people like me.

What most people don't seem to realize is that children really do get disinherited, and you don't even have to be stinking rich for this to happen. In my family, people seem to get put aside at a fairly fixed rate, and it is my constant fear that I am headed there myself. My parents are still annoyed with me over a suicide attempt I made after university—a complete accident, truly—and I haven't seen any allowance since then except in the direst of emergencies. I left my unimportant investment-banking secretarial job seven months ago, and have fallen behind in my rent. I am also deeply in debt.

The only way to get around this problem completely is by being illegitimate to begin with. Such is the lucky fate of my aunt and uncle Jung and Key, fraternal twins five years my senior. They are the result of an affair between my late grandfather in his waning years and his mistress, who was the old-maid daughter of one of his political associates.

Jung and Key moved to New York a few years before I did. We have lived in Korea on and off, have been educated at international schools, and speak the hybrid American/Commonwealth English that is the lingua franca of such schools. We were all sent to the States for university and remained here.

Jung is widely regarded as an extraordinary beauty, though I honestly never saw what the big deal was. I suppose it's because she's tall and thin yet busty, with the pointy chin and nose that Koreans covet so much and a widow's peak. Key, her own brother, is constantly admiring her breasts.

She owns a sleek, inky Italian greyhound, with papers proving that one of its ancestors appeared in a painting by Velázquez. A previous boyfriend imported the dog for her from Harrods. He gave her a Velázquez, too—not the painting itself, but a study in charcoal, now long gone.

Jung is often mistaken for being half-Caucasian, which among Koreans is a great compliment.

SIX WEEKS AGO, on April Fools' Day, Jung rang up asking to meet with me, on urgent business. She said, "Today, twelve-thirty. Meet me at Sheepshanks, 550 West Thirty-ninth."

"But that's really far away for me, Jung. Can't we at least meet on the East Side?"

"And what else were you planning to do today, in between your napping and your Winston Churchill breakfast special?"

"That's totally unfair," I said. "Churchill had three scotches before noon, whereas I'm not even up at noon, so which of us is the more sober lunch date, do you suppose, he or I?"

Sheepshanks was a singularly uncharming pub next to a cab dispatcher. Jung likes lunching at such venues during the daytime, since she doesn't like to be spotted by her coworkers drinking midday.

She was already seated when I arrived, and I saw that she had ordered her usual, a shot of vodka and a cup of coffee. "I like alternating between upsies and downsies," she would say.

She waved in greeting, eyes bleary from the vodka shot. I ordered a Mojito, was told gruffly that they didn't mix cocktails, then ordered a scotch and soda.

"Will you be wanting that in a sake cup?" asked our waiter with a silly grin.

Jung responded, "Hey, you Papist, I think your cabbage is boiling over." I blanched in horror until I realized this was some sort of long-standing bantering ritual.

The waiter returned shortly with my scotch. The tables were sticky and the coasters wouldn't budge from where the waiter had placed them, so I had to drink with my left hand. I kept spilling.

"Jung, what's that weird gray foamy stuff all over the ceiling; is that asbestos?" I said, looking around me. "Where do you even hear about these places? Why are we here?"

"We're incognito," said Jung. "I want to help you out, with your financial and other problems. I'm going to introduce you to a woman I know named Nausika Tartakov. She's an *ogresse*." She butted out her cigarette, though she had just lit it. The lit tip fell on the table and Jung swiped it onto her lap, absently.

"An *ogresse*?" I asked. "Does she have only one eye?"

"An *ogresse* is what the French used to call a woman who made social introductions. She wants to meet you. Don't worry; she knows you and I look nothing alike."

"Thanks, that is a comfort. I take it she's a matchmaker?"

"Of sorts. Listen to this." She pulled a pamphlet with a blank white cover from her leather tote, cleared her throat, and began to read:

Desmoiselles, this is a new Belle Époque. We are witnessing the resurgence of breeding, and when this sort of thing happens, it means that money wishes to be coupled with title. Hence a new trend among the extraordinarily wealthy: *grandes horizontales*, as they were once called, or, more familiarly, courtesans.

"Where'd you get that?" I asked, trying to take the pamphlet from her. She slapped my hand away and continued reading:

In fin-de-siècle France, courtesans were highly respected. They could attend any high-profile social event on the arm of their employer, and not be worried about public scorn. In fact, the gentlemen used to arrange the courtesanship contracts with the girls' mothers.

Desmoiselles, be one of the privileged few. Take advantage of this opportunity before the bloom falls off the rose.

Jung put the pamphlet back in her tote.

"Why are you showing me this?" I asked.

"See if you can guess."

I felt the scotch crawling back up my throat. "For you?"

She shook her head no with an exaggerated arc.

"Me, then?"

She nodded.

"Jung, this is jaw-droppingly insulting."

"Absolutely not. Jude, this is a revival of fortune for our sort, though not perhaps in the manner we would have liked."

"Sounds a bit off," I said suspiciously. Jung was prone to spinning pointlessly elaborate falsehoods. Once she told me in grisly detail how her friend had died in a fire; later, it emerged that Jung had merely had a falling-out with her friend and didn't want to admit it.

Jung said, "There's no pressure. Before you dismiss it, though, I should tell you that one of the courtesans, a friend of mine, is being set up with her own antique gallery on Madison Avenue. The client and you would have no claim on each other after two years, then you give each other the heave-ho, and your debt is cleared and you can keep all the money the bloke gives you." Her bravado flagged a bit. "In fairness, I should tell you that it does come with a sting. You have to get your tubes tied during the time you're with him, so you can't get pregnant. Supposedly you can get that procedure reversed later. Is that true, do you think?"

"Why so extreme? Why not the pill?"

"The pill isn't fail-safe. And it causes water retention. Men don't like that."

"I see. Are you doing this yourself, becoming a courtesan?"

"No need," she said while sipping her drink, her voice vibrating inside the glass. "But think of it, Jude—it's a job in which you'll be valued for who you are, and not for actual performance. It's a family tradition. In a manner of speaking."

5. If you were to lose family members other than your partner/spouse (e.g., parents, siblings), would you regret being childless?
___YES___NO___NOT APPLICABLE

Was it possible to fail this test? I wished I had someone to confer with about this, but Jung had refused to come with me to the clinic. "Too icky," she said. I don't see her as often as I used to. A few weeks ago, she fell head over heels for someone in her apartment building. After their first date, she told me, "I'm in love. I want to throw up."

A short woman with wiry hair and wiry glasses entered the examination room. This was Dr. Spero. I told her, "I don't understand this questionnaire. I thought this procedure was reversible."

She replied, "A tubal ligation involves snipping the fallopian tubes, and is permanent. We can also knot or clip the tubes, which can be undone later, but pregnancy is never one hundred percent guaranteed. That's why we have the questionnaire."

"So is it more like ninety-nine percent?" I suddenly noticed her very bad makeup job. What brown-eyed person wears blue eye pencil?

Dr. Spero continued, "If you're aiming for ninety-nine percent, you should not be considering this at all. I really can't recommend this for someone who's never had children, particularly one so young. I'm sure you're aware that there are many other methods of birth control that are very reliable. You need to consider this decision in terms of the bigger scheme of things. You have to weigh your partner's desires against God's design. You might be ending your family history, forever."

How could I make her understand?

"Our family line has ended," I said.

2

The Ogresse

Beware of enterprises that require new clothes.

—Henry David Thoreau

My aunt Jung introduced me, as she had promised, to Nausika Tartakov, a Russian immigrant in her late thirties. Rumor has it that Madame Tartakov falsely claimed Jewish ancestry when she was seeking refugee status in the United States. She was publicly exposed when she attended someone's Passover seder, at which she declared that Passover was the Jewish celebration of the crucifixion of Jesus.

Formerly a ballerina in Russia, now she worked as a dance instructor at New York's premier dance studio, and at one point taught the tango to a certain well-known Italian-American actor for a big Hollywood movie. She married one of the many dance pupils who had fallen in love with her, and who, by good fortune, was wealthy and had angina. He left his young widow a beautiful four-story town house on East Sixty-second Street, but little else, as his legacy had been largely swallowed up by debts.

The year her husband died, Madame Tartakov started Tartakov Translation Services. On paper, everything is aboveboard; her corporation is registered with the IRS, she pays taxes, and she sponsors her employees for H1 visas so they can work in the United States legally. And, I am told, they do a fair amount of actual translation.

I visited Madame Tartakov at said town house.

"Come in," she said, leading me through a foyer of gently rotting flowers. She was very slight, maybe five feet one; lissom with a bird-like bone structure; and had dark, boyishly cut hair. Her cheekbones jutted out sharply from her tiny face, accented with wide slants of rouge that paralleled her upturned, almost Asiatic eyes.

Her breasts were perfectly spherical, full, compact, and immobile. On her body frame, they appeared at once too large and yet too small, depending on how you looked at them. I imagined she would have to wear a little girl's bra but with large cups.

"Stop staring at my chest," she said shrilly. "Ah, you are blushing, that's very cute. Men like that. Sit down."

I was completely in the thrall of this heavily perfumed, diminutive harpy.

"What is your background?" she said.

I turned to look at the wall behind me and said, "Pink floral wallpaper with some cherrywood molding."

Madame Tartakov guffawed sarcastically. "HAW. HAW. NOBODY LIKES THE COMEDIENNE, OKAY?"

"Sorry," I said. "Background. Okay. I'm descended from the last Korean royal dynasty."

"Mmm." She nodded approvingly. "LET'S HAVE A LOOK," she yelled into my face. She held my chin between her forefinger and thumb, the way one might examine a cat's teeth, and said, "You have to massage your gingiva more often."

"My *what*?"

"Gingiva, your gingiva. Why you cross your legs suddenly? I mean this, here, what is called?" She opened her mouth and tapped on the tobacco-stained, semigangrenous flesh surrounding her teeth.

I felt slightly queasy. "My gums?" I asked.

"Your gums. Yes. Also, teeth need to bleaching. And use Blistex. Your lips, they're going to bleed all over me.

"Good skin, but need emulsifier. Good nose; most Oriental girls have too flat nose. Eyes have too much red. Use Visine. And too small, you looking like squinting.

"You blink too much. You are maybe allergical to your contact lenses; we have to get you a more wind-passing kind. [I think she meant more porous.] Breasts mediocre. Have you tried Rogaine? No, just for hair thicken. Good thighs, but this waist! You having the menses now or something? Annoying voice. Don't talk when you're making love."

Up to this point I had been ambivalent about becoming a courtesan, but she had pulled a cosmetic-saleswoman trick on me. She pitted my insecurities in a bloody battle against my vanity. I didn't want to be turned down on account of not being pretty enough. If only she had not engaged in this criticism, I might have turned and run, and there might have been no tale here to tell.

"Do you have any venereal disease?" she asked.

"Who can say," I said.

"My girls are clean. I will send you to the doctor. The same doctor will also do the snip-snip. You know about this, yes?"

"Snip-snip? I thought it was just *tying* my tubes."

"Whatever. Do I look like doctor to you? Your education is good, is important. You must be a lady. Must *be*, not *seem*. Do you know the difference between summer and winter truffle? What is significance of Caravaggio? What is the number of Muses, times the number of Furies? Good. I cannot be bothered to train. You play piano? Good, I have baby grand in parlor. You can practice.

"Poise you lack totally, and you have arrogant face. And you walk wrong. Pick up your feet. Heel, toe, heel toe. Show me. That's good. No, keep your fingers closed when you walk. Why your fingers spread? You think you playing guitar? GUITAR, GUITAR, GUITAR!"

"I take it you had some assistance in writing your advertising pamphlet?" I said.

"Shut up," she said. "Take off shoes. Good, no foot fungus. Okay. But not this kind of cheap-o shoes."

"These are Bruno Maglis."

"You look like stewardess, okay? Most of these men don't really want too much sex from you. They can get that somewhere else. Because honestly, darling, no one would really pay to have sex with most of my girls, if it were just sex."

"Then why do we have to have our tubes tied?" I asked.

"Birth-control pill make you into bloating. Also, is for no trouble later, with baby. Sometimes girls get desperate. Trust me, I have learned this the hard way. Don't worry; I pay for you to untie tubes later when your contract is done, and you can breed as much as you like.

"Fee for Madame Tartakov paid monthly by men. I don't take your money, except of course what you will owe me. Korean and Russian is the same; I not try to cheat you, if I remember. Madame Tartakov takes care of her girls.

"I give you clothes and jewelry; you pay me later. All designer label, but no logo showing. You can wear Chanel, but no big *C* all over the place. No Louis Vuitton with the *LV* all over bag. Label is for Russian mobster's girlfriend, not for courtesan.

"You live here with me and some of the other girls; no rent until later. Big room with nice big terrace. High-speed Internet broadband.

"But I have rules. You do not bring men here. This is not cathouse I am running here. Okay? *Ceci n'est pas un bordel.** All fucking is outside. No sex in this house. NO SEX, NO SEX, NO SEX." She jabbed my arm three times for emphasis.

"Ow," I said, rubbing my arm.

"What is this 'ow'? Why so fragile? You must to toughen; sometimes the men swap partners. Don't tell me you've never done that before."

"This sounds vile," I said.

"How much debt you have?" she asked.

---

*"This is not a bordello." Madame Tartakov had the Russian ballerina's penchant for blabbing in French. My reasons for engaging in this same habit are my own.

"Debt? I never really calculated. Let me have a think."

Madame Tartakov smiled wickedly. "Is very bad. America is country of credit, you know. How can you let this happen? You cannot buy anything now. No car, no house. You cannot even to pay plane ticket in cash now, you know that?"

She was right. I had just been turned down for a mobile-phone plan, of all things.

"So how much debt?" she pressed.

I mumbled the amount.

"Cannot hear," she said.

"At least fifty-five thousand dollars."

Madame Tartakov didn't bat an eye. No doubt she was accustomed to dealing in much larger figures. "Your family doesn't help you?"

"That's sort of the origin of the problem. You see, I borrowed against my expectations, and then it turned out I wasn't coming into any money."

"What expectation? You mean inheritance?"

"Right. I thought we had money—no, truthfully, I was always confused about that. I guess we used to, and we don't anymore. But by the time I figured this out I was already heavily in debt."

She said, "I take care of all of it. I pay off all your debt. Is loan, with interest."

"How much interest?" I asked.

"Is no matter, because if you work for me two years, debt is clear. And you make money on top of that, too. Debt-free, you can start all over again. So what will it be?" She began to pick her teeth with the corner of a napkin. "Will it be Madame Tartakov, or debtor's prison?"

"I still need to think about it," I said.

"Whatever. You can have trial period. Live here few weeks, then decide. Here is doctor's number. You have to be approve by doctor for tubal ligation or you no working for me anyway. So just do checkup, okay?"

. . .

I HAVE ALREADY told you about the checkup with Dr. Spero. Subsequently, I turned the decision over in my head for two weeks, taking advantage of Madame Tartakov's trial period. I stayed at her house on Sixty-second Street, no strings attached—for the time being.

During this two-week idyll, I had very little interaction with Madame. She gave ballroom-dancing lessons from the afternoon to late at night, and she was gone on the weekends, too, at professional ballroom-dancing championships around the country. She had trophies all over the sitting room, along with some photos from her days as a ballerina in Russia.

The trial period was a cunning idea on Madame's part, for the house was exquisitely comfortable. It had four stories in all. The kitchen occupied the entire basement level, its dankness and darkness giving it the feeling of a Victorian scullery, except that it had a Sub-Zero refrigerator and all the top-of-the-line appliances. A long pine table with beer-hall benches took up nearly the full width of the room; this was meant as a servants' dining area, but it was so cozy that the girls ate there most nights, rather than in the upstairs dining room.

On the ground floor, behind a set of heavy white double doors, was an enormous, sunny parlor containing two baby grand pianos. This, along with most of the house's furnishings, had been purchased by the first Mrs. Hunsecker (Madame Tartakov being the second Mrs. Hunsecker, though she never took the name). You could tell straight away which wife was responsible for which home furnishing. The first wife was very fond of Queen Anne–style furniture, English garden chintz, and the sort of toile wallpaper that features people in three-corner hats milking cows. Madame Tartakov, meanwhile, made her stamp on the house by squeezing in Roche Bobois furniture wherever she could, which was not objectionable except insofar as it matched so poorly with the previous decor that even my father would have noticed. Madame Tartakov also had an immense collection of Murano glassware, displayed in nearly every room of the house. The upper two stories consisted of seven bedrooms and five bathrooms, occupied by Madame and eleven of the most charming girls you could ever hope to meet.

THE FIRST TIME I saw all the girls seated in the parlor, I was very intimidated. Their complexions were glowing and clear and perfectly shaded; their cheeks were so like marzipan peaches that you wanted to bite them.

The girls were not exceedingly pretty, however, which was greatly comforting to me. Rather, they possessed other qualities that would make even the shallowest, most uncouth of men see further than skin-deep. They had a grace so innate that their occasional drunkenness or loss of temper could not wither it; even the way they opened jars was charming. It was the sort of charm that was most apparent when the girls were completely silent and still. They kept their eyes locked on you when you spoke to them, yet at the same time they had a constant faraway look that made you always try a little harder to get their undivided attention. Their singular gift was that they inspired, in anyone who encountered them, the desire to be surrounded by them always.

Their backgrounds made them all the more irresistible. The Scottish courtesan was descended from both Ethelred the Unready and the Thane of Cawdor, the fellow mentioned in *Macbeth*. Heike, a German girl, was the daughter of some impecunious Freiherr. The Walloon descended from Charlemagne. The Romanian girl called Minna was related to Vlad the Impaler, the historical figure upon whom Count Dracula was supposedly based.

None of the girl's families had had money for at least two generations. Many of their family homes were relinquished long ago and converted to ill-frequented museums. Poor Heike grew up not being allowed to venture downstairs in her own house from April to October of any given year, when the entire ground floor was rented out for private functions. It's been her family's main source of income for half a century.

Heike was assigned to be my roommate, and (I suspect) was given the task of convincing me to join Madame Tartakov's stable.

Heike was different from the other girls, a full head taller and big-boned. She had short hair, in the Vidal Sassoon vein, in violation of an unspoken rule that courtesans must have hair of shoulder length or longer. She cut her own hair, using those dull safety scissors that schoolchildren use to cut paper, and smeared her coif with wax every morning until she looked like a candle wick. She eschewed tony togs in favor of Cyndi Lauper wear—petticoats and striped knee socks with a lingerie top and a jean jacket thrown over it. She never shaved her underarms. Madame was always harping on everyone else's appearance, but she wouldn't dream of challenging Heike, I was told.

Nor did Heike share the kept woman's love of jewelry. "I don't like to look like a Christmas tree," she said.

For my first ten days in the house, Heike skirted around the issue of my extending my stay. It was I who broached the subject one night, as we lay in our beds. I asked, "Didn't you have reservations about getting a tubal ligation?"

"Are you kidding?" she said. "I would have entered into this contract just for the surgery. If it turns out to be irreversible, so much the better. I have no maternal instincts at all. Do you?"

"I suppose not," I said, recalling the many times I had to feign interest in people's babies. "But I don't like the idea of . . . Some of the most important families from Paris to Istanbul are represented in this house, and you're all infertile, at least temporarily. It's almost like a conspiracy to exterminate blue bloods everywhere."

Heike said sternly, "All of our families have been in a state of entropy for generations. What would our offspring have to look forward to, being bullied by the new ruling class?"

That remark affected me greatly.

Growing up aristo is not really what most people think it is. Especially for those who are blue-blooded but no longer part of the ruling class. Your power is all gone, but your responsibilities remain the same.

By way of analogy: Someone terribly important takes you out to lunch. What agony it is trying to determine the proper ordering strategy! Your host has remarked on his low opinion of the tenderloin, so you can't order that, or else it would look as though you did not value his opinion. You can't order the rib-eye steak, because it is the most expensive item on the menu. The sardines are not an option, because they are smelly and you would be too distracted by the task of filleting them to pay attention to the conversation. In the end, you have the chicken salad. And you hate chicken salad. But in terms of price, odor, and general inoffensiveness, it is your best option.

You have to apply the same degree of strategy and intrigue for every single thing you do. Growing up as an aristo with no power or money: you're getting a free lunch, but you can't even enjoy it.

Despite the fact that your family has no fortune, you are not given many options to earn one. Commerce of any kind is unacceptable. Law is all right in the vague theoretical sense, but not as a practicing lawyer. The arts are mandatory hobbies, but are not a respectable career path. In my family, the medical profession is out. "Strictly for immigrants and upstarts," my father would say. He once got into a disagreement with his gastroenterologist and told him, "You're not really a doctor. Not so long ago, only doctors of philosophy were bestowed the honorific of 'Doctor.' That tradition ought to be revived. You should be called Mr. So-and-so, not Dr. So-and-so." You are expected to perform reasonably well in school, yet you must accomplish this without getting dark circles under your eyes.

On top of all that, aristo parents place restrictions on the kinds of friends their children are allowed to have: friends must be from the right sort of family, which means those families that engage in all the above prejudices. But a family that is snobby enough to pass muster is probably too snobby to let their child be friends with you.

Most people envision aristos as being social butterflies and attending parties constantly. That may have been true at one point, but in the latter day, more often than not, old families without money are extremely antisocial, even agoraphobic. They are at once too proud and too ashamed to consort with outsiders.

From the day you are born until the day you leave home for university, you never have a friend over at your house for dinner. Your parents' absurd explanation is that they don't have liability insurance. To avoid having to return invitations, they forbid you, on pain of thrashing, to eat or drink anything other than water at a friend's house. Anyone who starts to become close to you is put off sooner or later by your coldness and your inability to give or receive hospitality. But no matter, because by early adolescence you have been fully indoctrinated in the belief that anyone outside your family is second-rate.

Consequently, your kin become your best friends. You don't spend too much time worrying about your future because you are too stupid to understand that while your family may be important, it is no longer influential. By the time you realize your mistake, it is too late. Which brings us to the present day: twenty-six, poor, congenitally incapable of holding down a job, and very lonely.

Very few people can understand what that's like. But now Madame Tartakov was giving me the opportunity to be surrounded by people who would understand me. At long, long last.

Just as my two-week trial period at Madame Tartakov's was drawing to a close, the Fates stepped in to seal the deal. The diabolical manager of my apartment building finally let the ax fall, and got me evicted. Never mind why. But it meant that I could never rent again in the city.

I entered my apartment for one last time, packed the rest of my belongings, and left, but not before stuffing the toilet with rubbish and then flooding it.

When I arrived at Madame Tartakov's, she smiled, took my head into her perfumey bosom, and commanded, "CRY." I affected sobbing noises, and then sneezed into her chest. I was allergic to her perfume. She yelled, *"Merde!"* and pushed me away.

3

THE ANTHOLOGY OF PROS

I AM TEN TIMES prettier than my intelligence would warrant, and ten times cleverer than such a lovely girl has any right to be. This has been the origin of all my life's sorrows, for one attribute gets me only so far before the other undermines it.

In particular, I have been victimized by men who like brainy girls. Of the manifold ways that a woman can be objectified, by far the worst is to be wanted for her mind.

I am sick of nervy brain fetishists, mouth breathers whispering amorous effluvia into their pillows. Such men have the unmerited reputation of being gentle and deep, but in fact they are more narcissistic than any other type of male. Their pursuit of their intellectual equal is an exercise in self-congratulation. To wit, a Frankish boy once told me, "I find your correct use of the subjunctive to be highly erotic."

Why does this happen so often? We can draw answers from the Mozart opera *The Magic Flute*. One of the characters, named Papageno, wears a parrot costume and plays the glockenspiel. He spends the whole first act longing to find a lady-love with whom to share his nest. And when he does find her, it's none other than Papagena, who, as the name suggests, is the mirror image of himself: a lady in a parrot costume who parrots him in her behavior. Love is inherently narcissistic. You fall in love most easily with yourself.

But the dynamic between a courtesan and her companion is completely different. It has to be. It is a culture built upon the man's adulation of the woman.

I booked an appointment with Dr. Spero, snip-snip, and for six weeks my barren womb recuperated tranquilly at Madame Tartakov's house.

During this idyll, Heike undertook the task of educating me.

"Repeat after me," she said one day when she was walking me through the "Precious Modern Objects" unit of her lesson plan. She held up a large pink glass bowl decorated with green glass flowers, one of Madame's tchotchkes. She said, with rolling *R*s, *"Reticello."*

"Reticello," I repeated.

"And why is it called that?" she said.

"Because of the reticulum design on the glass," I said with an air of tedium. "Heike, what man would care about my knowledge of Venetian glass?"

"Say 'Murano glass,' and you'd be surprised how often you can slip it into conversation," said Heike. "*Um Gottes Willen,* what are you doing? Stop that!"

"What? I just scratched my nose. The *side* of my nose. It's not like I was picking it."

"That's not the point. You have to contain your movements, Judith. You can't let it all just hang out. Like your laugh, for example. It's too loud, and definitely don't clap your hands together when you laugh; nothing is that funny."

Odd; my parents have been telling me the same thing for years. Little did they know how useful their comments would prove in a bordello.

Heike continued, "Okay, now feel these ridges—"

There was a crash. She had passed me the bowl without my expecting it, and it slipped out of my hands.

"Verdammte Scheisse," she said.* "You'd better let me say I dropped that or Madame will add it to your tab."

One day Heike showed me pictures of her family castle in Büdingen. "Oh, is this your sister's wedding?" I asked, as some of the photos were of a wedding party.

"I don't know those people, actually," she said. "We often let out the castle for weddings. You will get married there one day, yes? We'll all be your bridesmaids."

The thought of a wedding party full of courtesans made me think of an old joke. "Have you heard this one?" I asked Heike. "Three professors working on the *Oxford English Dictionary* spot a group of women of ill repute. They argue over what such a group should be called. One professor suggested, 'a jam of tarts.' Another suggested, 'a collection of trollopes.' But they all agreed the third professor's suggestion was best: 'an anthology of pros.'"

"Das ist ja Klasse!" exclaimed Heike.** "That is what we shall call ourselves. Madame Tartakov's Anthology of Pros."

We lived in Arcadia, this Anthology of Pros, this International House of Prostitutes.

DURING THIS TIME, I saw little of Madame. Occasionally she would pass me in the kitchen, slap my bottom, and say things like, "Stop eating all my fig jam."

Toward the end of my recovery, however, she began to take a deeper interest in my personal habits. Once we got into a little tiff, because she had thrown out my shampoo and replaced it with products of her own choosing.

"IS BULLSHIT, YOUR SHAMPOO," she yelled. I would soon learn that this was her natural speaking voice. "What for do you want to smell like eggnog?"

*[Common expletive.]
**"Cool."

"But it's from Switzerland," I said insistently.

"In this house, only Kérastase product for hair," she said.

Then one Tuesday night in late July, she announced, "Is time. Tomorrow I auction off your maidenhood."

"My maidenhood?"

"Is manner of speaking."

She spent all of the next day preparing me. She hollered, "On counter is very brown bananas. Peel and put in your bra. No only overnight, then you throw banana away; you don't meet a man while you wear fruit in your bra, stupid girl. Will make the breasts float; is old trick of Gabor sisters. Then bath at three o'clock. Then I exfoliate your back, because you will wear Dolce & Gabbana dress tomorrow night, who is backless. Wear girdle." She pinched my middle.

"No way am I wearing a girdle," I said, covering my waist protectively.

"Aphrodite's secret to seducing men was magic girdle. You are surprised I know this, but I know. Wear La Perla bra and panties." The latter had set her back four hundred dollars, for which she was presumably expecting reimbursement at some later date.

"Why the La Perla? I have to have sex with him tonight? The weather's too hot."

"No, darling. Why you American girls always wear pretty dress, ugly underwear? Is bullshit. When bell rings, no coming down stairs like young hussy. You wait in room until I call you down to parlor."

At six I was summoned to the sitting room to meet a man bearing a Bacchic expression. He had fine facial bones tapering to a small chin, very full lips, and eyes so glistening they appeared almost to be dipped in glycerine. He wore a white Tolstoyan shirt with billowy sleeves and a wide collar that exposed part of his chest. Except for his slightly glam-rock effeminacy, he had the manner of the corsair about him. We were startled to see each other.

Madame said, "Judith, please meet Mr. Yevgeny Slivovitz. Is classical violinist, but not faggot. And you, Slivovitz, this is Judith." I would later learn that in such situations, it is customary for the man to be introduced by his full name, and a courtesan only by her first name.

Madame Tartakov continued, "Princeton graduate!"

"Yale, damn it," I corrected indignantly.

She barreled on. "Very knowledgeable for opera and classical music, also literature, art. Is next to line for Korean throne."

"It's not quite like that," I tried to explain, but she cut me off.

"Is cheeky," she continued, "but virtuous, more or less. And she likes to eat." She pinched my middle.

"That's okay, so do I," said Yevgeny. I was always very susceptible to voices, and Yevgeny's captured my heart instantly. Voice teachers will always tell you to sing not from the throat but from the diaphragm; Yevgeny's voice seemed to come from someplace deeper still. It resonated from his whole body like the sound of a flamenco guitar.

"Ah, see, Slivovitz, she blushes!" spat Madame into Yevgeny's face. "Is first time for both of you, this arrangement. This girl satisfactory for you, Yevgeny? Lovely, no? If she loses some weight."

"She is the very picture of good health," he said, winking at me rakishly.

4

THE WIDENING OF ONE OF HER PARTS

*Comment une fille peut-elle être assez simple pour croire que la
vertu puisse dépendre d'un peu plus ou d'un peu moins de largeur
dans une des parties de son corps?*
How could a maiden be so naïve as to believe that her virtue
depends upon the widening or narrowing of one of her body
parts?

—MARQUIS DE SADE, *JUSTINE*

YEVGENY was not so much handsome as irresistible. For our first
meeting, on a midsummer night, Yevgeny and I dined at Pantagruel.
To my great discomfort, we were seated at a table in the center of the
room. We were surrounded by a circumference of eyes, all fixed on
Yevgeny. The waiter who took our aperitif order looked triumphant
as he approached us, as if he'd just won the rock-paper-scissors contest to determine who would have the privilege of waiting on
Yevgeny. He actually giggled as he announced the specials, ignored
my remark that it was too early in the year for Elbe truffles, and took
only Yevgeny's drink order. Yevgeny had to call him back to the table
to order my Kir Royal, at which point the waiter apologized only to
Yevgeny. When the drinks arrived, the tray shook and the waiter

mumbled, "I'm so stupid." When Yevgeny said, "Not to worry," I really thought the waiter was going to faint. Being with Yevgeny was ten times worse than being with Jung.

But I could express no discomfort; I had to remain insouciant and desirable. Not sure how to achieve this, I sat dumbly while Yevgeny told me about his background. His father was once a great professor in Yugoslavia; now he owns several Internet cafés. His mother was a Hungarian, from the noble Esterhazy clan.

After another waiter arrived to take our dinner order (this one behaved himself), I found my tongue. "Madame tells me you have an apartment in Paris; on the Île St. Louis," I said.

"That's my friend's flat," he said. "I stay there sometimes."

"By 'friend' I assume you mean 'wife.'"

He shrugged.

"Is your wife beautiful?" I asked.

"Very," he said.

I choked on my water. "My fault for asking, really. In that case, why did you enter a courtesanal contract?"

"She keeps a cold bed."

"A what? Oh."

I delicately dabbed the water I had dribbled on my face and changed the subject. "Do you do concerts often?"

"Just twice a year or so," he said.

"So seldom?" I said.

"It's hard," he said. "I'm not gay."

"What does that have to do with anything?"

"My God, everything! Why do you think J— B— gets bookings all over the place? You can't play with an orchestra these days unless you're willing to sleep with the conductor."

My brow furrowed. I said, "I thought . . . I read somewhere that most of these orchestras do blind auditions, behind a screen."

That remark clearly made him uncomfortable. This was not going well. He began to focus on the nosegay arrangement on the table.

The waiter arrived with our food. We both sprang on the poor man, so grateful were we that he relieved us from having to interact with each other. He placed a plate of steamed mussels before Yevgeny and a *terrine de canard* before me.

"Fuckin' A," I said, distractedly. "I just realized I ordered a duck dish for both my appetizer and the main course." Covering my mouth in horror, I said, "I'm so sorry about the swearing. That's not very decorous. It just came out. I guess Madame's spit and polish didn't quite work."

Yevgeny laughed, a beautiful low, throaty laugh. "You needn't feel so guarded," he said. The ice had been broken at last.

Feeling I could reveal a little more, I said, "I was a classically trained pianist, you know."

"What happened?"

"When I was thirteen, I entered a competition sponsored by this big bank in Seoul. The *Pathétique* Sonata was my entry. After an uninterrupted winning streak in the qualifying rounds, I didn't even place in the top five. My parents were so humiliated they made me quit."

"At least you were trained properly. I find it astonishing how many people are so accomplished in other ways but cannot play an instrument. It's a dead giveaway that someone is nouveau riche—if they have a good, expensive education, travel extensively, speak several languages, but don't have a classical-music education. It's irrecoverable."

I heard the bright clarion of recognition, signaling a kindred spirit. "Yes," I said. "I have always thought so."

He used one mussel shell as tweezers to pull out the flesh of another mussel, Belgian-style. This gesture endeared him to me; one can surely make a great many assumptions about a man who knows how to eat mussels.

He said, "Maybe we shouldn't rush into things. Maybe we'll just do this kind of thing, meeting up for dinner, just casually, okay?" But his voice dripped with innuendo.

Over coffee, he told me he had gotten us a room at the Mark.

. . .

IN OUR HOTEL ROOM, Yevgeny walked over to the chair where I sat, and said with that hypnotic voice, "Don't be nervous," and leaned down to kiss my forehead. He did this so gingerly that I was unprepared for the violence with which he grabbed my shoulders and pulled me off my chair. I continued to clutch my champagne glass, though its contents had spilled.

Yevgeny said, "Put down the glass."

"I'm not ready," I said, flushed with panic.

He then leaned toward me and bit down hard on the back of my hand, forcing me to release the glass onto the carpet.

I cried out. My hand throbbed, the pain centering around two rows of white indentations that formed a small ellipse under my knuckles. He pushed me onto the thick carpet, which was wet with champagne. In a disingenuous gesture to fend him off, I gently kicked at his *entre-jambe*. But where I expected to feel cloth, there was none; at some point or other, he had stealthily undone his Ermenegildo Zegna trousers.

He sank to his knees over me. That was how Yevgeny and I first had commerce.

Afterward, we moved to the bed, where I lay on my tummy smoking, propped up on my elbows. When you're a paid companion, you can smoke in bed.

He lay next to me, using the hotel stationery to blot the champagne stain on the knee area of his trousers. Then he turned to face me and said, "What makes two people from decent families do this sort of thing?"

I said, "Everyone should have the companionship they feel they deserve, even if they have to go through a woman like Madame Tartakov to find it."

"I suppose," he said. He lay flat on his back and rested his head in his palms so that his elbows jutted sideways. "I hope you're not offended by my question. This is delightful. But I admit I'm kind of disappointed."

"Why?" I thought I might cry.

"Don't look at me like that. All I meant was that in bed, you feel like any other woman. Well, except for a few things, I guess. Your skin is almost powdery. He looked at my backside with detachment. "It looks like a sculpture."

"A Michelangelo or a deformed Henry Moore head?" I asked.

He said, "Your skin is very . . . taut."

"Taut."

"Yeah, I mean, there's just the right amount of skin for the body you have."

"Why? Do other girls have large patches of their innards exposed?"

"And the other thing is——" He pulled my forearm to his nose and took an exaggerated whiff. "You have no odor."

"You are Pygmalion in reverse," I said. You don't want the statue to be a woman; you want the woman to be a statue."

"No, I want the statue to be a whore."

"That would make sex very painful for you."

MADAME WAS GOOD at what she did; it was a marvel to witness such multifarious competence as mother, manager, landlady, mollycoddler to the most persnickety girls imaginable, dancer, businesswoman, and teacher of deportment and grooming. She worked hard to make the courtesan arrangement comfortable and sanitized for all parties. In addition to her rules forbidding gentleman callers, she had a no-swearing rule (from which she herself was exempt); each infraction was penalized at ten dollars. Even her payment scheme was designed to be free of iniquity. After all, it's not as if Yevgeny left cash on the hotel dresser each morning. He paid Madame Tartakov, and she gave me pocket money after deducting her own cut and my debt repayment. A meager biweekly check was issued from Tartakov Translation Services to Judith M. Lee, with the option of direct deposit. It was almost like being a salaried employee.

When Yevgeny and I spent time together, much of it was devoted to discussing our own exceptionalism.

"I thought you said you were poor," he told me one day after I'd mentioned the details of my schooling and innumerable private lessons.

"No. I said we had *no money,*" I corrected. "There's a big difference. Homeless people are poor. Aristocrats have no money." I was talking out of my ass. He seemed pleased, however. He was getting his money's worth.

And I learned so much from him. He took me to wine tastings, where I helped him pronounce the Clos and Schloss names, but he knew more about wines than anyone else I'd ever met.

We usually met at the St. Estèphe Hotel, in a suite that happened to have a piano. He would explain to me why classical pianists prefer Steinway whereas jazz pianists almost invariably choose Yamaha; why it is that when a piano is tuned, it is flattened on the fifth; why viola players are stupid. It was these conversations that made me begin to grow quite attached to him, nearly to worship him.

But my enthrallment became complete one sultry evening in late summer. His wife was away that weekend, so he invited me to his almost-penthouse apartment near Lincoln Center (his building has three penthouses, which is impossible by definition because there can be only one; hence, "almost-penthouse"). It was exactly the sort of place I'd imagined a concert musician would have, decorated with a combination of French antiques and sleek modern Italian lounge furniture—the kind that's red and wavy and takes up entirely too much space for the number of people that it's supposed to sit. He had a grand piano strewn with sheet music ("Only idiots put photos and statues on their pianos," Yevgeny told me. "Everyone knows that compromises the sound"). He had dozens of metronomes collected from all over Europe; photos of himself standing alongside Sir Neville Marriner and Daniel Barenboim; open boxes of resin for bow maintenance; a Yamaha electric piano with headphones attached; books on music theory, which were piled on ceiling-high bookshelves accessible by a rolling ladder; Italian and German dictionaries; every violin he'd ever had since he was four years old—seventeen violins in total, most of which he had acquired after meeting his moneybags wife.

He showed me his beautiful instruments. He said, "This bow alone cost me—if I may be indelicate—fifty thousand dollars at auction. What is most tragic and unfair is that the price of violins is driven up artificially by wealthy collectors who know nothing about music. Thus the world's best violins are out of reach for most musicians. These ignoramus petits bourgeois are destroyers of culture."

"Yes, yes," I said, in rapturous agreement.

"I think that the world would be much better off if we reintroduced a patronage system, don't you think? We need another family like the Medicis."

"Yes, oh, yes," I said. I could not believe my luck at having found a man who shared my values so exactly.

"Barring that, however, people like me are stuck having to marry well in order to keep our art alive. You do understand that, Judith? How I so wish things were different." He looked at me forlornly.

Deeply moved, I said, "Play something for me."

Yevgeny nodded. He rubbed resin on his bow (the fifty-thousand-dollar bow), placed a violin under his chin, and from that moment he was like a man possessed. First he frowned, as if the facial tension were necessary for keeping his instrument in place. Then he raised his bow gracefully and brought it down softly on the strings, playing Tchaikovsky's Violin Concerto in D Major. The third movement of that piece is incredibly fast (*allegro vivacissimo*, Yevgeny would later explain), and he played with the vigor of a Gypsy, his face contorting as though he were in a powerful wind tunnel. He grimaced as one in intense pain. When his bow came down hard on the strings, I could feel it in my loins.

When he finished, he opened his eyes; the trance had ended. He blinked at me as if startled to see me there.

I wept.

5

HARVARD MAN

You can always tell a Harvard man, but you can't tell him much.

—AN ANCIENT PROVERB

ONE OF THE HALLMARKS of a civilized person is that he must often spend a great deal more time with people he loathes than with people whose company he enjoys.

This is particularly true in America, where it is considered unsporting to dislike someone without cause. In Europe—maybe not now, but once upon a time—"enemies" were a socially recognized reality among gentlefolk. Enemies would not be expected to make nice with each other; they'd perhaps acknowledge each other cordially, but that was all that was required of them. No one ever forced them to try to get along.

Thorsten Sithole, a friend of Key's, was just such a person. I didn't understand why Key found Thor an appropriate companion. Thor descended from *Mayflower* stock, but if it weren't for his father's connections, he would be working as a nightclub bouncer, not as the investment banker that he is. He refers to the coital act as "hiding the salami." He refers to female undergrads as "coeds" and to all taxi drivers as "Mohammed," regardless of their ethnicity.

Key and Thor had gone to Harvard together, where they had

formed a fraternity of sorts, devoted to being mean to ugly or fat girls. Of all the mythology surrounding their organization, their favorite anecdote concerned a girl who showed up at one of their Halloween parties in a red cape with a black bustier underneath. She claimed that she was costumed as "Super-Ho, the superhero slut," and no one could figure out who she was or how she had found out about the party. When she started having an epileptic seizure, triggered by seven tequila slammers, the boys considered calling an ambulance. They worried, however, that they might somehow be held liable for her state, so they instead rolled her out onto the street and left her for dead.

Thor graduated from university a year later than he was supposed to. His sophomore year, he got hold of letterhead stationery from the Harvard Admissions Office and forged a rejection letter to one of his friends at Taft who had applied to Harvard that year. Thor was suspended for a year, which he spent giving scuba lessons in the Maldives.

He professed to be an expert on all subjects and would never admit to being wrong, even in the presence of an undisputed expert on a given subject. Thor would correct blind people about Braille. He would insist that cold water was *not* the best method for cleaning menstrual blood off a pair of knickers.

The mutual animosity between Thor and me is one of the cohesive forces of our little group. A well-designed social circle requires enemies as much as it requires friends.

Our group consisted of me, Jung, Key, Thor, and Scheherazade, my roommate from Yale. Among the five of us, there are more factions and intrigues than there are members. Thor has, at different points, been obsessed with Scheherazade (or Zadie, as she is called), with Jung, and—I strongly suspect—with Key. But never with me. Jung and Zadie don't like each other much, so they stand as counterpart to me and Thor, though the latter antagonism is much more pronounced.

. . .

ONE SATURDAY IN AUGUST, Thor held a small cocktail party. Jung, Key, and I headed to his apartment together. As we waited for the elevator in Thor's lobby, Jung started to fiddle with my hair, smoothing it down, pulling at different strands. "You always manage to look so, you know, *mal soignée*," she said.

I said, "Who cares? It's just Thor and the usual gang, isn't it?"

Jung's eyes darted worrisomely.

"Oh, no, Jung, is this one of your setup thingies? Is someone here meant for me?"

"Your bra strap is showing," she said, reaching into my blouse and adjusting it.

I yelped. "Your hands are cold."

Jung said, "Goddammit, how old are you? Don't you know how to wear a bra?"

Key said, "Hey, can I try?" and reached, mercifully, not for my blouse but for Jung's. With rapid reflexes, she grabbed his wrist and twisted it violently. Key and Jung started wrestling and struggling, giggling and squealing. The twins were always embarrassing me in this fashion.

"Come on, you guys," I said through clenched teeth, glancing shamefully at the doorman, who was picking his nose and bearing an "ah, young love" expression on his face.

We let ourselves into Thor's apartment and walked through the foyer, which was strewn with scrimshaw and other nautical knick-knacks, harking back to some ancestor of his, who had been a whaling tycoon in Nantucket.

A half dozen assorted tired-looking folk were assembled in Thor's living room. Thor sat with his back to the door, his sunburned, muscular neck bulging from a tight button-down shirt. He looked like a strangulation victim. He was reading aloud to his guests from his beat-up childhood copy of the book *White Fang*.

He intoned hammily; " 'But White Fang could not get at the soft underside of the throat. The bulldog stood too short, while its massive jaws were an added protection. White Fang darted in and out unscathed, while Cherokee's wounds increased. Both sides of his neck and head were ripped and slashed. . . .'"

The small assembly in the parlor looked as if they'd been trapped for hours in an elevator. Zadie's head was buried in her lap; another guest was loosening his tie. It was as if Thor wanted to hammer home his two irreducible traits: his being a WASP and his being an asshole.

Jung cleared her throat. The guests were clearly relieved at our arrival. "Are the lushes here already?" said Thor. He rose clunkily from his oxblood leather armchair, put down his book, and came to the door, greeting me and Jung in his usual fashion of greeting women, by kissing us each on the hand while biting our knuckles.

"I'll decant another bottle," he said. "Like Martin Luther."

"Martin Luther?" Key asked.

"Yeah, you know, what he had to do when he was on trial. He said, 'Here I stand.'"

"*Recant,* not *decant,* you fuck-tard," said Key. Thor shrugged his massive shoulders.

"This new, Thor?" Jung asked as she knelt on the foyer floor and lifted up the corner of a rug to examine the tightness of the weave, a compulsive and annoying habit of hers. She said, "Nice Oriental rug."

"Don't talk about me as if I'm not even here," yelled an exuberant and studiously disheveled Zadie, who sat on a cushion on the floor, throwing her arms into the air. She feels obligated to sit on the floor a lot, because she's half Middle Eastern, I guess. I walked over to her and we air-kissed twice, then bumped our heads because she always insists on kissing three times, left cheek, then right, then left again; I had tried to pull away before the third kiss, to no avail.

Scheherazade Haboush is a luscious pseudo-Sapphic specimen. She has long sepia hair, naturally crimped in perfectly symmetrical ramen-noodle waves. She was wearing one of her silk scarfy headband things, which made her look like a slender Corinthian column, with her hair sticking upward at the roots and sloping downward over her shoulders. She has deep-set Semitic eyes accented above and below by a smudge of charcoal pencil—she tends to Orientalize herself in that way, though she is only *half* Middle Eastern. She comes from an old, established family on both sides. Zadie's father is in the Lebanese senate; her mother is a Park Avenue socialite. Her parents divorced when she was five, and her mother took Zadie back with her to live in America.

Our sophomore year at Yale, Zadie was chosen to appear nude in *Playboy* magazine's "Girls of the Ivy League" issue. She was offered five hundred dollars. The Yale Women's Center offered to match that fee for her *not* to appear in *Playboy,* so *Playboy* upped the offer to one thousand dollars. This bidding war continued to the twenty-five-hundred-dollar mark, an offer the Women's Center could not afford to match. Zadie's *Playboy* photo shows her sitting spread-eagle on her dorm-room bed, fondling one breast while reading Sartre's *Being and Nothingness.*

Zadie and I were inseparable for a time, but these friendships with nonblood relatives have a way of not lasting very long for me. We had a falling-out two years ago, from which we never fully recovered. It arose over Risa, a maid whom we shared, back when I could afford hired help. Zadie had referred Risa to me; Zadie had her on Mondays, and I had her on Fridays. That year, I gave Risa a Christmas bonus and a small pay raise, plus time and a half for coming around on a Sunday to clean up after my Christmas party.

"You backstabber!" Zadie shouted at me over the phone. "I'm the one who introduced you to Risa, and now you're trying to win her loyalties."

Some harsh words were exchanged. I later told Jung about what an idiot Zadie had been, and Jung replied, "I hate to admit this, but Zadie's right. You shouldn't have done something so sneaky. Didn't your mother teach you anything about household staff etiquette?"

"My mother never had to share her maid. She never gave pay raises, either."

Jung sighed. "Modern times. Learn to adjust, and apologize to Zadie, even if she is a hysteric."

"But she insists I give up Risa," I said.

Jung was silent for a moment. "That's different," she finally said. "It is as hard to find a good maid as it is to find a good husband."

"So what do I do?"

"You'll have to choose between your friend and your maid."

Against my better nature, I chose Zadie. But, as I said, things became awkward between us.

And then, last year, she came out.

This is how it happened: Zadie, Thor, Key, Jung, and I were sitting in a booth at a truly awful midtown diner. Thor was telling us about the interview questions that his investment bank asked job candidates, which included brainteasers.

He said, "Here's one we're not supposed to ask anymore, for reasons that will become apparent. Let's say four of us are at my beach house at the Hamptons for the weekend. Jung, me, Key, and Zadie."

"What about me?" I asked.

"Fine, you can come, Jude, but only to mix drinks. Anyway, the four of us want to have sex. I mean, not all of us, but all heterosexual combinations must have sex. But there are only two condoms. How can all the four combinations copulate, with the stipulation that you can only touch the side of a condom if it is unused, or if it has been touched only by your own fluids? In other words, no commingling of juices is permitted. How can all the heterosexual couples have safe sex?"*

---

*Incidentally, the correct answer, which took us about an hour to get, is as follows: Man A must wear two condoms simultaneously to have sex with Woman X. Then Man A removes the top condom and gives it to Man B. Man A is now wearing a condom that is clean on the outside, and that has touched only his own fluids on the inside. Man B then has sex with Woman X, putting the clean side of the second condom on his penis, and inserting it into Woman X, since the outside of that condom has touched only her fluids. Simultaneously, Man A proceeds to have sex with Woman Y. Then, Man A removes his condom, which now has two soiled sides. Man B then puts the soiled condom over the one he is already wearing, ensuring that the side of the second condom that has touched Woman Y remains on the outside. Man B then has sex with Woman Y. Have fun. Amaze your friends.

Jung said, "What makes you think that being in the Hamptons would somehow induce me to sleep with you, Thor? Not to mention my own brother."

"Okay, it's two HYPOTHETICAL heterosexual couples. Christ."

We all had many objections to both the question and the answer. Mine was: Why am I not being included in this tryst? Jung's was: You shouldn't reuse condoms. Key's was: I hate the Hamptons. Zadie's was this: Why only heterosexual pairings?

Thor replied, "It's not a political statement; it's just the way the question is worded. You can't change the format of the question."

Zadie said abruptly, "I'm a lesbian. I thought you ought to know."

THOR'S PARTY was like all of his parties: a license for him to colonize everyone. He embarked on a new topic, about various steaks he'd eaten throughout the world.

I already wanted to go home.

Jung said, "Who's this new doorman in your lobby, Thor? Why'd they pick an old white guy? How does that keep you safe? Doormen should be big, black, scary guys."

"Is *la négritude* inherently scary?" slurred Zadie.

Apropos of nothing, Key said from the chaise longue, "So I have a question. What is this expression, HYP? Harvard-Yale-Princeton? Why are we all lumped together? Does anyone actually know any Princetonians?"

We all admitted that we did not.

"This conversation is really déclassé," I said. "But since we're on the subject, who's going to the Yale-Harvard football game this year? I need a ride."

Thor said, "The vaunted Harvard-Yale rivalry is unilateral on Yale's part. It is unacknowledged by Harvard. In any case, it's called the Harvard-Yale game, you distressing woman, not the Yale-Harvard game." I shot him a disgusted look.

Zadie, who was now standing and doing some kind of inebriated whirling-dervish routine, said, "Are you listening to yourself, Thorsten? Do they not teach the concept of irony at Harvard?"

"No, but they do have a course called The Concept of Dread." The speaker was a young man sitting uncomfortably in the corner, whom I had not previously noticed. He had tight, curly brown hair and wore a chocolate-brown sweater with toothpaste flecks on it, beige corduroy trousers, brown shoes, and brown trouser socks. He had some sort of worrisome-looking black canvas pouch, the kind that bike messengers carry. He continued, "It's the title of a Kierkegaard book. A joke has been made. You are not expected to laugh."

No one did.

Thor said, "Excuse me. This pretentious young man is Joshua Spinoza, my new stepcousin, my old lech of a grandfather having married Joshua's grandmother just six months ago. Joshua is a philosophy Ph.D. candidate at Columbia. His family stands in firm defiance of the notion that education can help you break the cycle of poverty."

Joshua nodded at me solemnly in greeting. I did the same.

I once saw a poster of the Soviet chess master Garry Kasparov from 1985, when he was in his early twenties. Joshua brought him so much to mind that I nearly swooned. Joshua had those same eyes that were at once paranoid and arrogant, the same large forehead that suggested a highly developed frontal lobe, and the same full lips that created a hint of a shadow just above the chin. Okay, fine, I didn't just *see* the Kasparov poster; it hung in my bedroom for years.

At this point Zadie took me by the hand and announced to the room, "I'm borrowing Jude for a minute, everybody," as if anyone cared. I glanced once more at Joshua, who raised his eyebrows at me as he drank from his glass.

Zadie pulled me into Thor's bedroom, shut the door, and lit a cigarette.

The way Zadie smoked was so appealing that it would make an asthmatic want to start up, which is in fact what happened freshman year to some of the girls on our floor.

She had that red, red lipstick that all lady smokers should have; the kind that leaves a telltale stain on the cigarette, the sort of damning evidence that destroys a man's alibi. And instead of simply expelling the smoke as other people did, Zadie let it crawl out of her mouth like creeping ivy. "What's happening?" I said. "Are you in love with me?"

"No, you know I'm in love with Nat. You met him. He's the roommate of the woman who shares my painting studio. . . . You seem confused."

"Nat? It really has been a long time since I last saw you. You're back to dating boys now?"

"No. Natalie is the full name, but she goes by 'he.'"

"Transsexual?"

"No. Did you have a stroke? She *goes* by 'he.' It's a choice."

"Oh, right, I remember now. Your Bastille Day party." I scrunched up my nose disapprovingly. Zadie had recently sponsored an exhibit featuring Nat's artwork, consisting of found objects Natalie had cobbled together. It was so pretentious that I mistook a thermostat on the wall for being part of the exhibit.

I said, "She—he's using you, you know. You're using each other. He sponges off of you financially and in return offers you some sort of authenticity you feel you lack. Zadie, you're not even gay."

"Of course I'm gay. Why wouldn't I be gay?" She looked insulted. "Do you really think a courtesan is in a position to accuse others of financial sponging?" She pursed her lips smugly.

"Aha," I said, not sure whether I was pleased or annoyed that she knew. "Jung told you, I take it?"

She nodded.

"And what do you think?"

She said, "Your nails have never looked better. I guess anything that gets you started on a beauty regimen can't be all that bad."

"Can't you be serious?" I said.

She patted the bed, urging me to sit with her. "Seriously, then, you've got to spend less time with your aunt and uncle. They wield far too much influence over you."

I sat at the edge of the bed and leaned back on my hands. I said, "I'm having a hard time countenancing the fact that at this very moment I am being chastened by Miss January 1993."

At the mention of her photo shoot, she spread her legs a little, as if by reflex. She said, "That's different. I was just posing. Literally and figuratively."

Zadie continued to puff away recumbently. She said, "I know this is a sore subject, but there are always your parents. If you'd just suck up and be nice to them once in a while you'd be surprised how generous they can be."

"How kind of you to remind me that all parents are just an endless font of cash. But it's not just about the money."

"No, you're right. It's about deliberately throwing away your talents just because you're pissy about not having serfs."

"On the contrary, my talents have never been put to better use."

"Why must you pretend to be shallow?"

"This is dreary, Zadie. Let's go join the others."

We were still on the bed; she sat up slowly, anchoring her arm on my knee for support. I moved my leg away from her hand, only to realize that in doing so I was exposing my undergarments. She said, "Oh, my God. Is that a garter belt?" Ignoring my protests, she lifted up the hem of my skirt. She snapped the strap that attached the belt to the stocking.

"Ouch," I said. "Those are a gift, sort of, from Madame Tartakov, the *ogresse*."

Zadie traced her finger along the lace at the top of my stockings. She undid one of the snaps. Her hands were cold from the drink she had been holding earlier.

I clamped my legs together, accidentally trapping her hand between my thighs; then I leaped off the bed. I said, "If you really want to help me with my life, give me one of your ciggies, please. I'm out."

. . .

I HAD MY FIRST real conversation with Joshua after he came out of the loo. I hid my cigarette behind my back as he spotted me. We were both embarrassed; I because of my cigarette, he because he'd just come from the toilet and the water was still flushing. He was much taller than he had appeared while sitting.

With feigned casualness, he began to chide, "Why are you hiding your cigarette? You've been smoking in front of all of us this whole time."

"Promise not to tell?" I leaned toward him conspiratorially and continued, "I bummed a cigarette off Scheherazade, but it's a David-off Light, and I loathe that brand. But etiquette requires that a cigarette, once poached from another person, must be finished. So I was about to flush it down the toilet to hide the evidence."

He furrowed his brow, took the cigarette from my hand, and flushed it for me. How gallant. "Seems like an awful lot of trouble," he said. "There shouldn't be such elaborate etiquette s-s-surrounding a vice."

My family had always regarded stuttering as a revolting defect, but I found it endearing in this case. It was an imperfection that suited him well, like a beauty mark.

"All vices have codes of etiquette," I said.

Anyone in the employ of Tartakov Translation Services can tell you that.

There was an uncomfortable lull.

I said, "I can't really take this conversation further until you introduce yourself. The man has to do it first, you realize."

"Oh, sorry. I'm Josh."

I took his extended hand. "So I heard, Joshua of Morningside Heights," I said. He glared. I continued, "And I am Judith."

Pulling his hand from me, he crossed his arms in a hostile pose and said, "Am I mistaken in thinking that you have a very unforgiving nature? I shudder to think what opinion you might have of me."

"And why should I think so ill of you, sir?"

"No reason particularly. But I'm also a grad student and a pauper, as Thor pointed out with his usual delicacy. I don't play golf."

"Golf!" I tittered in an affected manner, covering my mouth with my hands. "Of what consequence is golf?"

"I don't know. It seemed as good a socio-economic determinant as any."

"Golf is an 'economic' determinant, but not a 'socio' one," I said. "Socio-economic is a misleading hyphenation of two totally unrelated concepts, like Greco-Roman."

"Then what constitutes the right sort of person, in your opinion, if not money?"

I said, "Can I share with you something that Thackeray wrote on the subject?" I straightened my posture, preparing to recite. "It's in his novel *Barry Lyndon*. Ahem. One of the characters, a nobleman, says, ' "My friends are the best. Not the most virtuous, or indeed the least virtuous, nor the cleverest, nor the stupidest, nor the best-born, but the best. In other words, people about whom there is no question." And that is how I define good breeding, Joshua. That is how I define aristocracy. It isn't any one thing; it's the right combination of many things."

"I don't see what that has to do with forcing yourself to finish a Davidoff Light. But, in any case, you're quoting from *Vanity Fair*, not *Barry Lyndon*. Do you just collect quotations?"

I blushed hotly. I have used that line many times in conversation and have never been called on it before.

He said, "I didn't mean that as a barb. I mean that if you were . . . *more* familiar with your social satires, you would know that they're all about how money and class are inseparably linked." I noticed that his stutter seemed to disappear as he grew adversarial.

"Nonsense. My family hasn't any money. And we are, if one can be forgiven for saying this, distinguished."

"But at one point your family did have money, did they not?"

"Yes, but everyone can say about their family that they once had money."

"Everyone? What utter rot." He seemed genuinely offended. His mouth curled into an unattractive grimace.

"At any rate, it wasn't like that for aristocrats in Korea."

"I'm rather confused. Are we talking about Korea, or Britain during the Napoleonic wars?"

"All the soccer-playing nations of the world are in agreement on this matter," I said.

Joshua gave me the hairy eyeball. "Meaning, everyone except America, I presume. Droll, but not accurate."

"Fine. In Korean terms, then. My ancestors were among the intellectual elite. We had to take exams to hold our place as the king's royal advisers. Like a whole fleet of Henry Kissingers, but not geniuses. While it is true that we were related to the *king*—" At the mention of that last word, Joshua shifted his eyes to the right, as if looking to an imaginary friend for succor. I continued, "Nonetheless, we couldn't have amounted to much without passing those exams. Money played a minimal role in it, really."

Joshua said skeptically, "Fair enough. Do you consider yourself an intellectual, then?"

"An intellectual? God, no! Blech! I'm the opposite of an intellectual. I'm an aesthete. The only thing worse than being a racial minority in this country is being an intellectual. American intellectuals are the most bitter, humorless, self-segregating bunch of whiners. They're always in cahoots with the working classes against the aristocracy. I suppose it's not really their fault, either. How could they possibly turn out to be well-adjusted when the moment they say something important, everyone looks at them as if they've just farted. Do you not find this a hostile environment?"

"Is there nothing you admire about America?" he asked, his grimace deepening.

"Yes, like, it's bad to peach on people." I was completely serious. I was relieved that no one had told Joshua what I did for a living.

" 'Peach?' This isn't Eton. I assume you mean 'tattle.' " Joshua began to chew aggressively on an ice cube he had in his mouth. I shivered.

"Right-o," I said, which made him put more ice in his mouth. "In Anglo-American culture, it's considered a sin above all other sins to rat someone out. No matter what the person you're peaching on has done, it is far more ignoble to be the one to expose him."

"You must be very unhappy here, if that's all that ties you to the land in which you make your home." He tipped his glass to his mouth, sucked in another ice cube, and began to chew on it.

I startled him by exclaiming, "Cup holders! The movie theaters in America have cup holders. American cars have them, too. That's a nice feature, don't you find?"

Joshua said cryptically, "If you studied your Greek tragedies, you would know that whatever it is you are pushing away with your flippancy will come back to bite you on the ass."

I nearly smiled, but stopped myself by pressing my tongue against the inside of my cheek. I was finding this man's abuse irresistible. Before I could ask Joshua to explain himself, however, Thor stumbled over to us, smiling smarmily. "Am I interrupting something?" he said.

"No, I'm glad you happened by," I said. "I've been meaning to ask you why you are serving a Napa Valley sparkling wine with the word *unfiltered* emblazoned diagonally across the label? It bloody well better be unfiltered. Presumably the wine doesn't contain paint chips either; why not just mention that, while they're at it."

Thor said, "That's what happens when your wine industry doesn't have an Appellation d'Origine Contrôlée. But I'm not the one who provided that bottle. Joshua did."

I was deeply embarrassed.

Joshua said coolly, "For a minute there, I was beginning to wonder how you two could be friends; now I understand."

Thor chuckled. "Young stepcousin, it's very easy to offend you, I find. It's like clubbing a seal."

"Clubbing a seal?" said Joshua, cringing slightly. "I don't think I like the way you people talk." He looked in his glass for more ice, but he had already consumed the last of it.

"What do you mean, 'you people'?" I asked.

"I mean, people who are addicted to elitism and cruelty."

I was more deeply affected by his comment than I wanted to admit. "Excuse me, I think I see someone over there I know," I said abruptly, leaving a disapproving Joshua in the corner with Thor, who was already developing that nail-polish-remover smell of someone who'd started drinking the day before.

As I walked away, I turned my head slightly to look at Joshua, who was wiping Thor's spit off his face. Thus distracted, I tripped on the edge of Thor's Oriental rug. My knee buckled; my drink spilled. "I'm fine!" I yelled, my voice cracking as I straightened out my gait like a newborn colt.

Joshua recited with a strong tone of sarcasm: " 'She walks in beauty, like the n-n-night.' "

Thor guffawed wetly.

I made myself a strong something-or-other at Thor's bar, and took it to the kitchen, where I slurped it quickly and listened in on the various conversations taking place in the sitting room.

THOR: Okay, any music requests?

ZADIE: Do you have "Mmm Bop"?

JUNG: "Ring of Fire."

THOR: Any music requests from someone who isn't a complete ass-clown? No? Okay, then I'm putting on the Bach Nuremberg Concertos.

KEY: Brandenburg, you moron, not Nuremberg. Bach did not write the soundtrack for the Nazi war-crime tribunals.

ZADIE: Hey, Jung, I heard you know a lot about knives.

JUNG: *(testily)* What's that supposed to mean?

ZADIE: I'm deciding between Henckels and Wüsthof. Do you have any suggestions? Someone told me that with Henckels you never need a sharpener. But I assume a gourmand like you would find that an abomination.

JUNG: A knife you don't have to sharpen is one for which you will never develop affection and therefore *point*less.

JOSHUA: It is socially irresponsible to make puns. A pun is a trivi-
alization of the instability of language. *(Awkward silence, then)*
I was just kidding.

ZADIE: *(awkward silence, then)* Anyone wanna see a picture of me
with short hair?

JUNG: *(whispering)* Joshua has the worst sense of humor, Thor.
And for fuck's sake, he *stutters*. I'm no longer sure this was such
a good idea. Did Joshua say anything about Judith?

THOR: *(not whispering)* Yeah, he said, "You told me she was pretty,
Thor. Imagine my disappointment."

JUNG: Shit, why would you go and tell him something like that *(hits
Thor in the arm)*. Judith's sort of plain-pretty, like a governess.
Those who are told that she's pretty in advance of meeting her
are always disappointed. It's better to understate it a bit.

THOR: Don't yell at me. I never said Jude was pretty, exactly. I said
she has a face that a gay man would call very beautiful.

JUNG: Joshua is gay?

THOR: No. It's just a manner of speaking. At any rate, it was a losing proposition. They're both too high on themselves to notice
each other.

At the point in the evening at which Thor and Key began raiding
through the medicine cabinet to find things to pulverize and snort, I
prepared to slip out of the party.

Joshua, the only sober person in the room, intercepted me. "Help
me with my coat," I commanded.

"Why, are you too drunk to put it on yourself?" he asked, bewildered.

I stomped my foot. He held up my coat, turning it this way and
that, not quite sure what to do with it. I had to coach him: "I can't get
my arm in the sleeve if you hold it like that. No, you can't just let one
side drop to the floor. Now straighten out the collar."

"Can I drop you off somewhere?" Joshua said.

"Do you have a car?"

"No, I meant, I meant that I could walk you to the subway station. It's not far. I could ride alongside you on my bike."

I stared at him motionlessly for a moment before realizing that he was taking the piss out of me. To stop myself from smiling, I said, "You are so tacky I can hardly breathe."

But he smelled wonderful, like tea and cumin.

He looked confused. I shook his hand nimbly and said, "Good-bye, Joshua. I doubt very much that we will meet again." I made an about-face and departed very stylishly, waving at him with the back of my hand while my back was turned to him, and closed the door. Fine exit. But I realized I had to go back. I knocked on Thor's front door, and Joshua opened it. "I'm wearing someone else's coat," I muttered, avoiding eye contact.

6

A Treatise on Lactation

My mother told me only one story when I was a child, the same one over and over again. It's a Korean folk tale about a farmer who lived in a small village with his wife and son. One day, a beautiful stallion wandered into the farmer's lands, and the farmer was able to claim it for himself. "How lucky you are!" the villagers cried. But then the son, attempting to tame the horse, fell violently to the ground when the horse bucked, and the boy broke both his legs. "How unlucky you are!" the villagers cried. Some weeks later, the local feudal lord declared war against a neighboring fiefdom, and the lord's men went from house to house, recruiting all able-bodied young men to join in the battle. The village mothers wept inconsolably, but the farmer's family was spared this sorrow, since their son's injury rendered him useless to the army. "How lucky you are!" the villagers cried.

The rest of my story continues in the same vein. The lessons I was told to draw from this were twofold: (1) only an idiot gets excited about good or bad news; and (2) you can stay out of trouble by being just a little incompetent.

In the early 1940s, when Korea was still a colony of Japan, my paternal grandfather was a viceroy, overseeing a province of Korea for his colonial masters. He was, in a sense, an Uncle Tom. Frustrated to be assigned to such a backwater, he longed for promotion to a larger city. But then, in 1945, Korea gained independence from Japan. After that, my grandfather's allegiance to the Japanese might have put him in jeopardy. The three men immediately above him in rank were persecuted as traitors by the provisional government and either disappeared mysteriously or were hanged. But, happily, my grandfather was too low-ranking to be considered a real threat, and his life was spared. He was saved by his own failure.

So what happens when lucky is really unlucky, and genius is really stupidity, and fair is foul, and foul is fair? It means that all words are emptied of meaning.

All the girls in the Anthology of Pros understood this. Even as they clung to their blue-blooded heritage, they were unwilling to accept the emptiness and fatality that went with it. In order to be free, they had to orphan themselves. And here we are.

KEPT WOMEN are very agreeable company. They are very good cooks, I find. You'd think the opposite would be the case; that we'd be so accustomed to being taken out to restaurants that there'd be no occasion for us to learn to cook. But, as I learned from the other girls, one has to support oneself in between men, and the only way a girl can afford to eat cheaply yet maintain her spoiled palate is to learn to reproduce those dishes at home. Puttanesca sauce, of course, derives from the derogatory Italian word for prostitute.

The girls cook for one another a few times a week. Justine, the pixie-voiced half-French, half-Belgian, makes a lot of fish: salt-crusted bass, skate with champagne butter sauce, and the like. Heike, like all good Frankfurters, has a penchant for Italian food, particularly Bolognese. The Scottish girl won't cook for us because once we all asked her to make us meat pies and she got really offended. I make French and Korean food, but not together, because we all agree that fusion cuisine is strictly for losers.

On Friday nights, when most of the girls are lounging at Madame Tartakov's (men with kept women spend Friday nights with their own families), we congregate around the sitting room banging out tunes on the piano; Heike, the German baroness, sings Schubert lieder, and

Giovanna sings from Verdi. This always devolves into an iterative argument on the merits of German opera versus Italian opera.

The other day, we were discussing places we would be willing to live when we grew up.

I said, "Anywhere in Europe except for Poland."

The half-Walloon girl said, "Anywhere in Europe except for Poland and the Netherlands, because the Dutch are stupid and unfriendly."

Giovanna said, "Anywhere in Europe except for Poland and Milan, because the Lombardi are so bigoted, and they're not even really Italian anyway."

"I *hate* bigots," Justine added, to which we all emphatically agreed.

Heike said, "Anywhere but Poland or Austria."

"What is wrong with Poland?" asked Tonya, a member of the Sobieski clan.

"Poles are anti-Semitic," said Heike, the German, with irony.

I'VE BECOME CHUMMY with Heike, though she has the German's obsession with fresh air and insists on leaving our bedroom windows open all day long, even though this practice has permitted leaves and caterpillars to blow in from the ivy that surrounds the window. She also won't let me turn on the air conditioner. "Air conditioners are very lethal," she says.

One August evening when some of the girls were lounging in the parlor, Heike asked the room at large, "Do you know what all the girls in the Anthology of Pros have in common?" She was on the chintz easy chair, sipping at the caipirinha she had just made for herself. Lime wedges hit her nose as she tipped the glass to her mouth. I was stretched out on Madame's buffalo-hide sofa, flipping through the multilingual array of *Vogue* magazines the girls had left in the magazine rack over the years. Some of the other girls were engaged in a French variant of hearts, playing for money, and I sulked a bit at being left out. Madame Tartakov had forbidden me to play games of chance with the other girls, because I proved myself unlucky at cards, and Madame was worried I would prioritize my debts to the girls over my debts to her.

"Are you talking to me?" I said. I was engrossed in a magazine quiz, "How Many Real Friends Do You Have?" with questions like, "Excluding relatives and lovers, how many people know your birthday offhand?" I wasn't doing too well.

Heike said, "I've got something I want you to see," and clomped up the stairs clad in her lingerie and hiking boots. Shortly after, she ran back down clutching some papers.

"Not so much noise when you walk, Heike," said Justine in her elfin voice. "We're all trying to count cards."

"Read," Heike commanded, passing me a document.

A Treatise on Lactation
by Heike Freifrau von Grünesosse

Aristocrats the world over have a tie that binds them: they are descended from hundreds of generations of people who suckled at the teat of a hired peasant woman.

For throughout the Eurasian land mass, aristocrats were not nursed by their own mothers, but rather by wet-nurses, which is peculiar, given the traditional aristocratic obsession with keeping the blood line uncontaminated. The peasant milk coursing through the veins of alleged blue bloods may explain why they are dying out. All just so their vain mothers wouldn't become saggy-titted.

I winced at her imagery.

"What, you found grammatical errors, didn't you?" said Heike, looking mildly distressed.

"No, your English is astonishing, as usual. But, uh, what is this for? Some kind of religious tract?"

"It's the introduction for my doctoral thesis. I've come upon a topic, finally."

"Your WHAT?"

"I'm a Ph.D. candidate at Columbia. I thought you knew."

"No, I DIDN'T," I said, which prompted commands from the card players to keep my voice down. I looked over the first few paragraphs again. "If this is an academic paper, though, I don't think you can get away with being so . . . opinionated."

"It's okay to be opinionated in women's studies. Keep reading."

Wet-nursing was deleterious not only for the class that employed them, but also for the wet-nurses themselves. They were not allowed to breast-feed their own babies, who then had to drink cow's milk, not properly sterilized. These babies often perished.

Wet-nursing, one might argue, was a form of prostitution. At one time, wet-nursing was the highest-paid female profession in Europe. Yet these women were treated wretchedly. As far back as 2000 B.C., in ancient Babylon, the Code of Hammurabi literally set in stone that if an infant in the charge of a wet-nurse perished, and the wet-nurse continued to service another child, the woman's breasts would be cut off.

I nodded approvingly. "It's a good start, very energetic. But how did you end up in the Anthology of Pros? Did you drop out of Columbia?"

"No, technically I'm ABD, meaning, I'm finished with All But Dissertation. My funding ran out, so here I am. Originally, I was going to write about courtesans. But the wet-nurse idea is more original, don't you think? Or is it just stupid?"

She had misinterpreted my expression for skepticism, when in fact I was merely distracted. One subject had invaded my thoughts for days now, almost to the exclusion of all else. It had given me a low-grade fever. I said, "Columbia, is it? Do you know Joshua Spinoza in the philosophy department?"

"Name sounds familiar, but I'm not certain. Why? You want me to talk to him on your behalf? God, you look sick."

"Oh, no, please don't approach him. He's just some bookish malcontent who accuses me of being snobby, even though he's even snobbier, albeit in a different way. Arrogant, critical . . . No, really, don't say anything to him; I want nothing to do with him."

Down Eros, Up Mars

IF YOU EVER tell someone you never want to see him again, you are bound to run into him within a fortnight. It's worse than that: you are bound to be paired with him for an impromptu debate on a topic you do not understand, for which you have had no preparation. And worse still: your debate partner is a stutterer.

It so happened that Joshua and I were both vying for membership at the Young Crotonia Club, a sort of singles group disguised as a discussion society, held at one of the tony, mahogany-paneled club buildings near Grand Central Terminal. It offers fencing lessons and quarterly Scottish balls, and has a small, pretty library that houses, among other things, issues of *The New Yorker* dating back to the 1920s.

The membership applications are reviewed every September. One of the requirements for prospective members is that they participate in three debates, for which the topics and partners are chosen just thirty minutes prior. For my first debate, I was paired with Josh. We stood awkwardly next to each other as the club officer led us in the official opening song for club meetings, "Gaudeamus Igitur," a traditional Latin student song.

The club president announced the commencement of round seven of the Initiates' Debate Series.

One of the club officers read out the topic: " 'Resolved: The United States Should Take Greater Measures to Ensure Stability in

Chad.' Mr. Eustace Diamond and Ms. Rebecca Sedley will take the pro position. Mr. Joshua Spinoza and Ms. Judith Lee will take the con position. You have thirty minutes to prepare. All other members of the audience are welcome to these lovely Bellinis our staff has prepared. Please return to your seats when you hear the gavel."

Joshua and I were sent to a curtained-off corner of the auditorium. We sat in silence at two schoolroom desks, the kind that have armrests attached. I chewed on a nail; Joshua drummed his fingers on the armrest. We kept up this stalling for five minutes before Joshua finally asked, "Hey, Judith, where is Chad?"

I said, "Hey, Spinoza, I thought you were the big brainiac here."

"Hey, Judith, I'm just a philosopher."

"What are you even doing at a private club? Isn't this a bit snooty for your blood?"

"They book really good speakers," he said. "Jürgen Habermas is coming here in February; it may be the last chance I get to see him before he dies."

"And another thing. Why did you tell Thor that I wasn't pretty?" I had blindsided him.

"What? I never said that," he replied, looking a bit cagey.

"He seems to think you did. *Disappointed* was the word, I think."

"I was just trying to get him to mind his own b-business, that's all. There was some scheme to set you up with me, and I detest those sorts of things, because the people who arrange them feel that they then possess the couple. And if you must know, I didn't say you weren't pretty. Thor bungled it as always. I said you were *contemptible*."

I was greatly relieved. "Really? That's all? You swear?"

"Really. Now, what do you know about Chad?"

We argued about the location of Chad until the club officer struck the gavel three times, announcing our doom.

Filled with dread, Joshua and I took our seats at one of the two tables on the stage; it was made of a stately oak that mocked our underpreparedness. Joshua and I paid no attention to the first pro argument because we were scribbling notes to each other, like: "We're fucked." "I know."

I was to deliver the first cross-examination. "Help me!!!" I wrote, underscoring it three times and tearing the page with the pen. This was fun.

He wrote, "Will make you note cards, but don't know specifics."

When my name was called, I pushed back my massive chair, which screeched as it slid, and stood up to cross-examine the other side. I cleared my throat and began, "I wonder whether the gentleman has considered the long-term consequences of the, uh, plan he has laid out, with respect to America's unpopularity in eastern . . . western . . . in that region." I glanced at Joshua's notes and barreled through. "Is the gentleman not concerned that his plan is indicative of a messy Interpol?"

I leaned over to Joshua, seething. *"What?"*

He whispered indignantly, "It doesn't say 'messy Interpol'! It's shorthand for 'messianic interventionist policies.'"

"What?"

Joshua clutched his head, unable or unwilling to help me further. I resumed with the cross-ex. "Indicative of messianic . . . I'm sorry. I can't do this."

"Thank you, Ms. Lee," said the moderator, smiling condescendingly.

I turned to face my opponents. "I'm offering you a draw," I said. They looked at me with exasperation and disgust.

Joshua had removed his glasses and was now pinching the bridge of his nose. But under his hand he was concealing a smile. The edges of his eyes crinkled adorably into premature crow's-feet.

There were a half dozen more debates, after which it became clear that Joshua and I hadn't a prayer at being anointed Young Crotonians. Accepting our defeat, we disbanded with the others into the study for cocktails. Over the mediocre Crotonia Club wine, which I think was some relabeled Málaga, I said to Joshua, "What do you do with your life otherwise, or is contempt a full-time hobby?"

Joshua spat up his wine. "I'm teaching the odd class at Columbia to maintain my embarrassingly meager stipend, while on the endless quest for a dissertation topic."

"Ah. Well, I wonder how many Crotonia members are students."

"Is this your way of asking how I could afford it? They have a reduced-fee schedule for students. I am able to get away with a great deal, in fact, based on student discounts. Any museum in New York is practically free for me, and Columbia sets aside a block of tickets in the Family Circle for performances at the Metropolitan Opera. Would you like to go to *La Bohème* next Thursday? Franco Zeffirelli designed the sets."

I pursed my lips to stop myself from beaming. "I'd love to," I said. "I've never sat in Family Circle before. Is that above Mezzanine?"

"Ha-ha," he said. "A little higher up."

"Why not meet me under the left-hand Chagall?"

"The what?"

"The Chagall on the left-hand side. There are two Chagalls in the lobby; you know that, right?"

"Actually, I haven't really ever been to the Met. But I do listen to a lot of opera."

Oh, dear. Joshua's knowledge of opera, as his knowledge of everything else, was strictly theoretical.

8

THE MARROW SUCKER

I SPENT ALL of Thursday getting ready for the Met, employing all the beauty tips Madame had given me for my first meeting with Yevgeny—banana breasts and all. I wore a sheer silk plum gown that I'd bought at Morgana le Fay in SoHo. Over it I wore a white cashmere cape with a hood. I wore plum sandals with satin ribbons that I tied and crossed around my ankle, and carried a tiny beaded handbag.

By prior arrangement, I met Joshua below the left-side Chagall. I was somewhat taken aback by his attire. He wore the same all-brown outfit he'd worn the night I met him at Thor's party, with the toothpaste flecks still on his sweater. And he was finishing a large *pickle* brought in from some nearby street vendor. He saw me and waved with a mustard-stained hand. A death fugue played in my head.

My internal mood music was interrupted by the Met orchestra xylophone, sounding the last seating call for the first act, and Joshua led me up the red-carpeted stairs. As the crowd ascended the staircase, the ladies in ermine were the first to leave us, taking their seats in Orchestra. Then the ladies with Tiffany necklaces, but who were of the younger, antifur generation, went off to the mezzanine level. Slowly, gradually, all the people dressed like me receded, until I was surrounded only by people dressed like Joshua. Even the girls who looked as though they were wearing their old prom dresses had already taken their seats. My stomach was turning. It was Dante's *Inferno,* inverted: the higher you climb, the worse your seats, the worse the refreshments, the scruffier the crowd. We had passed the Good Champagne Zone thirty steps ago, and from the looks of it, I was going to have to drink a Heidsieck during intermission, unless I could somehow persuade Joshua to steal downstairs to the Mezzanine bar, which I didn't want to risk unless he had somehow brought a change of clothing.

We took our seats, and I saw that I was surrounded entirely by students, who were staring at me.

"Are you okay?" asked Josh. "You look a little queasy."

"Oh, just, uh, vertigo. We're a bit high up. But it's delightful, though; this way I get to see the whole stage. You know, I hate it when I'm sitting too close and, um, have to keep turning my head to follow the action."

Even with my opera glasses, I could hardly see a thing. Looking so far downward at the stage was making me dizzy and I had to lean back in my seat.

Joshua's behavior was mortifying. He kept humming through the arias, and applauded at inappropriate moments, as if we were at a rodeo. A few times he turned to me and said things like, "She's the last of the lyric sop—sopranos."

"Shhh," I said, but he was not the only one talking. Some woman with her hair in a chignon was gabbing at full volume to the man next to her.

I leaned over and whispered loudly in the woman's direction, "I don't know how you people do things at Disney on Ice, but here you keep silent during the performance." In the shadows I could see the silhouetted head turning to glare at me several times during the performance. I contemplated how wrong a chignon hairdo was for someone like her, whose head was proportionally so much larger than her body. She and I exchanged silent, invisible hate flares.

After act two, we sauntered out to the lobby and Joshua said, "That seemed kind of abrupt. The couples meet, one guy buys his girlfriend a bonnet, and it's over? Isn't Mimì supposed to die? It's just as well. Let's have a nice stroll, shall we?"

My jaw dropped. My stomach fell. "You're kidding, right?"

"You mean, because it's too hot for a stroll?"

"No, it's *intermission*. What is wrong with you, Spinoza?"

"Oh," he said. "But everyone got up to leave, and there were cur-curtain calls—three, in fact—and people were throwing flowers onstage, so naturally I thought it was over."

I anesthetized myself with Heidsieck, then sulkily followed Joshua to watch the second half of the opera. At the end, when consumptive Mimì was coughing up her little lungs, everyone around me started coughing, too, as if in sympathy, or maybe they had colds and had been holding in their phlegm until they felt that Mimì could camou-flage their coughs. Poor people have colds all the time, it seems. I guess that's why domestic help are always taking sick leave.

During the five curtain calls, the audience stood to do their usual indiscriminate, mindless, and unmerited standing ovation. As the applause died down, someone booed. Very loudly. Good for him.

"How unbelievably rude," said Joshua, standing up. "Let's have our stroll now."

I said, "Spinoza, have you ever been blackmailed before?"

"No. Why?" He looked terrified.

"Because if you don't feed me, I'm going home."

"Oh." We stood among the exiting crowds, who were undoubt-edly on their way to nice restaurants with their nice dates. Joshua half-smiled and said, "How about if I make you dinner?"

I brightened. "No man has ever cooked for me," I said.

Just moments later, Joshua and several people surrounding us were stunned by the sound of my yelling at the top of my lungs. A woman had stepped on my sandaled foot with her stiletto heel. She was still standing next to me, a cigarette in her mouth, fishing in her purse for a lighter.

"An apology seems to be what's called for," I said to her. "That was no accident."

She looked at me contemptuously and cupped her hand over her lighter. She was wearing a bizarre, baggy blue acetate pantsuit that looked like a karate outfit. It was the woman with the huge head whom I had shushed during the opera.

"If it wasn't an accident, I don't need to say sorry," she said, looking off to the side and smoking her cigarette with ferocious drags.

That is a gauntlet, is it not?

"When you talk to me, you look me in the face," I said.

"Get away from me," she said, though her eyes betrayed a glimmer of fear that beckoned me to crush her.

"I will follow you all night until you apologize," I said, breathing fire.

"Come on, let's go," said Joshua, gently grabbing my elbow. I must have looked like a madwoman, because when he looked into my face he appeared frightened, and let me go.

"I'm calling the police," the woman said.

I said, "I relish the thought. Who do you think they're going to believe: me, or a first-generation white-collar acetate slag? They'll come here and see that it's *you* who looks out of place here, not me. They'll look at the two of us and know that it was you who instigated this. These people are my people, not yours," I said, gesturing the crowd at large. Those within hearing distance recoiled.

I couldn't stop. "DO YOU EVEN KNOW WHAT COUNTRY THIS OPERA TOOK PLACE IN? COULD YOU LOCATE IT ON A MAP? WHO DO YOU THINK YOU'RE FOOLING BY SHOWING UP TO AN OPERA, YOU PARVENUE!"

At that moment a man smelling of CK One appeared at the woman's side. "Sorry it took so long in the john," he said to her. "Is something going on here?"

Joshua grabbed my elbow, harder this time, and dragged me away from the exit, past the fountain, and cut in front of a line of dozens of people to usurp a taxi, where we took refuge.

"One hundred tenth and Amsterdam," said Joshua to the driver.

I was hyperventilating. "You should have let me finish," I said bitterly, adjusting my wrap.

"Finish? What were you going to do, stand around and slap each other all night? Judith, you thought I was some philistine for thinking the opera was over at intermission, and yet here you are practically getting into a street fight. And you weren't making much sense. What do you mean, can she locate France on a map? It was just one bizarre non sequitur after another."

"She was like a bag lady coming into my house uninvited."

"Lincoln Center is not your house."

"It's more mine than it is hers."

"Judith, you're pretending you were taking some high moral stance, when the fact is that was the most *un*aristocratic display I have ever seen. You just looked stupid," Joshua said sternly.

I hated him for saying that. Facing the window, I said, "My whole class is getting their asses handed to them by common trollops, and you expect me to just take it."

Joshua said, almost menacingly, "I never want to hear you use your class as a justification for putting someone down."

"You won't have to hear it, you supercilious asshole," I said, tears streaming down my face. "I want to get out of this cab!" I made a gesture to open the door.

Joshua grabbed my hand. "Judith, no! The car is moving!"

"I don't care!" I screamed, reaching for the door handle.

Joshua grabbed both my arms and held them forcefully to my sides. I tried to wriggle free but I could not; I was surprised by how very strong he was, given his wiry appearance.

Our cabdriver, who had been babbling to someone in Urdu over his mobile phone, interrupted his call to shout at Joshua, "Next time leave your woman at home." We ignored him.

"You're hurting me," I said to Joshua.

"You're hurting yourself," Joshua said.

"If you let go, I promise I won't try to open the door."

Joshua loosened his grip. "Well, we're at my place anyway," he said. "Driver, just pull up here please. Thanks."

The driver pulled up accordingly and Joshua sat there, doing nothing.

"Joshua, you're on the curbside. You have to get out first."

"Um, Judith," he said sheepishly.

"You're kidding," I said. "You can't pay the driver?"

Joshua shook his head. "A cab wasn't in the budget. But I had no choice, it seems."

I nodded. I fished scrunched-up bills from the bottom of my pill-box-size purse, which was not designed for people whose dates were cash-poor.

We walked four flights of stairs to his student hovel, which was sort of quaint, with the predictable collection of abstruse books with broken spines, and Aubrey Beardsley posters on the walls. And, oh my God, hanging in the corridor leading to the bedroom was the same Garry Kasparov poster I used to have in my dorm room. I looked at it again and saw that my initial impression of their similarity was not mistaken; the two looked so much alike that it almost seemed narcissistic for Joshua to have the poster up in his own apartment.

I took a seat on Joshua's sofa. My face was stinging with wet salt; I didn't realize how much I had cried.

Joshua silently went to the kitchen and brought me a glass of water.

"Thank you," I said, somewhat touched. I was dehydrated; it was kind of him to notice. "I almost got killed," I said plaintively.

He seemed unmoved. "No, you didn't. Drink," he said, standing over me.

I emptied the glass. I wished he would sit next to me. But he did not; he just waited for me to finish my water, then he took my glass from my hand and went back into the kitchen.

I heard Joshua opening his larder. "I believe I promised the lady dinner," he said.

I was still sore that he didn't come to my defense at the Met. I said, "I think the opera should only sell season subscription packages, not tickets to individual shows. That would keep out the dilettantes."

Joshua said, "It would keep me out as well. You realize that." He appeared in the door frame that connected the kitchen to the living room. He was holding boxes of pasta and crackers. He said, "You know, even if this were the time and place where duels were appropriate, you still shouldn't have done what you did. Not only because you're girls. Dueling was only legal if both parties were aristocrats. If you had shot her in a duel, you would have been killing your social inferior, which would have been a crime. I'm almost certain of it. I can look it up if you want. I have a book on nineteenth-century European social history somewhere."

Was he serious? "If you have to look it up, it means you don't really know what you're talking about," I said. My upper lip was quivering; Joshua became blurry as my eyes filled, once more, with hot tears.

Joshua walked to the sofa and stood over me. "I'm really sorry," he said awkwardly. "I didn't mean to sound so . . ."

"It's not you," I said, pressing my tear ducts in an attempt to clog them. "I was just so mad."

Joshua nodded. "The adrenaline is probably wearing off all at once now."

"If you're such a sensitive guy, why aren't you getting me a Kleenex?" I snapped. Stupid nerd; how could someone with so much natural understanding not attend to these sorts of details? Yevgeny had French linen handkerchiefs on his person at all times.

"I was just about to," said Joshua, who ducked into his bathroom. "I just thought I shouldn't leave you alone with all these, uh, *sharp* pens lying around. Okay. Here we go."

He reemerged and handed me a white crumpled wad.

"This is toilet paper!" I snapped, bawling into the linty, scented clump.

"I'm sorry! That's all I have," said Joshua, looking tense. "I guess I should make myself useful somehow." He went into his kitchen again. "Okay, do you want roasted garlic, mushroom, or alfredo?"

That question brought my crying to a sudden halt. I peered into the kitchen. To my horror, he was reading off labels of Prego spaghetti sauce. "Garlic," I said. I had a sudden desire for halitosis.

As we sat at a collapsible card table before two steaming bowls of capellini alle Prego, Joshua asked me, "What's wrong?"

I examined the bowls from which we were eating the pasta and said, "Are these café au lait bowls? What a charming notion." I think I showed admirable restraint in not asking why we were using old jam jars as water glasses.

"Is that it? You know, for someone who's so hung up on etiquette, you're pretty rude. I'm not even sure why I'm bothering with you, except I promised you dinner and I always keep my promises."

"I'm not rude; I'm mean," I said.

Joshua half-smiled, exclaimed, "Hoo!" and pantomimed wiping sweat from his brow. The gesture was somehow cute.

He said, "Did you at least enjoy the opera? Aside from your scrape with death." He twirled pasta on his fork, dropped it, and twirled it again.

"Oh, truly," I said ebulliently. "It was a wonderful production. If I may say this, however, without offending my host, I never cared much for the plot of *La Bohème*. I find myself always sympathizing with the landlord. I hate bohemians. With a passion. I think those people should pay their rent. If they can't make a living as artists, then they should do something else. It's irresponsible not to earn a wage when your girlfriend is dying of tuberculosis." Or eating spaghetti sauce from a jar.

Joshua smiled fiendishly. "Interesting, interesting. I'm getting an altogether different impression from you than I did from our initial meeting. Your observations are, if I may say this, a bit bourgeois-sounding. I would have thought a blue blood would eschew the notion that people have to abandon the arts for money. What if I were to tell you that Henri Murger, who wrote the book upon which *La Bohème* was based, lived precisely such a life as we saw tonight onstage? If he had gone out and found a real job, as you appear to be proposing, we would have no *La Bohème*."

You pedant, you intermission leaver, I thought. Aloud, I said, "The world would not be greatly impoverished without this oeuvre."

Joshua continued, "And what sort of career would you suggest for Mimì or Musette—prostitution?"

That last bit caught me off guard. I coughed suddenly, with red particulate matter flying out of my mouth.

He continued to twirl his pasta on his fork, not yet having taken a single bite. He said, "Maybe money is more important to you than you let on. I'm genuinely concerned that you think I'm too poor to take seriously."

"You're too serious not to be taken seriously," I said.

"In the interests of full disclosure, I should mention that I saw you once a few months before we met at Thor's party."

" 'In the interests of full disclosure'? Are you afraid I'll sue you?"

"Maybe I should be, because it's a little creepy. I followed you. Just for a bit, and just within Coliseum Books. I saw you there one Sunday, holding a copy of Hans-Georg Gadamer's *Wahrheit und Methode,* and a copy of *The Rules: How to Attract and Win Mr. Right.*"

"That wasn't me," I said, my skin tingling with embarrassment.

"And I remember thinking that your expression reminded me of Jane Eyre."

"That social-climbing domestic, for God's sake?"

"You didn't buy *The Rules.* Only *Wahrheit und Methode.*"

"I'm telling you, that wasn't me."

Suddenly I was overwhelmed with a sense of well-being; it took me a moment to realize that it was because of an earthy, nutty smell that had begun to fill the tiny loft. The fragrance had taken me unawares, like being awoken from a bad dream by a concerned kitten licking your face.

"That's an unusual odor," I said. "Like burned armpit with nutmeg."

"I'm roasting veal marrow," Joshua said. "You didn't really think I was just going to serve you spaghetti, did you? I imagine you did. You were spot-on about the nutmeg, incidentally. Good nose. And a well-shaped one, too. In the nineteenth century, that would have meant a lot more than it does now."

"Some compliment," I said.

Joshua was intently preoccupied with the state of his marrow. He walked over to the oven, opened the door, and used a pot holder to slide out the heavy cast-iron pan that held the marrow. "It's ready," he said, lifting the pan and placing it on the range. "Ever had marrow before?" he asked.

"No," I said, eyeing the pan with suspicion and disgust. The cylindrical bone slices looked like a thigh dissection, and the roasting had given them a crackled, desiccated look, the macabre effect brought to a head by the droplets of burned blood that spotted the pan.

I said, "Joshua, I don't mean to be rude, but are you sure you know what you're doing? Aren't those bones meant for making soup stock? There's no meat on them at all."

Joshua said, "One misses out on a lot by focusing on the m-meat. Would you please slice the bread? Thumb's width or so?"

He brought the cast-iron pan to the table and placed it on a ratty pot holder. We returned to our seats. Joshua said, "It's what's inside the bone that interests us. You just scoop out the marrow and spread it on the bread."

My knife made blood-curdling noises as it scraped against the bone. I spread the gritty, greasy paste on the bread, took a bite, closed my eyes, and thought of England. But I was surprised by joy. It was like some sort of Willy Wonka candy, magically evolving into every sinfully delicious, savory flavor imaginable. At the tip of the tongue, it tasted like fresh creamery butter; then, foie gras; then, crème brûlée; and finally, like demi-glace, like the essence of a hundred cows spread on a single slice of bread.

"So?" said Joshua.

"Oh, my God," I said.

Joshua, having finished the contents of one bone fragment, now took the hollowed-out cylinder and brought it to his lips. Unaware of anything else around him, he took a few licks around the periphery of the bone, then pressed his tongue into the hollow, lapping it up. He then sealed his mouth over the hollow and began sucking noisily and passionately, releasing his lips occasionally to dart his tongue around the bone. Burned marrow juices dripped from the corner of his mouth.

"Ah," I gasped involuntarily, embarrassed at being so obvious in what was already becoming an overwrought metaphor.

By the time we were finished eating, I was prepared to give myself over to Joshua entirely. Such a sensuous display from such a clod. But as I sat across from him, waiting for him to reach for my hand, he shattered the moment with inane, nervous banter. He said, "Hey, those are really nice opera glasses, by the way. Do you know where I could get something like that cheaply?"

"You can have mine," I said, deflated.

"That's really generous," he said. "Thank you so much."

"Certainly," I said, taking them out of my handbag, which was slung over the chair. My brief swooning was supplanted by the usual horror with which I associate him. He wasn't supposed to actually accept the opera glasses; I just compulsively offer people any item of mine they compliment. I was raised that way. Could he not discern that?

"I'd better be pushing off," I said, getting very depressed. Joshua wanted to see me home on the subway; I insisted on a cab, which I then had to pay for, yet again.

"Wow. This yours?" he said when he saw the town house.

"Just a room on the third floor. It's really nice, though."

"Can I see?"

"Truthfully, my landlady doesn't allow me to have gentleman callers after six P.M." I also had a bad stomachache, but ladies don't admit things like that.

Joshua nodded approvingly. "That's adorable. I love that. Very chaste. I feel like I'm dating Nancy Drew or something."

"I've had a lovely time," I said. "Thank you so much." I saw that Joshua's usual sanctimonious expression had given way to solemnity. He touched my upper arm. I braced myself for what would surely be a clumsy kiss.

"Your arms are badly bruised," he said, scrutinizing the three rosy contusions. "I must have done that in the cab when I was trying to restrain you."

Embarrassed at being reminded of my behavior, I pulled my arm away from him and lost my balance slightly. "Good night," I said, anticlimactically. When I turned to enter the house, I caught my heel over the door frame and fell face-forward into the foyer, banging up my knee very painfully in the process. "I'm fine! Bye! Thanks for the bone!" I yelled, slithering indoors on my belly. I shut the door behind me, still prostrate. I slammed the door on my foot.

As I walked up to my room, I pressed my hand down on my chest to stop my heart from pounding. How could I have completely lost my head over bone marrow?

THE FOLLOWING WEEKEND, I met up with Yevgeny at a suite at the Royalton. We ordered up vichyssoise and oysters and champagne from room service and ate them in bed before the television. Though I shouldn't have been drinking, really, as it had begun to give me horrific stomach cramps. Yevgeny had cut his finger on an oyster shell and was sucking sensually at the wound.

I said, "Yevgeny, have you ever heard of someone leaving an opera at intermission because he thought it was over?"

"No, but I have booed at operas because they were so awful there was no other way to respond. This production of *La Bohème* at the Met, for example. Saw it on Thursday. Simply dreadful."

I coughed; champagne bubbles went up my nose. "Booed?" I asked. "You actually stood and booed?"

"The woman scheduled to sing the part of Mimì bowed out because, rumor has it, she claimed she was having her period and it was bloating her vocal cords. She was replaced by some ridiculously ugly cow who was the most unconvincing consumptive I've ever seen, not to mention completely unbelievable as a lovely young thing."

"Ugly cow? You can't even see the players' faces at the Met," I said. "Particularly if someone steals your opera glasses."

"You can see everything from where I sit," said Yevgeny proudly. "My wife has a well-situated, cozy box. Though not nearly as cozy as yours." He put his hand between my legs and gave a squeeze. "Ow," I said, thinking about Joshua's objection to puns. Was this the sort of thing he was talking about?

Yevgeny continued, "It's our obligation as members of the upper class to vocalize dissatisfaction with a production, to boo if necessary. Noblesse oblige, my dear, doesn't just mean helping out the unfortunate; it also means stamping out mediocrity. Each time a member of the nobility fails to boo at a bad production, he diminishes his role as patron of the arts. Once we stop taking our responsibility seriously, we might as well leave opera-going to the nouveau riche poseurs."

"Yes, yes!" I whispered gratefully, leaning toward Yevgeny and resting my head on his shoulder. How desperately I wished that it were Yevgeny who had accompanied me to the Met instead of Joshua. Yevgeny would have come to my defense against that woman with the stiletto heels. My feelings for Joshua had been conveniently chased out, a disastrous *mésalliance* averted.

9

GIRLS AND THE FAMILIES WHO ARE INDIFFERENT TO THEM

MY MOTHER'S BLOODLINE is perhaps even purer than my father's, but it didn't help her nearly as much as it helped him. The benefits of lineage require a patriarch, and my mother's family had none. My maternal grandfather died before my mother was born, my great-grandfather died when my mother was three years old, and my grandmother's five brothers had all died before the age of twenty. "Men are weak and superfluous," their mother would say. "They know this; that's what makes them so frightened." It was exceedingly rare to find a household consisting of three generations of women. Their manless state put them outside the caste system, somewhat. They were still considered gentlewomen, but, being relieved of any civic or social responsibilities, they had very little engagement with the outside world.

While my father's family escaped the war in relative comfort, my mother's family was stripped bare. She could express emotion only when talking about tragedy, so as a child I often asked her to tell stories about her childhood. Her misery became my lullaby.

My mother was only six years old when the Korean War started on June 25, 1950. Her ancestors had been landowners and gentleman farmers, and they lived in sylvan splendor among their apple and pear orchards, two hours' drive southwest of Seoul. Flocks of geese served as their alarm system, honking in unison whenever anyone approached the house. My mother drank fresh goat's milk every morning.

My mother remembers that when the war broke out, my grandmother started wearing a money belt under her clothes, and made her two daughters do the same. They had to burn down all their orchards, because of the possibility that enemy soldiers could take refuge in them. The danger had not yet reached the countryside, but one could never be too prepared. A good thing, too, because several weeks later, a neighbor came running into their kitchen to tell them that the Communist North Korean soldiers had been about the village, looking for my grandmother. They were rounding up all the decadent landowners and taking over their houses.

When her mother—my grandmother—packed up baskets of food and took her children out of the house, she thought they were going on a picnic, until they started to pass by piles of corpses.

They traveled on foot to hide in the countryside. After just a few days my grandmother decided that they might as well return home, since it seemed that families without men to recruit for soldiering were relatively safe. "So you see, it was lucky that all the men were dead," my mother would say. Just like the farmer in the parable: bad news is actually good news, and vice versa, until they all whir into an indistinctly gray, listless life.

When my mother's family finally returned to their home, they found that it had been ransacked and everything had been stolen. But not by Communists—by their own neighbors, or at least that's what they deduced when they spotted some of their china in a friend's cupboard one day. Even the family photos were missing. My mother chiefly missed a newborn baby goat, adorable and precious even when he emerged, slicked with blood, from his mother's womb. Before she had left home, the goat had just learned to walk without hobbling.

Through the basement window of their house my mother watched the B-29 planes deposit bombs. She said that it looked as though a bird were laying eggs from the sky, four at a time. My mother returned to the same elementary school she had been attending, only by this time the Communists had occupied their village and they were being taught to sing patriotic North Korean songs.

During this process of changing powers, many civilians were murdered by both armies. Among the people who lost their lives was a relative of ours, a very famous painter, a talent that would bring his doom. During the North Korean regime, he was forced to paint a poster denouncing the South Korean president. Later, when the South Korean army recaptured their town, the painter was shot without a trial because of this poster he had made under duress.

Shortly after the Communists had reoccupied their village, they fled once more. They subsisted on tinned lima beans that had been provided by the U.S. Army. To this day my mother can't bear the sight of beans.

AFTER THE WAR was over, my mother shared a room with her sister, mother, and grandmother. Long after they were asleep, my mother would study by candlelight, so as not to awaken them. She rarely went out with friends and never even had a birthday party, because her birthday always fell too close to midterm exams. When she was a teen, the local cinema had a special promotion, offering free entry to a Sandra Dee movie to any girl who had the same birthday as Sandra Dee, which my mother did. She desperately wanted to go, but she couldn't spare even two hours from her studies. She once told me, in a moment of rare excitement, "My first day in America, I actually spotted Sandra Dee, walking a standard poodle in front of the Carlyle in New York. I assumed that I would see a movie star every day thenceforth, but it never happened again."

My mother turned down suitors who intended to live out their lives in Korea. She was fatalistic about this sacrifice; she said, "In those days, a woman could get a Ph.D., or she could get married, but not both." In spite of her Dresden doll looks and good family background, she was considered unweddable.

So when she met my father, a movie-star handsome, charming youth from a noble family, she could not believe her good fortune. My father wanted to see my mother constantly, and was utterly frustrated that he could not reach her by phone, as all the phone lines in her part of the city had been destroyed during the war and had never been repaired. What my father did to remedy the situation was positively Arthurian in its gallantry; he asked his father, a member of the Korean presidential cabinet, to have phone lines installed in my mother's neighborhood.

It is difficult for me to imagine my mother as happy, let alone amorous. These stories she told me of her past had the irreality of biblical parables.

I happen to know that she never wanted children. But to be married and childless was unthinkable for her generation, so she put it off as long as she could, then succumbed.

I once overheard my mother telling my aunt, "My whole marriage still runs on the afterglow of our first four years of marriage; after that, everything went irretrievably sour."

After their first four years of marriage, I was born.

She began screaming at me almost immediately thereafter. She thought that children were supposed to be fully formed adults in miniature, and she couldn't understand why she had to teach me things, be it multiplication tables or how often a person was supposed to bathe or why it was wrong to steal. The drawings I brought home from school were met with derision. When I was in first grade or so, when we were still living in Connecticut, the teacher had us do an "All About Me" booklet, wherein we were supposed to write about our hobbies and aspirations: a song of ourselves. My execution of the assignment resulted in my teacher calling my mother for an emergency meeting.

In response to the question "How would you describe your personality?" I had written, "Irresponsible, Ungrateful, Lazy." My teacher, Ms. Robertson—dear, dear woman—was greatly concerned. So was my mother, but for different reasons. My mother made me apologize for having embarrassed her in this fashion, and she ordered me to explain to Ms. Robertson that I just had a strange sense of humor. My teacher didn't believe my explanation; I could see it in her eyes, and she paid special attention to me after that. She and I used to have lunch together once a week, alone in the classroom, but only for a month or so: my mother, unable to countenance her humiliation, put me in a different school. A few months ago, my mother sent me a parcel containing said "All About Me" book, as well as all the photo albums containing photos of me. The accompanying note said, "I don't want these here. Please take them."

I had thought that my mother was just one of those women who couldn't juggle a career and a family. But things between her and me got even worse when we moved back to Korea and she stopped working, at my father's behest. I was ten. Her famous temper withered away, and she became just as cold as she had once been hot. Her life spirit was sapped. Unwavering, however, was her constant criticism, only now it became less aggressive, more underhanded and snide.

I didn't have the heart to fight with her anymore. Nor did I have the energy; I had entered the Korean school system, where the teachers thrashed me within an inch of my life on a regular basis, a fact that my mother met with equanimity.

I ALWAYS ENVIED Jung and Key, assuming that bastards could never be disappointed with family. They were orphaned at a young age, their father (my grandfather) having died shortly before their birth, their mother having died a year after. The twins were separated and shuttled around to different members of their mother's family for years; finally being settled upon one unhappy aunt.

Only Key showed Jung kindness during this brief period they lived with their aunt. He was devoted to his sister. They were now five years old, and, having never known about Jung before, Key was past any notions of jealousy or sibling rivalry—an easy matter for him, since he was the clear favorite of the household. Jung's unchecked early years had made her untamed and feral, like a female Heathcliff. The maid would chase after her with a comb, to no avail; Jung's hair was so tangled and matted that it had to be cut to be manageable.

Jung transformed under Key's doting care. While most boys his age shunned their sisters from play, Key always included Jung during playtime with his friends. Constantly surrounded by boys, Jung dropped her rough-and-tumble defenses and evolved into a delightful hybrid of tomboy and coquette. She adored her brother, even though everyone's golden-boy treatment of him would have given Jung every cause to hate him.

This idyll was not to last, however. When the children turned nine, their late mother's family separated the twins once more, for reasons unknown. The children were shipped off to different boarding schools—England, Switzerland, America. Aside from school holidays, the siblings were never in the same country at the same time, no matter how many times they got kicked out of one school and had to be sent to another. And so it remained until it came time to choose a university, when the siblings agreed that, by hook or by crook, they would both be in the same city. Key entered Harvard; Jung entered Wellesley, forty minutes' drive from her brother. The two have been nearly inseparable ever since. They so esteem each other's opinion that the slightest hint of disapproval from one will make the other drop what he or she is doing—be it a job, friend, or lover.

Or even a spouse. For his junior year abroad at Harvard, Key went to France chasing after a rumor that Asian men were much sought-after sexual objects, after the release of *L'Amant*, the movie adaptation of that lugubrious Marguerite Duras novel of the same name. Key resembled Tony Leung, the handsome, fine-boned actor who played the wealthy Chinese merchant, and used the likeness to great advantage. My dear uncle wrote to his sister that he would not be returning to America, as he had married a lovely French girl just eleven days after meeting her. Jung was inconsolable. She missed her final exams at Wellesley to fly out to Montpellier, and returned to Boston three days later with her brother.

Extricating himself from the marriage was no trouble at all; the couple had married in a church but it was never registered officially with the *hôtel de ville*: the girl was fifteen. Key never had a girlfriend after that, at least none I've met.

Key was soft, which was a delightful trait when he was a child. But over time, his softness became mealy and fungal, until he seemed like a rotted-out, if stately, yacht. Jung, however, had started out hard, and this worked to her advantage—over time, she became shiny and polished like beach glass.

When I was little, I would see Jung and Key at the odd family event, where they were treated with a dismissive, superficial acknowledgment. As the twins were provided for by their mother's family (wealthier than our own), they never made claims on the dwindled Lee fortune, which is perhaps why the Lees tolerated them at all. The twins were always more preened than the rest of us, and observed all family rituals to the letter. I absolutely worshipped Jung and counted the days until some funeral would allow me to be in her awesome presence. I think that part of what helped Jung survive her childhood, aside from the love of her brother, was the knowledge that she was descended from an important and illustrious family, particularly on her father's side—my side, the Lee side. The fact of her illegitimacy only strengthened her fascination with her birthright. She and her brother seemed to shrug off the tacit scorn from the Lees, which made them seem all the more gracious in my eyes. They understood that love, while probably a very nice thing indeed, was not the glue that held families like ours together. The Lee name is stronger than love.

This is what helped Jung get through those winter vacations at boarding school, when she would be stuck in the dorm with all the other kids whose parents didn't want them home for Christmas. They were an assortment of Eurotrash and American tycoon scions who were banished by evil stepmothers. Jung became their ringleader, convincing them that to be disowned was a status symbol; it meant that your family was old enough and important enough to be concerned about your sullying the family name.

During those isolated winters, those kids would form a small-scale *Lord of the Flies*–type microcosm, with the kinds of drugs and sex orgies and senseless persecution that would have made Caligula blush. One winter, at Jung's school in New Hampshire, an Italian kid died accidentally during an erotic asphyxiation session. That particular academy mandated thenceforth that no students would be permitted to stay in the dormitory during winter break. Consequently, Jung's maternal relatives made her change to a different boarding school that did stay open for Christmas. All that trouble just so they wouldn't have to see her for three additional weeks of the year. She started up the same bacchanal at her new school, too, again as the ringleader of blue-blood decadence.

IN THE FIRST WEEK of October Jung rang me up.

"Did Yevgeny give you any credit cards?" Jung asked.

"Yeah, how did you know?"

"That's how it works. Courtesans get limited cash but unlimited credit. It's to prevent your becoming independent. If you disappear or displease them, they cancel the cards. But you only have store cards, right? No Visa, Amex, or MasterCard, right?"

"Indeed. Bergdorf, Henri Bendel, Barneys, that sort of thing. All boutique stores."

"See? That's because they don't want you running off to buy a car, or whatever. They only want you to buy things that make you pretty. Wanna take me shopping? Don't worry, I won't go overboard. Just some shoes."

I agreed.

We met up at the beauty salon at Bergdorf's for a hydrodermic facial. We didn't have an appointment, but Jung knew someone there, as usual, and got us adjacent slabs. We lay there like corpses in a morgue, being prodded by a woman in a lab coat. This was our masseuse, who insisted on being called a skin analyst.

Hydrodermics are offered only in a few places outside of Paris; Jung has been getting them every six weeks since she was thirteen. The masseuse runs electricity through the skin, or something, and the currents force dirt out of the pores the way a storm makes earthworms leave the ground. It leaves a strange tin-foil taste in your mouth.

Lying on the slab, I said, "Hey, Jung, why do you need me to take you shopping? Doesn't your new boyfriend, John Locke, or whatever, give you credit cards? How do you know him again?"

"Emerson," she mumbled, trying to keep her face motionless for the masseuse. "His name is Emerson, and he's my upstairs neighbor. He doesn't give me credit cards because it's not like that with us."

"Indeed? Must be serious," I said.

"Don't mention Emerson to anyone," she said menacingly. "Especially not to my brother. If this gets out, I'll know you were the leak."

"What's to mention? You always tell me that if I don't keep this or that to myself, you'll cut my head off, and then you never actually tell me anything."

"I'll tell you later," said Jung sternly.

"Let's talk about me, then," I said. "Joshua hasn't called since I saw him at the Met. I think it's because I got into one of my bad-temper scrapes."

"Who's Joshua?" said Jung. "Oh, the one-act wonder? Who cares."

"Or maybe it's something else that turned him off. I'm really worried. Do you happen to remember whether I was unusually bloated or something that second week in September?"

The masseuse interrupted, "Both of you, stop talking or you'll jiggle your pores." She added in my direction, "Yours are cavernous, especially."

As we lay quietly, my thoughts wandered to another piece of dermatological advice I once received twelve years ago, in Seoul, Korea.

I am fourteen: three years have elapsed since we moved here from the States. I bite into a peach. The piece in my mouth appears still to be attached to the peach, by some sort of umbilical cord, stretched taut. It is a worm. Still very much alive, it chooses to align its fortunes with the larger of the two pieces of peach. It extracts its tail from the piece in my mouth and retreats into the nearly whole peach in my hand. I drop the fruit and run around the room spitting and shrieking in disgust.

"Stop screaming and stop spitting on my carpet," my mother commands. "It's just a peach worm. In the old days they used to say that eating peach worms were good for your complexion. It would be unwise to pass on any such opportunity."

Appearance was paramount to my mother, which is not remarkable except that it was a strange lesson for her to come away with after a lifetime of suffering.

AFTER THE FACIAL, Jung and I went, scrubbed and ruddy-faced, to the shoe department. Jung felt instantly at home, but I have never liked shopping at Bergdorf's, and I find the shoe department particularly nauseating. It's full of uppity monied types who spend all their time at the gym, but, ha-ha, no amount of exercise can hide their ankles, wide as all outdoors, which these ladies try unsuccessfully to stuff into strappy shoes. The balls of their feet balance precariously on pin-thin stiletto heels, resembling a tennis ball on a golf tee.

"Do you have to look so damn hostile?" Jung said, picking out a pair of Christian Louboutin pumps for herself. "You having one of those imaginary altercations in your head again? Make yourself useful; try on some shoes."

I shook my head, whining, "I don't want more shoes. I just went shopping last week."

Jung sighed. "You amateur. You have to keep using the cards as much as possible, keep the balances high, so his records show a history of large purchases. That way, the store doesn't call Yevgeny to get his consent when you splurge. Plus, if you keep spending a lot and he keeps paying off the balances, they'll keep raising the credit limit on the card."

"You amaze me," I said. "This system has too many loopholes, though. What's to prevent me from using the cards to steal money from Yevgeny? I could buy a bunch of gift certificates and then redeem them for cash."

Jung shook her head. "They won't let you do that without calling Yevgeny first."

"How do you know all this?" I asked.

She shrugged. "A kept woman knows these things," she said.

"Why don't you just stop working?" I asked. "Haven't you saved any of the money all those men gave you? Or the allowance from your family, at least?"

"Kept women don't save money. It's not our way."

Jung taught me long ago that in order to attract wealth, you have to project an image of wealth. You have to join clubs, attend balls, wear nice clothes, and, most important, upgrade continually. Jung says it is like the property ladder: you start off with the best you can get at the time. Then you use that boyfriend's money to pretty yourself, and use his connections to meet someone better. Jung got on the ladder at age sixteen; while at boarding school in New Hampshire, she was tooling around with a Boston banker in his thirties who made *only* a hundred thousand a year. He outfitted her so nicely that she was able to run off with his boss a mere four months later. And so on and so on, ever upward, for more than a decade. Her last boyfriend, the one prior to the upstairs neighbor, was of the Cisneros clan, one of the wealthiest and most powerful families in Venezuela.

After I paid for our shoes, Jung and I went to Bemelmans Bar in the Carlyle. We ordered glasses of Veuve. Hers was free; I had to pay for mine.

"I always get my drinks free," she said in a singsong voice.

"I know," I said, seething at the injustice of it.

"You know what it is? It's my *boobs*. Having a pretty face will get you a good table, but you can't get free stuff unless you've got the *chest*."

"I'll bet," I said.

"Don't you just hate it when guys stare at your *rack* while they're talking to you? I'm like, 'Hey, my face is up here.' I guess you don't know what I'm talking about, though."

"It must really be a nuisance," I said.

"Oh, it is," she said without a hint of irony. "My body is a size four, but I have to buy a size six dress just to accommodate my *bust*."

Losing patience, I said, "Size four, my ass."

She choked on her cigarette smoke as she laughed. "Hey, no need for that. You're probably not doing so badly yourself in the free stuff department. Any jewelry from Yevgeny yet?"

"No," I said. "Just dresses, and, oh, this Burberry coat." I put my thumbs under the lapels and posed jauntily.

She scrunched up her face in an expression of incredulity. "A bloody raincoat?"

"It's a Burberry."

"It's a raincoat." It did sound pretty foolish when she put it like that, but I wasn't about to admit that.

I said, "There's time for jewelry later on; maybe he's building up to it."

"No, no, no," Jung said. "Being a courtesan is like being a professional athlete. Your payoff has to be all at the front end, because you have to retire before age thirty-five."

"Jung, maybe I don't care about jewelry."

She said, "You may not care, but Yevgeny should. What is this, amateur hour? He has clearly never kept a woman before, otherwise he would understand that he has to buy you jewelry in order to signal to other men that you are kept. It is a parade of vanities, a Vanity Fair." As she spoke, she fingered her own Cartier choker. "And now I'll tell you a secret. You must swear never to tell anyone, okay?"

"Not this again, Jung? Either tell me or don't tell me, and then let it go."

Jung nodded and leaned across the table, whispering, "Emerson is Korean."

I screamed, "What?" I was met with the scornful glances of our fellow patrons.

"Not just Korean, but the son of a friend of our family, absolutely the right sort. A member of the Vanderbilt four hundred, or whatever the Korean equivalent would be."

"What kind of Korean is named Emerson?" I asked. "And which part of it is meant to be a secret? Wouldn't your family be over the moon?"

"All will reveal itself in time."

10

KRAUTS AND DOUBTS

MY FRETTING about not being in communication with Joshua came to an embarrassing halt after less than a fortnight.

Apparently, someone came by the house last week and hand-delivered a large envelope. Giovanna had signed for it and forgot to mention it to anyone. Some four days later, one of the other girls noticed it lying around the foyer, opened it, and informed Madame Tartakov, who was out of town at a dance competition. Madame called the house phone and asked to speak to me. She shat bricks as she explained that the contents of the envelope had to be translated from German to English. A legitimate job for Tartakov Translation Services.

"What has this to do with me?" I asked. "Go tell Heike."

"Heike is with her client. You are only one speaking German besides her."

I froze. "What's the job?"

"How would I know? You stupid girls don't show me my own mail. It is from old associate of mine. Is needed by six A.M. tomorrow."

"I never said I could translate from German," I said.

After some exchanges of the "YES, YOU DID," "No, I didn't" variety, I begged her to get me an extension on the translation job.

"Simply tell the truth," I said, "and explain that Giovanna forgot to deliver the document and that we need more time for Heike to become available."

"The IRS thinks this is translation service I am running," she said. "If I refuse or delay jobs we will all go to jail for sure." After demurring a bit, she very reluctantly offered to shave two hundred dollars off my debt if I would do this for her. I had twelve hours.

I agreed. But I knew I couldn't do it alone. The document was in some kind of dense financial language, and I could never get through it by the following morning, flipping through the dictionary all night long.

I needed help. But within my limited social circle, there were only a few people I could burden with an imposition of this magnitude. And only one of those people had an entire bookcase full of books in German.

I picked up the phone and dialed the number that I had so presumptuously committed to memory.

"I STILL DON'T UNDERSTAND," Joshua said. "Madame Tartakov is your landlady, or your boss, or what?"

"Both," I said.

We were seated in Madame Tartakov's basement kitchen, where I was heating up some *boeuf en daube* that I had made for dinner the night before. It hadn't been that difficult to convince him to come, which was surprising in light of our turbulent first date. Even the most unassuming of men will succumb to the slightest appeal to their intellect. So much so that Joshua was willing to spend his Saturday pulling an all-nighter to translate this document for me, for the small price of my keeping him fed and caffeinated.

I was taking a great risk in bringing Joshua to the house, but given the time constraints, I had little choice. At the slightest whiff of a male presence, six of the girls found a reason to happen into the kitchen within a twenty-minute period. They winked and smiled at me; I rolled my eyes to give them the impression that I did not care.

Joshua missed these gesticulations, as he was wrapped up in his own discomfort at being a toothpaste-stained nebbish among potpourri and silk and smooth elbows. He was clearly overwhelmed by the girls' brand of aggressively floral femininity.

When the last of the girls had left the kitchen, Joshua asked, "How did your landlady happen to find this whole b-b-bevy of very fragrant girls from different countries?"

"I don't know," I said. "I imagine she's well connected through her late husband. Or from her days in the ballet."

"Aren't there other places people can go for that kind of service? I mean, places that are more . . . professional?"

My heart pounded. What did he mean, "that kind of service"?

"I mean, they're just fancy girls. They're not really trained as translators."

The muse for liars, strengthened by my success heretofore, was singing louder to me now. I said, "Tartakov Translation Services helps people with things that no one else can do. The wife of a Saudi oil baron might just be lonely and want a *dame de compagnie* who speaks her language. Or some dignitary's wife wants to plan a big dinner party, and needs someone to communicate with the caterer and musicians. These are high-end, personal services that require very refined girls, not just linguists. A normal translator doesn't have the vocab to translate, you know, the names of different kinds of antique chairs."

Joshua fingered the rim of his water glass. He said, "I still don't understand why you all live together. In the same house."

"Rich people want things when they want them, Joshua. Day or night." I had said the right thing, as it tapped into his resentment of the privileged classes.

"Of course," he said, nodding vigorously. And I was out of danger, for the most part.

He took a bite of the food I had put before him. "This is really good stew," he said.

"It's not stew," I nearly shrieked. "It's *boeuf en daube*."

After Joshua finished eating three platefuls of my food, which greatly pleased me, we went upstairs to the parlor to begin work. I tried to work alongside him for the first half hour, but he said he'd be better off going it alone. So he sat on the sofa with his laptop, and I took out my sewing basket and sat in the armchair mending some of my clothes, which fascinated him nearly to distraction.

We exchanged smiling glances as we undertook our respective tasks. It was like being an old-fashioned husband and wife, and the harmony of it was very agreeable.

Joshua was working swiftly, though he made frequent use of the German-English dictionary. He nodded to himself now and then, satisfied with his work. Then, sometime into the third hour, Joshua said, "This can't be right. Judith, did you look carefully at this document?"

"No. What's wrong?" I said, pricking my finger with the sewing needle out of nervousness. Had I actually been stupid enough to ask him to translate something that made it obvious what sort of work we did here?

"If I'm not mistaken, and I'm pretty sure I'm not, this document is an illegal offer of shares for an IPO of a German company called Struwwelpeter Industries GmbH. You know, an initial public offering."

"I worked at a bank; I know what a fucking IPO is," I said.

"The author of this paper is trying to sell shares of Struwwelpeter to American investors, without registering with the Securities and Exchange Commission."

"Oh, is that all?" I said, much relieved.

" 'Is that all?' " mocked Joshua. "Judith, this is highly fraudulent. Is that what Tartakov Translation Services is all about? For dubious documents that people don't want a legitimate translation service to see?"

I wanted to take issue with his claim, but I was silent, deciding it was better that he bark up this tree than that he pursue another one.

"Please, Joshua, I'll get into so much trouble if you don't do this for me."

"I didn't say I wasn't going to do it. Who knows, maybe there's more to this than is apparent here. I'm no finance expert. I could be wrong. It happens."

While he plodded on, I kept his teacup full and even rubbed his neck a bit as I mused at how extraordinary it was that he was doing this favor for me.

Joshua finished translating the job at half past four in the morning; he handed me a disk and packed his bag. I was sorry to see him go, though I could think of no excuse to force him to stay, besides which I would likely get in trouble if he stayed till morning.

We stood facing each other in the parlor. The lateness of the hour made everything seem sultry. I had become attuned to tiny sounds, like the whirring of his computer as it shut itself down, and my heartbeat, accelerated by coffee. I opened the door; we stood in the doorway a minute, sharing silent complicity in the dubious task just performed.

"What are you two doing?" came a female voice from a silhouette approaching the house. I froze, thinking Madame Tartakov had returned early, but in fact it was Heike, come home at last.

"We're doing *your* job," I said with false irritation.

Heike clomped up the stairs to her room waving tiredly and said, "I'm sorry, but I'm not going to remember any of this."

Joshua and I were once more alone at the doorstep.

"Have I seen that girl somewhere before? Her face and voice are really familiar."

"Heike? I doubt it." He had probably seen her at Columbia, but it seemed best not to draw attention to any connection he might have to any of Tartakov's girls.

Joshua said, "You're probably wondering why I'm being so nice to you when you've been so unpleasant to me."

"I wasn't thinking that at all," I lied.

"I've been giving this a good deal of thought. When I first met you, I thought that your obsession with correct form was a bit odious. But I decided that this trait was an indication that you were the sort of person who tried to be careful about things. Most people aren't careful."

I stood there waiting for something to happen, only to have him say "Good night," unlatch the wrought-iron fence, and walk briskly into the indigo night.

Being a complete obsessive fool, I sat up until breakfast looking up *correct* and *form* and *careful* and *obsession* and *odious* in the *Oxford English Dictionary,* and pondering all the possible nuances of his parting words to me.

11

A MEDITATION ON POOR BOYS

THE TRUTH was that Joshua was correct in his initial assessment of me at Thor's party. I do care about money. It's not something I'm proud of. I don't require a great deal, mind you; this is a common misconception that people have about me. I don't need to sit in a private box at the Met, though certainly that would be nice. But I do have many needs about which I cannot be flexible.

I am healthy, but not robust. It's the princess-and-the-pea problem, one of the chief downsides of my lineage. I have dust allergies, and thus require two HEPA air filters in my room, which have cartridges that are expensive and must be replaced frequently. I am also allergic to household cleaning agents, and therefore require the services of a maid, which Madame Tartakov pays for but adds to my growing debt. I go into an asthmatic fit if I'm anywhere near furniture made of particle board, which contains formaldehyde, so all my furniture has to be solid wood, and preferably antique, as I am also allergic to new varnishes and the sawdust that one often finds in new furniture. I was even allergic to the door to the room that Heike and I share; it's made of particle board, and one humid night the door released its toxic vapors into the air and I woke up covered with hives. Madame Tartakov replaced the door, adding it to my tab.

My father once said, "Allergies are an ailment arising from migration. That's why all Americans have allergies; it doesn't happen to those who stay where they belong. If you had stayed in Korea all your life, this never would have happened to you."

Twice weekly I see a therapist who charges $220 an hour, and that's her reduced rate. Depression: Zoloft, 20 mg daily. To counteract fatigue caused by Zoloft: Adderall, 10 mg. To counteract insomnia caused by Adderall: Ativan, 1 mg. I have no insurance to cover this. I have very sensitive feet, which means that I can buy only shoes made by Bruno Magli, whose superior tanning processes allow the leather to stretch with the wearer's foot. I have chronic insomnia, as I have said, so I have special mattresses and pillows. Because of my skin sensitivities, my bedsheets have to have a thread count of greater than 380 threads per square inch; otherwise, no kidding, I wake up with a full-body rug burn. My frailty requires no extravagances, but rather a lot of little expenses that add up. To save money, I pluck my eyebrows by myself.

My need for money arises from far more than just my health: for a racial minority in this country, there is no gray area between the peasant and the upper middle. Last year, I was doing some laundry in a nearby launderette when an elderly woman came up to me and said, "Give me a roll of quarters for a twenty."

I said, "This is the Kazantzakis Laundry. Do I look like a Kazantzakis to you?"

"You just look like you work here," said the woman. "Can you change this twenty or do I take my business elsewhere?"

I put a quart of bleach into this woman's dark laundry when she wasn't looking.

I would be a courtesan my whole life to a man fifty times worse than Yevgeny if it meant I would never again be mistaken for a laundress.

IT IS THURSDAY, and I have a hectic afternoon ahead; first, coffee with Joshua, then Yevgeny later on.

"I think I sorted out who Joshua is," Heike said as she pulled bobby pins from my hair; she had set it for me the night before and now she was smoothing out the curls. "I was in a class with him at Columbia, Ethics and Gender Equality. He's totally brilliant, very intense, if you go for that sort of thing. But he brushes his teeth constantly, before and after each class. And he has toothpaste *Flecken* all over his shirt, always."

"Yes, I know," I moaned.

Heike said, "Did you ever notice he looks like Garry Kasparov? Except not as suave. Joshua seemed a little like brown flour—*unraffiniert?* Unrefined?"

"Trust me, this has not escaped my notice," I said. "In fact, I'm just not sure at all about this Joshua character. First of all: he wants to meet for coffee. Come on. Should a girl in a silk dress have to sit at a sticky Formica table?"

ENTERING CAFÉ BUDAPEST, I squeezed between the tables looking for Joshua, my shopping bags brushing up against the other patrons. The shabby pseudobohemians with five-hundred-dollar glasses, rejoicing over their escape from suburbia, looked on with annoyance.

"Hi, Spinoza," I said, approaching his table, which was covered with papers. He didn't notice me because he was seated with, oh my God, a mousy Bolshevik girl with butt-hugging paint-stained jeans and a Walter Benjamin book in her hand. She said adenoidally, "You spilled my coffee all over my term paper."

"It shouldn't matter in the age of mechanical reproduction," I said, referring to an essay contained in the book she held. The girl actually pondered my words for a second, frowned, then left for the counter to refresh her coffee and flirt with the geek manning the register.

"Have I told you about Benjamin?" Joshua said, squinting as he tried to recall.

"No, you didn't tell me about Benjamin, for crying out loud. I read it on my own. Who was that?"

"Just a girl from Columbia," he said.

I looked over to the counter where she was leaning with her chin in her hand. Annoyingly, she wasn't actually that hideous; she had a sleek chestnut-brown ponytail and smooth skin with well-formed dimples on either side of her mouth.

"I guess she's so skinny because she's a Communist," I said.

Joshua, unamused, looked me up and down and said, "Do you never wear trousers, ever?"

"Meaning, what, like that girl's spark-plug-factory uniform? Bite me."

"Where would the upper classes be if they couldn't put people down," he said prudishly. "The master needs the slave. The slave doesn't need the master."

I harrumphed and took a seat. My silk dress fluttered inelegantly in the airstream that seeped from a hole in the vinyl chair cushion. It made a flatulent noise as I sat. I smoothed my hem over my knees.

"Hegel, I presume," I said.

Joshua nodded. "Right. Your froufrou costume notwithstanding, you're not as out of place here as you are trying to appear," Joshua said. "Have you considered going back to school?"

"I could do without the condescension."

"You studied philosophy before, right? You could continue your studies, get a Ph.D."

"And why would I want to do that?"

"Because right now you're just engaging in palaver. You've reached a level in your education at which it is very dangerous to stop."

I said, " 'A little learning is a dangerous thing; drink deep or taste not the Pierian Spring'?"

"Something like that. See what I mean? You have what is some-times referred to as a 'polite education.'"

"What's wrong with that? Polite is good."

"If you leave it at that, you will remain a dilettante."

"Says the man who leaves Lincoln Center at intermission because he thinks Puccini operas are supposed to end before the denouement."

"How m-m-many times do you intend to bring that up? Anyway, my observation wasn't meant as an insult. You have this problem because, and only because, you're so very clever." He blushed.

"One more remark like that, and my heart will harden to you for good," I said.

"Oh, come now, what is it with you? You'd rather I say that I am entranced by the swell of your bosom."

"Unrealistic, but that's the right idea," I said, shrugging. This was pointless.

Suddenly, his eyes became hard and determined; he took the cigarette from my hand, and butted it out in the ashtray before me. He leaned across the little table, gripped my head with both his hands, and kissed me. First gently, as one would expect from a sullen bookish type, then forcefully, then finally tugging my lower lip with his teeth. His smoldering look passed; the sullen expression returned, and he stared into his coffee.

Whence did this corsair appear, I wondered, breathlessly.

The atmosphere was shattered by the shrill voice of Bolshevik Girl, crying, "Joshua!" She ran from the counter to our table with some desperation, her long bushy ponytail swishing buoyantly. She tugged at Joshua's arm, whining, "Come on, we're going to be late for the lecture."

"What lecture?" I asked, seething.

The girl said smugly, "The French Department got Luce Irigiray to speak about Plato's Cave as a metaphor for the womb."

"You're right, Joshua," I said. "I'm missing out on so much by not continuing my education."

The girl frowned. The two of them walked out of the café with an enviable sense of purpose.

LATER THAT EVENING, Yevgeny was late coming to our room at the St. Estèphe. He strolled into our hotel room; I had settled in an hour

before and was sitting in a big fluffy bathrobe, watching *Cagney &
Lacey* reruns on the telly while painting my nails. "Sorry I had to cancel last time," he said. "Wife came into town at the last second. Maybe
this will induce you to forgive me?" He tossed a Tiffany & Co. box
on the bed. I opened the box; it was a Paloma Picasso necklace-and-
earring set—platinum and diamond—and exclusive to Tiffany. Not
extravagant by Jung's standards, but, as Thor pointed out so indelicately, a girl has to price herself realistically. Only Yevgeny under-
stands how bourgeois I really am inside. The very nature of our
relationship obviates the need for me to conceal such things from him.

"Wheee!!" I said with unfeigned abandon, leaping off the bed and
circling my arms around Yevgeny's neck. He helped me don the jewelry, these symbols of my captivity and his devotion. He gave me a
quick peck on the lips and said, "Lemme put my coat away. Continue
with what you were doing. Please."

I resumed painting my toenails. "Except that," said Yevgeny. "Feet
are repulsive. Don't get nail clippings all over the bed." Yevgeny sat
next to me on the bed, removing his shoes. "Oh, my God, what happened?" He grimaced. "Your pinky toenail is cleft down the middle."

"That's congenital," I said. "It signifies I'm descended from Han
Chinese. As opposed to Mongols, I mean."

"So the husband your parents picked out for you has a cleft toenail
also?"

"My parents do *not* have a husband picked out for me; come on.
I'm related to all the Korean persons of eligible breeding. We are all
consanguinés."

"Thanks for translating the English to French; that's really help-
ful," said Yevgeny sarcastically.

"I'm not in the mood for this, Spinoza."

"Who's Spinoza?"

Uh-oh. "A famous atheist."

"I'm sure my parents would have set up a wife for me, I mean, in
the old country and pre-Communism. Don't you find that a little
grim, the prospect of anyone marrying a near-stranger?"

"Not necessarily." I recited, " 'Happiness in marriage is entirely a matter of chance . . . it is better to know as little as possible of the defects of the person with whom you are to pass your life.' "

Yevgeny raised his eyebrows. "Confucius?" he asked.

"No, dummy, *Pride and Prejudice*," I said, very much irked. Joshua would not have made such a gaffe.

Yevgeny tucked himself under the bedcovers. "I don't think it's salutary for women to read so many novels," he said.

HOW DISTINCTLY I remember; it was in late November. I was at Joshua's apartment, the first time I had been there since the night he sucked so alarmingly at the veal marrow.

I was beginning to wonder why he invited me over; as soon as I arrived he became engrossed in a book called *The Kantian Sublime*. So I turned the television on at a loud volume, began channel surfing, and started to needle him about our last meeting.

"How was the vagina monologue?" I asked.

"The what?

"Didn't you go with that Bolshevik woman to some dubious lecture about how Plato is living in a vagina?"

"Oh, that," said Joshua, grimacing. "You're right, it was pretty intolerable. I was just going along to make nice with Sandy Snell."

For a second I misinterpreted "make nice" as "make love." Realizing my error offered some—but not total—relief. I said, "And what has this Smell creature done to merit your groveling obeisance?"

"It's *Snell*, not Smell. She had this wrong idea about me a while ago and I felt kind of guilty about it."

"By 'wrong idea,' I assume you mean the notion that you were romantically involved."

"Approximately and exactly. How did you know?" he said. Even a bookish man is still just a man; the facts of the Snell matter were stupidly obvious, yet Joshua trembled with the fear that I was clairvoyant.

"Please be someone whom I can respect," I said. "She is making you believe you are in her emotional debt for scorning her. That is her power over you. I know you just think I'm horrible and misanthropic, so you probably don't believe me."

He looked away, giving the appearance that his attention was elsewhere, but I'd come to notice that this meant he was ruminating. He said, "You practice what the French philosopher Paul Ricoeur would have called 'the hermeneutics of suspicion.'"

"Why are you always quoting at me like some troubadour? It's degrading."

"I'm trying to teach you to rhyme, as Doctor Faustus teaches Helen of Troy, so they can shout rhyming couplets at each other. Thereby representing the union of pure intellect with life."

I said, "You know how *Faust* ends: Intellect loses out. Life triumphs over philosophy."

"Did I tell you about *Faust* already," asked Joshua, face aglow. "That was a very good summary of the book's themes, Judith."

I said, "No, you arrogant prick. I've read fucking *Faust*. And why is it that whenever I say something erudite, you become simultaneously condescending and amorous?"

"Sorry, can't help it," Joshua said. He took the remote control from my hand and switched off the television.

"Hey," I objected.

He put down his book and turned sideways to face me, then reached under my skirt and undid one of the straps of my garter belt.

I choked with surprise at his lack of hesitation; even the slight tremor in his hand had magically steadied. "What about your Kant?" I asked.

"What about yours?" he said.

"What about your objection to puns?" I said, tingling.

He rolled up the sleeves of his oxford shirt, revealing the thin but sinewy forearms that had so forcefully restrained me in the cab that day we went to the opera. He put his hand on my knee, tucking his fingers just beneath my skirt hem.

I pushed away his hand with nervous excitement, then picked up an ugly IKEA cushion from the sofa and clutched it defensively.

He pried the cushion from my hands and threw it on the floor. He said, "You don't seem the 'close your eyes and think of England' type to me."

He placed both his hands on my knees and leaned toward me. The freshly laundered cotton smell from his shirt commingled with the smell of deodorant, and with that whiff of tea and cumin that seemed to be permanently ground into his sweat glands, I was ready to be enveloped by him.

Then he stood up.

"Where are you going? What's wrong?" I asked worriedly.

I was still sitting on the sofa. With a sloe-eyed expression, he stood over me, raised his right knee, and wedged it between mine, prying my legs apart.

He grabbed my legs just below the knees and slid me slightly forward in my seat toward him. He knelt on the floor, keeping my legs spread apart with his torso. He slid his hands up my thighs, leaned his head forward toward my chest, and looked up at me seductively, sticking out his tongue and flattening it against my nipple, through my dress. I was not wearing a brassiere.

"This is silk, you know," I said. "It's not supposed to get wet."

He continued to press his tongue on me until his saliva seeped through to my breast. I gasped.

He plunged his front teeth down. He tugged at the nipple, which was now almost dangerously sharp, then gently slid his teeth from side to side, as if testing a coin to see whether it was made of real gold. I clutched his hair. He slid over to the other breast to repeat the pattern. (Aside: Why do men always do to one breast what they have done to the other, right down to maintaining the identical rhythm, manner, and duration of attention paid to each tit? Is it a form of obsessive compulsion, as with those people who have to chew an equal number of times on either side of the mouth? And why does it apply only to breasts? I don't recall, for example, any gentleman caller who insisted on alternating sides with me on the sidewalk so that he could hold both my right and left hands.) While doing so, he slid his hand up my thigh, then down toward my knee, then up, then down, slowly, slowly drawing higher upward on my thigh. Finally he rested his fingers between my legs, massaging my stately pleasure dome.

He said, "The undergarments are silk as well. Well, you ruined those on your own, it seems. Might as well make the best of it."

I was startled at the violence of what came next. He bit down on the crotch area of my panties, grabbing only silk, not skin, and used his teeth to tear a hole into the fabric.

I cried out.

He used his powerful tongue to enlarge the opening he had torn in the panties. When my orifice was sufficiently accessible, he pressed his tongue sharply inside me, his saliva commingling with my own nether nectars. (Aside: I think Jung would be shocked to learn how skilled Joshua was at this. Bookish men have a great deal of stamina, I find, and, having been denied the satisfaction of their sexual curiosity in their adolescence, they develop an unending fantasy about taking long drinks from the Pierian Spring.)

I convulsed violently around his tongue. As I came, he bit down on my labia and made what former U.S. presidential candidate Ross Perot would have called a "giant sucking sound going southward."

After my selfish, long bout of ecstasy, Joshua kissed my inner thighs and gasped, startled. "Are you, uh, having your period? You're bleeding a bit down there."

I said, "No. You bit me. I felt you break the skin."

Joshua blanched with horror, but laughed. "Did I do that? I'm s-sorry."

He rose from the floor and lay down behind me on the sofa.

"We're finished?" I said. "Why? What about you?"

"Do you know about the myth of how Tiresias became blind? It's part of the Oedipus myth, but not mentioned in Sophocles."

"Joshua, you suck at pillow talk."

"Tiresias, the soothsayer, was originally a hermaphrodite. Zeus and Hera were having an argument as to who enjoyed sex more: men or women. They consulted Tiresias, who responded that sex was nine times more pleasurable for the woman. Zeus, angry at having lost the argument, punished Tiresias with blindness."

"So what's in it for you?" I asked.

Joshua petted the back of my neck. "That's how it is when you love someone. You joyfully give unreciprocated head."

I FELL INTO a deep sleep on the sofa, in Joshua's arms, fully clothed. I vaguely registered that he got up to brush his teeth and carried me over to the bed.

When I awoke the next morning, he was watching me from the foot of the bed, again brushing his teeth. I looked down and asked, "Why'd you put these flannel pajamas on me?"

Joshua took the toothbrush out of his mouth; foam dripped down his chin. He said, "I wanted you to be comfortable. Jude, what's the scar on your abdomen?"

"Appendectomy," I lied glibly.

Joshua nodded, splattering his trademark toothpaste flecks all over his clothes. "You wake up like a cartoon baby bird," he said, "stretching and yawning."

"Go spit in the sink," I said. "Oh, but first, hand me that hairbrush from my purse, will you?"

He sifted through the contents of my bag and produced my brush.

"Thanks," I said, taking the brush from him. I began to tame my hair with long strokes. Joshua removed the toothbrush from his mouth again and watched me groom myself.

"You are 'a lass unparalleled,'" he said.

"What's that from? Sophocles again?"

"Shakespeare, *Antony and Cleopatra*, act 5, scene 2."

Was I supposed to respond in kind? I reflected worriedly on Joshua's words: he wants us to communicate in couplets. In the end, it's the smarmy boys like Yevgeny who understand you best. I would never get a Tiffany box from Joshua; he's never so much as given me flowers. Not to mention: *Did I tell you about* Faust *already?*

And yet Joshua had one irrefutable advantage: I had always wanted a boyfriend who would watch me while I brushed my hair.

12

SUNDAY BRUNCH

JUNG WAS THROWING a small brunch party at her apartment. She had invited me, Joshua, Key, Thor, Zadie, and my friend Ezra Dwight, who was passing through town on his way to some family affair in New Hampshire with an estranged branch of the Dwights. He is my only childhood friend who still lives in Korea, and I haven't seen him since I left Seoul for university.

Ezra is descended from four consecutive generations of Dwights who have lived in Korea almost continuously since the late nineteenth century. The first set had originally arrived as Methodist missionaries, but were ousted from power by a competing American missionary family in some kind of Methodist-Baptist showdown. The Dwights, ever resourceful, established a profitable import-export concern, which was one of Korea's first foreign-run businesses. Over the generations, their New Hampshire twang evolved into a San Fernando Valley accent, which is inexplicable since the Dwights had very little contact with English speakers other than one another.

Ezra's parents thought it would be character building to put their pasty-white, big-nosed boy into the Korean public-school system. He speaks perfect Korean, including all the modern Seoul street slang; he can read thousands of Chinese characters; and he's a talented classical pianist to boot, going so far as to enroll in the most prestigious Korean music academy for high school. He went to university in the

States for the first year, at Juilliard, but, finding himself unable to stomach it, returned to Korea.

By no means handsome, he nonetheless found work in Korea as a fashion model, his smirking visage appearing in adverts for contact lenses and other products that drew attention to his round eyes. Now he works as a comedian on Korean television. He's not really very funny, unless you consider a white guy speaking Korean with a thick Seoul dialect to be in itself comical.

I am Ezra, and he is I, as seen through a *camera obscura:* he is the obverse of me. Having found that we didn't really belong in the country where it was most obvious we should have belonged, we swapped places. We will always be bonded to each other for that reason.

JUNG LIVES ON Seventy-eighth and Fifth, near the Sherry-Netherland Hotel Café, which is hands down the worst brunch place in Manhattan. On Sunday mornings you can see the idiotic lemmings queue up for brunch in the cold, as if in a Soviet bread line. Today the line was full of the *Sex and the City* crowd, the ones who believe that HBO has given them permission to discuss fellatio at breakfast.

As I entered Jung's building, the doorman stopped me. "You here for twelve-J?" he asked. "Tell the young man who lives there that I have something here for him," he said.

"It's a woman living up there, not a man," I said. "You mean her brother? I can just take whatever you have for him."

"No, that won't be necessary. Just have the young man come down."

When I got to Jung's apartment, I delivered the doorman's message.

"Oh, it's just my blow," Key said. "I'll be back."

Jung shouted, "No lines before dinner, Key, or I'll beat the bloody shit out of you. I didn't make a bloody lobster soufflé so that you could have a bloody nosebleed all over it."

I was the last to arrive; the others were already in their trademark poses. Thor was dangling around his pocket-watch chain to provoke Lucia, the Italian greyhound whose ancestor inspired Velázquez. Joshua waved to me from the sofa, looking dyspeptic. Ezra sported a David Cassidy haircut, amber-tinted glasses that looked like ski goggles, and a faded Ocean Pacific T-shirt with a blazer resembling a zoot suit.

I said, "You look like Eastern bloc Eurotrash. At least take off the shades."

Ezra said, "I don't need fashion advice from the girl who used to change her panty hose in the middle of a café."

I seethed to see that Zadie, the scheming hussy, had sandwiched herself right between Joshua and Ezra, her brown calves prominently exposed like two cedars of Lebanon. Her evening dress was inappropriate for brunch.

These people seemed to live in a world where it was perpetually after six P.M.

Zadie was drenched from the rain and the wet silk clung to her kneecaps, which formed a symmetry with the silk clinging likewise to her breasts. "Sorry about ruining your sofa, Jung," she said. "There's no getting around it. I'm *wet*."

Joshua looked down at his feet, and my *colère* increased as I saw that the tops of his ears were bright pink.

Ezra said abruptly, "Hey, what dreadful music they're playing in here, eh?" and pulled a CD out of his bag. "May I?" he asked Key, who was engaged in conversation with Thor. Key waved an assenting hand in Ezra's direction.

"Oh, really, Ezra. Led Zeppelin?" I said.

Ezra said, "It didn't seem to bother you in high school when you'd carry it around in your bag so you could ask cabdrivers to put it in their tape deck." Joshua spat out his prosecco and began choking, glancing at me with a smug, asphyxiated expression. Thor offered to thwack him on the back but Joshua waved him away.

When Joshua recovered, he asked, "So how do you two know each other?"

Ezra said, "At middle school in Seoul. We met in seventh grade. We were both *bubanjang,* even. That's class vice president, to you." He directed that last remark to Joshua, who grimaced. Ezra continued, "But Jude and I really bonded over shoplifting."

Joshua's eyes widened.

I said, "It's true, I'm afraid."

Joshua asked, "What were you stealing, exactly."

"A desk blotter," I said.

"White-out," Ezra said.

Joshua furrowed his brow. "You couldn't afford these items?"

"That wasn't the point," said Ezra. "Shoplifting is a rite of passage." Josh looked at me for confirmation. I shrugged.

My stomach started to cramp a tad. "'Scuse me," I said, running off to the loo. I had to pass through Jung's bedroom to get to the bathroom, and I scrunched my nose at Jung's always-unmade bed. Lucia came into the bedroom shortly behind me and jumped on the bed.

"Off, Lucia!" I shouted, knowing that Jung wouldn't want her there. Lucia pranced around the bed on her graceful, taut legs, then buried her head under the crumpled sheet.

"Bed not for doggies, Lucia!" I said, pulling the sheet off Lucia's head. As I did so, I noticed that Lucia had found a shiny blue object in the sheets and was now chewing it. "Bad!" I shouted, taking it upon myself to pry the item from her teeth. To my amusement, Lucia's little treasure was a torn condom wrapper, still damp from Nonoxynol-9. Ewww. I tossed the wrapper in the bin, chased Lucia off the bed, took some Tums from Jung's medicine cabinet, and returned to the sitting room.

Key came through the front door with an Altoids tin he had retrieved from Jung's doorman. "Score!" he shouted. Thor hooted approvingly.

Jung came over to Key and swiped the tin. "I'm confiscating this for now. And thanks for slamming the bloody door. Didn't I just say I'm making a soufflé? If it collapses, I'll kill you."

Ezra asked Joshua, "So you're Jude's new guy? Jung told me you're a violinist or something?" Joshua furrowed his brow and shook his head no.

I said loudly, "Joshua, did you know Ezra is a big television celebrity in Seoul?"

Ezra adopted an expansive, storytelling posture, sprawling his scrawny arms over the back of the sofa, and said, "Well, it's quite true, I suppose. I am most famous for a regular role I had on a Korean soap opera set in the nineteenth century. I played the real-life person-age of Henrik von Drosselmeyer, a Prussian who came to Korea in the late nineteenth century as a tradesman. Like me, he went native. He was appointed by the king to serve as Korea's vice foreign minis-ter. Not unlike Lawrence of Arabia. Incidentally, that king is an ancestor of Jude's." At which disclosure Joshua rolled his eyes.

Ezra continued, "Anyway, Koreans can never trust a foreigner for very long, and the Prussian was dismissed from his post after three years."

I added, "As was Ezra, incidentally, during the third season of the soap opera."

"Right, thanks," said Ezra, snatching the lit cigarette from my hands and taking a long drag. Joshua now looked completely repulsed.

Ezra said to him, "Hey, what's with you, dude? Is the floor warp-ing or something?"

Joshua said, "No, it's not. Uh, so, Ezra, Judith tells me you dropped out of Juilliard?"

Joshua smirked, not knowing that this was actually one of Ezra's favorite topics.

Ezra nodded. "Couldn't stand America after a lifetime abroad. Too much of this identity-crisis malarkey. In Korea, people have defined roles and thus know how to behave. Like, in America, maids don't do windows, right? In Korea, the maids do whatever you ask them to. They don't get all huffy like American maids do, because in

Korea maids are maids, and cobblers are cobblers. And aristocrats like Jude are aristocrats. You see what I mean?"

"Ezra," I said sternly, and he was silenced.

"Mmmm," said Joshua, chewing aggressively on an ice cube. I knew what he was thinking: that Ezra and I must be really tight to be able to communicate with a single word or glance.

I looked plaintively at Jung, who caught my glance and emerged from the kitchen, looking domestically imperious as she wielded a nine-inch chef's knife. "Can you men put on some soft porn or something? Jude and I want to talk." I waved good-bye to the room, winked at Joshua, who blushed, and followed Jung into the kitchen.

Jung closed the kitchen shutters to give us privacy from the others. "Want some wine?"

I shook my head. "Not in the middle of the day."

Jung put her hand to my brow. "You sick?"

"Not certain. Of late, I've been getting these bizarre stomachaches, and alcohol seems to exacerbate it. Although sometimes it just happens spontaneously, too. Nothing to worry about."

She didn't seem very concerned. She asked, "So, how's it going? Love triangle, I mean? Why didn't you tell me you were dating Joshua, you goose? I had to hear about it from Thor, of all people."

"A triangle would be a stable structure," I said, "whereas I'm simply two-timing in a hugely messy fashion."

"Did you ever figure out whether Joshua's speech impediment was hereditary? Like whether he has a cleft palate or a cognitive disorder?"

"Why is a little stutter indicative of defective genes?" I asked.

Jung said, "It's not just that. Joshua seems kind of tired to me. Tired, and yet uptight at the same time. But I don't know to whom it is I'm comparing him. You've never introduced us to Yevgeny. How can I help you make a decision if I've never met one of the two principal characters?"

"No way does Yevgeny meet members of my family. That is his wish, as well as mine. Joshua is the opposite. He is utterly take-home-able, except for his occasionally jaw-droppingly poor manners. I wish they could be meshed into the same person. Yevgeny is someone I would have found perfect five years ago, and Joshua is someone I will find perfect five years from now. Yevgeny is well-born and open and passionate and a musical prodigy and has bedroom eyes *all the time* and has that voice that makes my knees buckle, and is a gentleman, a flake, and a dilettante and lazy and dishonest. Joshua is brilliant and more conventionally handsome and tall and fascinating and gentlemanly in content, if not in form, but almost autistically self-involved."

"So date them both. There's nothing unique about your situation. If you had a better acquaintance with the world, you'd realize that. That's why Doctor Zhivago wouldn't leave Tonya for Lara, or vice versa. The two women existed as one in his mind."

"So when should I tell Joshua about Yevgeny? Or vice versa?"

"The time for such disclosures is *never*."

"Speaking of triangles," I whispered, "I found a condom wrapper in your bed. Or Lucia did, rather. Didn't you tell me that Emerson, or Waldo, or whatever, was sterile from a childhood bout of chicken pox and that you didn't use protection?"

She looked mortified. "Where is it? The condom wrapper?"

I said, "I folded it into a paper crane and displayed it on the mantelpiece. What do you think? I threw it away. Just tell me, though— are you cheating on Emerson?"

Jung began to wash the veal blood off her hands obsessively. She looked down, biting her lower lip, an expression I knew to mean that she was trying to decide whether to tell the truth.

She finally said, "Yes. I'm cheating. Don't say anything to anyone."

"As usual, I don't have enough information to disclose anything," I said.

Jung was clearly agitated, shaking spices into the sauce with frenetic vigor.

I said, "Jung, please tell me you're not making osso buco. For brunch? Isn't that a bit . . ."

"Show-offy? You think it's show-offy."

"No, I was going to say heavy. Why are you using fennel seed? It's going to taste like licorice."

"Stop goading me, Jude!" Jung, red-faced with irritation, banged the saucier forcefully with her tongs.

At that moment, Thor pulled open the kitchen shutters, in the process tearing them from their tracks. "Your place is falling apart, Jung," he said. "You're not going to get your security deposit back."

Jung, still tense from our conversation, composed herself quickly and said, "Thanks again for your help, you pricks."

We sat down to brunch; Jung brought out the lobster soufflé very, very slowly so as not to upset it. Thor, Key, and I applauded. That's what punctured the soufflé. Jung looked as if she were going to cry.

Key said, "It's okay, we're eating it anyway, see? Mmm, it's delicious. Lighter than ether, and I know my ether. Everyone, have some. Jung, it's okay. Everyone likes it, see?"

We all agreed it was the soufflé to end all soufflés, taking exaggerated bites. Jung seemed comforted, that is, until the second course, at which point Thor said, "Why does this osso buco taste like Good & Plenty?"

"I warned you about the fennel seed," I said, and Jung went into crying mode again, causing everyone to give me disapproving looks.

When Jung finally calmed down, Thor said, "I'd like to raise a glass to the newest and most frightening constellation in the heavens. I speak, of course, of the recent coupling between the castrating Virgo and the self-hating Jew."

" 'Virago,' not 'Virgo,' " I said.

"Half-Jewish, not Jewish," Joshua said.

Key sat up in his chair. "Jewish? Who's Jewish?"

"Oh, *now* we have the Dormouse's undivided attention?" Jung said.

Thor said, "I stand corrected. Half-Jewish, but fully self-hating."

"Are you a Levi or a Cohen?" Zadie asked Joshua in a patronizing voice. I gave her a dirty look.

"Neither," said Joshua. "Just a common-garden Jew."

"Are you Ashkenazi or Sephardi?" asked Zadie, clearly pleased with what she perceived as her erudition.

"Spinoza is a Sephardic name, but I'm mostly Ashkenazi," said Joshua, nervously overbuttering his bread.

"What's the other half, anyway?" Thor asked.

"Generic mongrel. Mother is mostly Irish," said Joshua.

"Good God," Ezra said.

Thor replied, "Yup. He's got potato eaters on both sides, I'm afraid; Irish on the one, towel head and Polish shtetl stock on the other." Thor shoveled piles of lyonnaise potatoes into his mouth as he spoke.

"Not far from the mark," said Joshua. I thought to myself, *Where are your balls, man?*

I said, "Thor, is your house haunted or something?"

Bewildered, he shook his head no.

I said, "Really? Because I can't think of any other reason why you won't stay at home in peace instead of spending every waking hour tooling around with people who can't stand you."

"Judith," said Joshua cajolingly. Was he taking Thor's side?

"It's okay, Joshua," said Thor, whose voice lacked its usual booming quality. I had clearly hurt him. "Judith's sense of humor is a bit of an acquired taste."

IF THIS WERE A PLAY, someone would have thrown down his napkin and stormed out. But in real life, luncheon parties are imprisoning. No matter how unpleasant the company or conversation gets, no one ever leaves.

After brunch, Key and Thor did a few lines of coke on the coffee table and then held a race to see whose mobile phones would wiggle across the table the fastest while in vibrator mode. Key's right nostril started to gush blood suddenly. He grabbed a couch cushion to stop the bleeding. Thor laughed uproariously.

"That table is oak," Jung said. "You didn't even use a coaster."

Suddenly, a horrific pang shot through my abdomen, as if I had eaten broken glass. I doubled over and fell to the floor, screaming.

"Shit, call an ambulance!" shouted Jung.

"No, really, Jung, I'm okay," said the ever-self-absorbed Key, whose nose was still bleeding.

"You've been in the ER a lot lately, according to this," said a youthful lady doctor, a Dr. Cha, who was an attending physician at the Mount Sinai Hospital emergency room.

"My body is very sensitive," I said, reclining on a narrow cot.

"So it seems," said Dr. Cha. "Do you know what irritable bowel syndrome is?"

I shook my head, my hair making a bristling sound against the cot.

"We're thinking that this is what you have, at least by process of elimination. That bit of unpleasantness earlier with the probe was to rule out other possibilities, like spastic colon."

I giggled at the term, and my stomach seared with fresh pain.

"Try not to laugh," said Dr. Cha. "Anyway, irritable bowel syndrome is what happens when you have very sensitive intestines, as you seem to. Irritation in the intestines leads to painful cramping, sometimes problems with waste elimination. It's not lethal, but as you see it is very painful and debilitating. It is often brought on by stress, which is why the disease is sometimes known as successful-woman's ulcer."

"Well, it can't be that," I said.

"Funny," said Dr. Cha. "But I think there may be triggering factors other than stress. The X-ray showed you have something on your fallopian tubes. Clips, I presume? Have you had your tubes tied?"

I nodded.

"And the abdominal pain started after you had your tubes tied?"

I nodded. "Is it that something's not fully healed in there? Because it's been almost four months now."

Dr. Cha said, "No, the tissue itself is fully healed, and the doctor did the job properly, such as it is. But it seems your organs are kind of squished together; it's not good or bad, it's just how your body is made. And your intestines, as I say, seem to be responding adversely to the intrusion created by the clips."

"Idiot," I muttered. Seeing her look of surprise, I added, "I'm talking about me, not you. Would the problem go away if I had the clips removed?"

Dr. Cha sighed. "It's hard to say. Most likely, yes, though you might still suffer from the trauma of a second surgery. But in theory, the pain should subside over time, if you get the clips removed."

"Can you do it here? Now?"

"I'm sorry, it's not really considered an emergency procedure. I can have you book an appointment with a colleague of mine. Your insurance should cover this."

I didn't have insurance. "Thanks anyway," I said. "I'll just take the meds for now; that'll work, won't it?"

"As a stopgap measure, yes. That's what most people with IBS do," said Dr. Cha. "Just try to stay away from stress and alcohol and try to eat more fiber. Here's some literature. In the short run, there's nothing serious to worry about. Over the long haul, though, you will have to get the clips removed. Oh, really nice lingerie, by the way."

Joshua, who had accompanied me to the emergency room, rode with me in a cab back to Madame Tartakov's.

"Please talk to me, Jude," said Joshua. "I'm worried sick."

"They think it might be a gallstone," I said. "Or my appendix."

"Didn't you say you had your appendix out already? That scar on your belly; you said that's what it was."

"Right, I forgot." I rested my head on his shoulder and pretended to sleep.

13

THE BALL IS ROUND, THE GAME LASTS NINETY MINUTES

Der Ball ist rund und das Spiel dauert 90 Minuten.
The ball is round and the game lasts 90 minutes.

—SEPP HERBERGER, GERMAN SOCCER PLAYER

THE DAY AFTER my visit to the ER, Madame Tartakov announced that all girls and their escorts would be attending the mandatory Demimondaine Winter Ball.

"What is this ball, exactly?" I said to Heike as she was getting dressed to meet her man Boswell. "Is it just for us girls and our escorts?"

"No, it's for everyone who's anyone in the demimonde. All the top New York *ogresses* send their girls. They rent out ballrooms and suites at the St. Estèphe. White tie. Really very fun."

The ball was held on the winter solstice. After the usual preening, I arrived at the St. Estèphe on Yevgeny's arm. He looked ripping in his tails, a black Oscar de la Renta with matte satin lapels. He looked like a young Daniel Barenboim. I proudly took my place next to him in a long queue outside the ballroom.

I pride myself on not being easily impressed, but now, peeking into the ballroom, I was completely floored. It was so vulgar that it had exceeded the boundaries of vulgarity and was almost elegant.

At such times one cannot give a proper description without making crass references to money: the centerpieces alone must have cost at least ten thousand dollars all told. Each floral arrangement consisted of the freshest ginger blossom, heliconia, and birds of paradise, in clusters so thick and tall that they drooped like palm trees over the seated diners. I would later learn that the flowers had been hand-delivered from Hawaii, and that the florist had escorted the flowers personally from Kauai to Honolulu to the St. Estèphe, to ensure that the delicate blossoms were not exposed to continental December weather for even a second.

Each table was recessed in the center and filled with a flat layer of real cherries, luscious but inaccessible, as they were sealed under a thick sheet of beveled glass.

"Oh, heavens, not a *champagne fountain,*" someone complained in a melodiously disapproving baritone.

I turned around to identify the speaker; it was the man standing next to Heike. They were five couples behind us and I beckoned them to cut behind us.

"No backsie cuts allowed, only frontsies," said the man standing behind me, who was wearing a white tie and tails.

I sighed and moved Heike and her companion to cut in front of us instead.

Heike introduced me and Yevgeny to Boswell. "Lovely dress," Boswell said to me, kissing my hand in greeting. "Raw silk, I presume?"

"Indeed," I said, a titillating suspicion rising within me.

He looked over Yevgeny's outfit. "Is this event white tie or black tie? Why are there people in both? They really ought to be more specific in the invitations; otherwise it makes everyone look like a bunch of vaudevillians."

"Speak for yourself," said Yevgeny, fingering his black tie.

Abruptly, he stood on his toes, eagerly peering into the ballroom. "Oh, look, we're being paired off," he said.

"Paired off? We're already paired off," I said innocently. But I had grasped Yevgeny's meaning. We were to be swapping partners.

In this atmosphere of tightly controlled mirth, it seemed fitting that the redistribution of partners was determined by a game of charades. The girls drew lots to determine the order of play. Immediately before her turn, each girl drew a slip of paper containing the item to be mimed. Whichever gentleman correctly guessed the answer was paired with the girl charading it. Her own client was of course excluded from play during her turn.

When my turn came up, I drew my item from a hat and chuckled. I squinted through a closed fist and made a crank-turning motion with my other hand.

"Film," someone shouted. I nodded.

Third word: I tried to look statuesque and pointed to myself.

A man in the audience shouted: "Acne." "Cellulite." I recognized the heckler as Jeremy, a particularly nasty fellow in mergers and acquisitions, who at one time or other was paired with Heike and was now with Justine.

Sighing, I picked up a book—one of the sanctioned props—and balanced it on my head.

"Charm school—charm," shouted Boswell. I nodded vigorously, silently praying for him to win.

Fifth word: I mimed making a martini. Spotting Yevgeny, I seized upon an idea. I began mimicking the jaunty way he would shoot out his shirt cuffs from his jacket sleeve in order to admire his cufflinks. Funny, until then I hadn't realized that Yevgeny was really . . .

"Bourgeois!" came a voice from the audience, completing my thought.

The same speaker followed quickly on the heels of his previous guess: *"The Discreet Charm of the Bourgeoisie!"* To my great relief and delight, the victor was Boswell.

. . .

"What do you think of all this?" Boswell asked me as he sat on an armchair in the St. Estèphe Hotel suite to which he and I had been assigned. I was sitting on the bed, massaging my feet and wondering about the very fair-skinned woman who got paired with Yevgeny.

Boswell lit a meerschaum pipe and adopted a patrician tone, speaking while biting down on the pipe stem. "Rather nelly affair, eh?"

I said, "Does your boyfriend approve of your smoking?" I lit a cigarette for myself.

Boswell sputtered, having accidentally inhaled his pipe smoke. As he expelled the smoke, it mingled with the smoke from my cigarette, forming a fog between us that rose slowly over our heads like a canopy.

I ran over to the courtesy bar and got Boswell a bottle of Evian. He nodded, gulping down the water until his coughing subsided. Face still crimson, he said, "Heike promised she wouldn't tell."

"She didn't," I said. "Heteros don't use the word *nelly*."

"Oh, fiddlesticks. I imagine ladies of the evening would become astute at such things." He banged the tobacco out of his elegant pipe, angry with it for its spectacular failure as a heterosexual disguise. He continued, "Heike is a front; my beard, as they say. My boss is a client of Madame Tartakov's; he's here tonight, somewhere. He suggested this courtesan arrangement to me, and it seemed such a delicious idea. I couldn't resist. It was easier than manufacturing a wife, at any rate."

I started rubbing my other foot, relieved beyond belief. I asked, "In this day and age, does a gay man really need a front?"

"You'd be surprised," he said, flipping through the *TV Guide*. "If you're at a white-shoe law firm and have the Church of Latter-day Saints as your chief client and you're up for senior partner, then, yes. Oh, look, they're doing a *Northern Exposure* marathon on channel fifty-six."

After a respectable period of time, which was two and a half *Northern Exposure* episodes, Boswell and I returned to the ballroom for the next part of the festivities. I tried to catch Yevgeny's eye; he was standing akimbo over a girl with pale, almost greenish skin, the one with whom he had been paired. She was slumped limply over a chair. Her face was smudged with green eye shadow mixed with blood; she looked like a melting cake. I was taken aback to see that the source of blood was her wrists, which were cut open. When I approached her, two men scooped her up and removed her from the room.

I gasped, but Yevgeny's plaintive glance silenced me. He was holding what looked like a garbage bag. He walked over to me, put his arm around my tensed frame, and whispered, "She did it to herself. I couldn't stop her." He kissed me on the forehead. I nodded and smiled warily.

THREE LETTERS FROM MY FATHER

MY FATHER called me one morning to tell me he had just arrived in New York, and was staying at the Helmsley. He had a meeting in Washington, he said, but he was in New York to pick up a suit he was having made. Did I want to meet him for lunch, since he was going to be around anyway?

Things between my parents and myself have been uncomfortable for nearly a decade, the evolution of which can be described in several letters.

My parents were never wild about the idea of my going to the States for university. My father handed me a letter as he saw me off at the airport before my freshman year. I read it on the plane.

August 26

My dear Judith,
    As you know, in the 1960s your mother and I went to America for school. As you are doing now. We were so very lonely, as you will be.
    I befriended a Japanese student, called Yoshihara, the only other Asian in my department. We cooked our native cuisines for each other, one time attempting to make soba noodles together. Yoshihara told me that the sauce would taste better with lemon juice, so we picked up a can of lemon Pledge from the store. Everything in

America came in cans. We didn't know it was furniture polish until we noticed the sauce tasted soapy. Is that not diverting?

Whenever the three of us met—Yoshihara and your mother and I—we would sit whispering in Harvard Square cafés and share all of our new discoveries about Americans. Over time, we came to agree upon several patterns which we deemed to be almost axiomatic:

1. When eating out in groups with Americans, do not offer to pay the whole bill. Americans will not fight you for it. They will take you at your word and expect you to pay the bill, and they may not reciprocate the treat at a later date.

2. When an American you meet for the first time suggests, "Let's do lunch," this may or may not mean that he wants to have lunch with you.

3. When you visit an American's house for the first time, he will give you a "tour" of the house, as if it is the Versailles. He will even show you his bedroom and his bathroom. You are expected to compliment the furnishings.

4. If you see a woman and man together socially, do not ask whether they are married, or even if they are dating.

5. If offered a drink, say yes the first time. If you refuse the first time, your chance is gone forever.

6. If you break something in an American's house or spill something on his clothes, peace will not be made until you offer to pay for it. They may not accept your money, but you must at least make an offer.

Learn this list, Judith, if your choice is to stay in America. You will not survive without it.

Americans have no fixed class system; anyone can rise and fall at any time. Status maintenance requires unceasing aggression, which is perhaps why they smoke marijuana constantly, even blue bloods.

In my student days in Boston, I befriended an American hippie called Ronald, who had dropped out of Harvard and was working in the bookstore of the Harvard Coop. He became fascinated with me and your mother, and he kept asking us questions about Zen Buddhism, about which I knew nothing. I explained to him that Korean aristocrats are never Buddhist.

"That's okay, too," he replied.

You see, Judith, when you are living in a foreign country, it becomes very difficult to judge people correctly.

I did eventually have to teach myself about Zen Buddhism, because I found it was the only way that I could make friends with Americans. I gave myself a crash course, reading the essays of Japanese spiritualist D. T. Suzuki, which of course were not available in Korean, only in English. I became something of a guru, and a small group of frizzy-topped Americans came to my apartment every weekend to nod solemnly and ask questions like, "Should we say some Oms?"

Shortly after completing my degree, I took a post with the Korean Consulate in New York. This part you no doubt remember. I ached to return to Korea, but your mother wouldn't hear of it. As you know, I finally wore down her resistance and we left America. I was all too glad to see the back of that place.

I don't understand why you choose this difficult life instead of returning to Korea, where your family has perks. We are fragile beings who cannot survive outside our native environment.

Regards,
Your father

By "perks," I think my father was referring to things like the citation he received from a disgraced Korean president three regimes ago. As one of the perks of the citation, my family now has lifetime immunity from being charged with traffic violations in Korea.

Similarly gnomic communications followed over the four years I was at school. Though I went home twice a year, my parents communicated their concerns only through letters.

The real tension began my senior year at Yale. I had failed a few classes and would not be receiving my degree on time.

The university was very good about letting delinquents like me save face before our families. On graduation day, I walked up to the podium like everyone else, shook the dean and the master's hands, and received a velvety portfolio, inside of which was a piece of paper that read, "As you know, your diploma is being withheld." Very smooth, very tactful, those WASPs.

After the ceremony my parents took me to dinner at a seafood restaurant in Old Saybrook, where people could bring their boats right up to the dock and come in for oysters that had been hickory-smoked under a layer of wet seaweed. My parents are very fond of Yankee restaurants.

We ate in silence. My mother took the videocassette out of the camcorder and gasped.

"*Aie,* I taped your graduation over the video head cleaner. I didn't realize it was in there. It's not going to come out at all."

"It's not important," my father said gruffly.

We stayed at a hotel that night. The next morning, my parents packed to fly back to Seoul. My father handed me an envelope, telling me not to look at it until after they left.

Later, in the hotel room, I opened the envelope, expecting to find a check, and instead found a hand-drawn line graph.

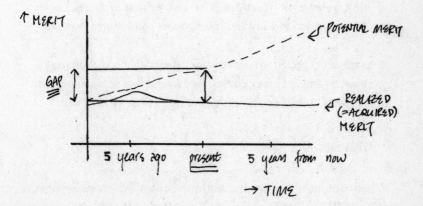

My dear Judith,

As shown above, I have charted your realized potential over time. You are (far) below your real capabilities. As you see, the line has stagnated for some time, and now, it has reached an ebb.

Some observations:

1. If you had studied rational choice theory you would know that people (or markets) do not behave stupidly. All markets are efficient. In other words, that the world has not awarded your achievements is not the world's fault, but rather your own.

2. To put it more simply, in a way that your crass American friends might understand, do not sell your stock at a low price. You were too impatient to wait for it to come around to the right price.

3. A few months ago Korean television broadcast a BBC documentary called *7-Up*. Do you know it? It is worth seeing. What you will learn from this program is that aristocrats in the West share many traits with us.

In the documentary, the difference between the upper-class children and the lower-class children is that the former group followed precisely the plan they had laid out at age seven. The public-school boy who sits with his legs crossed says that he intends to enter Trinity at Cambridge, and indeed he does. Meanwhile, the lower-class children either wholly missed their mark or exceeded their expectations admirably. The lesson to be learned is this: for our sort, your destiny, your telos [the word *telos* was written in Greek] is to become what you already are. It is no more complicated than that.

You are not expected to surpass your parents; that is the difference between us and the lower classes. Be grateful that you do not bear this burden. Achieve equilibrium, but don't drag us all down.

Regards,
Your father

I had trouble sleeping that night. I consumed a whole sheet of sleeping pills, probably eight or ten in all, and drank all the liquor from the minibar. I didn't do it all at once; just a little at a time, while watching television, all the episodes blurring into one montage as I faded in and out. The next day, the chambermaid found me lying unconscious, and I was sent to the emergency room.

The hotel called my parents in Seoul, having traced their phone number through their credit-card records. My mother called me at the hospital.

"Well?" she said.

"I think I slept through checkout time," I said. "Did the hotel charge us for an extra day?"

"I was so embarrassed when the hotel called. I'm sure they are laughing at us."

"Also, you should refuse to pay for the drinks I took from the minibar. Some of them had been opened already." I couldn't let her know that my heart was breaking.

"Are you crazy or something?"

"That's what I've been trying to tell you for years," I said.

"What you did was very inconsiderate," said my mother, hanging up.

In disbelief, I continued to hold the receiver to my ear long after the phone recording warned that the phone was off the hook. I clutched the phone to my chest and wailed. I was so dehydrated that no tears would fall.

I do understand why my mother would use the word *inconsiderate* to describe someone who has almost topped herself.

When I was in the sixth grade, puttering around my uncle's house in Seoul, I looked through my grandmother's photo albums and found a recurring image of a girl whom I could not identify, though she was the spitting image of my grandmother.

When I asked who the girl was, my grandmother slammed the book shut and said, "I imagine she's a friend of the family."

I asked my mother about this. She smiled wickedly and said, "That must be your aunt Yong-Ja." I could tell from my mother's expression that this was a story that would not portray her husband's family in a flattering light. She cautioned, "Don't tell anyone I told you this, particularly your father."

Yong-Ja, my mother proceeded to tell me, was the tallest and prettiest girl in the neighborhood, as dead girls always are. Disobeying her father's orders, she went to America at age eighteen, following some seedy American diplomat whom she had met in Seoul. She bore a son. After divorcing her husband, she tried to reconcile with her family, with results that proved unsatisfactory to all parties. While still in her thirties, she died under unexplained circumstances. Having ceased communications with her family long before, quite some time elapsed before anyone learned of her death. No one seemed to have a clear understanding of the details.

In Korea, for a child to die while her parents still live is the ultimate act of rebellion. Such a child is known ever after as an ungrateful child. It is the most grievous social crime a person can commit.

After my aunt's death, her family embarked on a Stalinist purging of her effects—her childhood violin, her books, every picture she had drawn, every letter she had written them. They never attempted to contact her son, whom none of us has ever met.

She was not given a headstone in the family cemetery. Proof of her existence remained only in those photos in which other family members also appeared, and even then only when she couldn't be cropped out.

That's how my family treated a woman who died accidentally. You can only imagine what they think of someone like me.

MY FATHER asked me to meet him at Remson's Steak House, a wood-paneled joint for alpha males who lunch. It was just the sort of impersonal setting he would choose. One would only ever go to Remson's for professional transactions. I felt like a secretary meeting her boss for lunch.

I looked over my outfit to make sure that my lapels were straight and that my blouse was tucked in, then entered the restaurant. The maître d' seated me with my father.

Dad was wearing a blue blazer over a hideous ensemble, most commonly associated with old WASPs and Korean golfers: plaid trousers, V-neck plaid sweater vest, and white turtleneck. I flushed with anticipation and relief; family was family. I bowed in greeting to my father.

My father was unresponsive. The first thing he said to me was: "Paul Castellano was shot here." People who are accustomed to having everyone's undivided attention, regardless of what they say, develop autistic speech patterns.

"Who?" I asked, dejectedly.

"Castellano, the head of the Gambino crime family. John Gotti shot him down in front of this restaurant."

"Poor him," I said.

Continuing his dialogue built on non sequiturs, he gestured at my blouse and asked, "Do you mind telling me what color that's supposed to be?"

I looked down at my shirt. "It's . . . mustard yellow, I guess."

"Is that what people are wearing these days? You look like a phone book."

It was true that I was deliberately wearing my frumpiest outfit. Nonetheless, I could not believe I was hearing this from the man who raids Arnold Palmer's wardrobe.

The waiter arrived, pulling along a cart with sample cuts of meat on it, wrapped in cellophane. He said, "I'd like to show you some of the cuts we have available today." He picked up a large slab of meat and held it before us. "Are either of you in training? Because if you are, we have a forty-eight-ounce porterhouse—"

My father interrupted, "Do you mean to tell me that I am selecting my steak from this cart?"

"Well, no, sir, you wouldn't want that. This is just for display. It's been sitting out all day."

"Precisely. Why are you showing me rotting meat? When did this restaurant begin this practice? You don't bring a cart to the table unless your intention is for us to select the specific item we wish to eat. Unless you have the cows here, this is senseless."

The waiter retreated. There was some whispering in the kitchen, then a different waiter emerged and approached our table. Face flushed, he explained that he would be taking over our table, as the previous waiter was indisposed.

"You shouldn't be so rude to people," I said once we were alone again. Clearly this was Joshua's influence. How strange that I should take Joshua's role when speaking with my father.

"If we show too much pity for our inferiors, they will take things away from us. They already have. This is not our world anymore. All the ease has gone out of it."

"What do you mean?" I said.

My father responded by dusting imaginary lint off his sleeve.

I don't know what his agenda was, but I had my own. Gathering strength, I said, "Hey, Dad, you know how you've always been harassing me about using your connections, like the guy at the World Bank, or the one at the UN? Do you think you could give them a call and see if they need someone?"

He said, "We must speak of other things first. Your cousin Min-Joon is very ill, I'm sure you've heard. Stomach cancer." Min-Joon is the cousin I mentioned at the beginning of this tale, the one whose first wife set herself aflame. He moved back to Korea some ten years ago, remarried, and now had two daughters.

"No, I hadn't heard."

"Yes, you have. I told you." When delivering bad news, my father would insist that he was merely repeating what you already knew.

"No, you didn't tell me."

"Life is nasty, brutish, and short," he said. "My candidate lost."

"Your candidate?"

"You know. Pay attention."

I looked down at my lap. What were we talking about now?

Our food arrived; we had each ordered a rib-eye, both prepared *bleu*. My father continued, "My high school classmate who ran for president. He just lost the election. He was going to make me a cabinet minister." He looked down at his plate.

"Oh, I'm sorry," I said, surprised. I had never seen him so disappointed.

"You know why my friend lost? He's too obviously aristocratic. Too privileged. No one likes that anymore, not even in Korea. So this simpering fool won instead, this peasant, this illiterate. He's going to destroy us. He wants to restructure my alma mater, on the grounds that it fosters elitism."

"That's horrible," I said, recalling how very proud he was of his schooling. How strange it was that this man, whom I so ill understood and who understood me just as poorly, was in fact my strongest ally in my struggle to preserve our way of life.

"For our sort, it will all go downhill from now on. Not just in Korea, but in the world at large."

"Father, what do you mean by 'from now on'? I can't think of any time in history or any place in the world where you could make people do your bidding just by being supercilious and rude to them."

My father used a piece of bread to sop up the beef blood on his plate. "You're mistaken. Democracy is destroying us. Everyone thinks they can be successful if they try; they don't have a sense of their limits. And it's completely disruptive to the fabric of society."

Stifling a laugh, I said, "I'm sorry." What was comical was that he was expressing my beliefs exactly. But it sounded ridiculous when he said it.

My father said, "What I'm trying to say is I can't help you; not with contacts, not with anything. This means you have to learn a trade."

I felt a panic attack coming on. "A trade? Like blacksmithing?" The words stuck like a big pill in my throat.

"And I was wrong about one thing: you do have to let them see the dark circles under your eyes. Modern society resents those for whom things come easy. For our sort, our proverbial goose is cooked, as they say."

He spent the remainder of lunch regaling me with the history of the Gambino crime syndicate, apparently some new interest of his. As he waved his fork around, blood from his steak dripped all over his plaid golfing vest.

When the waiter brought the check, I peeked over to see what my father was writing on the credit-card slip, and said, "Father, you can't leave a tip like that. It's too low. It's embarrassing."

"The tip should be on a sliding scale," argued my father, the man who lends money to underdeveloped nations. "If you have a cup of coffee, you leave a fifty percent tip, right? So therefore for a one-hundred-fifty-dollar meal you leave one percent."

My father was eyeing a kerosene lamp on the table, in the shape of a pewter pig. Without so much as a nod or wink, he removed it from the table and placed it in his horsehair-weave briefcase.

"Father!" I hissed. I looked around; the staff was studiously pretending not to have noticed. "Why would you covet such an item?" I asked, though I already knew the answer: his kleptomania was one of his silent gestures of contempt for those around him.

My father covered his mouth as he picked at his teeth with a toothpick.

As we got up to leave the restaurant, I discreetly slipped some cash into the waiter's hand to supplement my father's meager tip. Outside the restaurant's entrance, at the very spot where Paul Castellano was shot, my father and I shook hands. He does that only when we are in the West; never in Korea. He passed me an envelope. "Read this at home," he said.

"Why do you always give me letters when you see me?" I asked. "I never get letters from you in the post. Only when I'm physically right in front of you."

"What's wrong with my giving you letters?"

"To an onlooker it might appear as if you had trouble communicating with me."

"I'm your father. We don't have trouble communicating."

January 15

My dear Judith,

The news of your cousin's fatal illness has affected all of us deeply. I am writing this letter because I wish to clarify some things about which you have perhaps been ignorant.

Several years ago, I expressed perhaps too much condemnation of your being an utter mediocrity as a student at Yale. Now I must explain myself, not to apologize, mind you, but rather to demonstrate that I know that of which I speak.

I am a failure, too. But unlike you, I have chosen to settle in an environment wherein, until recently, my failures could be masked.

In Korea, as everywhere, aristocrats aren't really supposed to show effort. In America I think they call it the "Gentleman's C," but in Korea, it was more like the "Gentleman's F." In fact, two failing grades (which is what I had achieved) were called a double-holster, a sign of machismo and joie de vivre. So you and I have much in common.

But in America, your worth is measured by your performance—on what you do, not on who you are. So you understand now why I behaved as I did when you failed to graduate on time.

You had an aunt called Yong-Ja; I never told you about her. She was blessed with all the beauty and potential in the family. She ran away to America, seduced by the promise that she could create herself anew. But no one can really create oneself anew, Judith, and your aunt became deeply confused in the attempt. She became a showcase wife to an unfortunate sort of man, and when that marriage ended, she became a hermit from the shame of it. She died brokenhearted and alone.

I reiterate: in a foreign country, you lose your ability to judge people correctly. This miscalibration can be very costly. My dear Judith, leave that accursed country with all possible haste.

Regards,
Your father

P.S. Enclosed is a check. Buy yourself a proper shirt.

15

ZEYNEP ESCAPES

THAT EVENING Jung asked, very peculiarly, whether she could spend the night in my room, on an air mattress on the floor. Madame didn't have any restrictions on female overnight guests, so I agreed. I anticipated a pajama party for Heike, Jung, and me. But Jung stretched herself out on the air mattress and said wearily, "I really, truly, honestly just want to sleep. Please."

"Oh, that's not fun," I said. "Why'd you want to come over, anyhow?"

"I felt unsafe in my apartment."

"Oh?" said Heike. "Don't you live on Fifth Avenue?"

"Yeah, but . . . it's nothing," said Jung. "I'm in a new relationship, and . . . it starts all over again."

"What starts all over again?" asked Heike, leaning over the side of her bed to talk to Jung.

Jung said, "I just want to sleep, okay?" She lifted up the bedskirt and looked under my bed. "Hey, what's with all these Maison du Chocolat boxes? There must be thirty, forty of them here."

I rolled over on my tummy and leaned over the bed to see what Jung was doing. I said, "Oh. Those are all from Yevgeny. I never had the heart to tell him I hate chocolate. So now he keeps giving them to me."

Jung pulled out some of the boxes and examined the contents, finally settling on a white square-shaped bonbon and popping it into her mouth. "I guess it's like faking orgasm," she said. "Once you start doing it, you have to keep doing it. It's better to be honest about these things at the beginning."

I said, "I never took you for someone who regarded honesty as paramount."

She said, "Whatever. Can I finish off the dipped almonds? There are only two in the box."

"Take the whole lot," I said. "Why do men want so badly for their girls to like chocolate?"

I fell asleep to the sound of Jung licking chocolate from her fingers.

By the time Heike and I awoke the next morning, Jung was gone. But the heavy-heartedness she had brought with her lingered in the air, clashing with the incongruously sweet smell of chocolate.

Heike rolled over in her bed to face me. "Your aunt is very elegant," she said.

"So I've heard."

"But very unhappy. She's not good at hiding it. Neither are you. Speaking of which, is your stomach better? The irritable syndrome?"

"Irritable bowel syndrome. Not better, really. I have to have the clips surgically removed from my tubes, and I can't afford it. I got some money from my father, and I have a tiny bit of savings, but not enough."

Heike said, "*Weißt du was,* you probably have to find a secondary source of income that Madame and Yevgeny don't know about. Not just because she'll take the money, but because she'll never approve of your untying your tubes. I didn't know that could happen with your intestines. *Barbarisch.*"

I was hoarse from all the sotto voce chatter. I said, "All of us girls are prominent in some way, well connected. How can Madame be sure we won't use our influence to make trouble for her?"

Heike reached over to the nightstand for her cigarettes and said, "It's precisely because we are from important families that she has assurance of our discretion."

I said, "If you were to run away, leave the country without paying your debt, do you think she'd come after you?"

"Germans don't get into debt. That's not why I'm here, remember? But for you, for that amount of money, she probably would. It's not hard to find people these days. She seems rather resourceful to me. But maybe you're really wanting to run away from something else. Like this seeing two men at once; that would make anyone crazy."

"Heike . . . do you think all charming people are secretly cruel?"

"Cruel, how?"

"Hard to say exactly, though there was that strange incident at the courtesans' ball. What do you suppose really happened?"

"These are hard questions," Heike said cryptically. She put out her cigarette, turned her back to me, and went back to sleep.

Less than an hour later, Madame Tartakov began screaming at the top of her lungs. Her childhood operatic training was kicking in full force, sending shock waves through the tips of my nerves and waking me and all the other girls in the house. Everyone scurried out of their rooms and congregated in the third-floor corridor, clad in their array of curlers, cotton moisturizing gloves, and fancy sleepwear. Had Heike not extinguished her cigarette properly and started a fire? But I didn't smell smoke. Or was I going to get in trouble for letting Jung sleep over? I scrambled to get a defense together in my head.

Madame Tartakov stood at the end of the corridor closest to the stairwell. She was fierce of expression, and stuck her arm straight up in the air, holding in her hand a piece of paper that looked as though it had been strangled.

"WHO KNEW ABOUT THIS?" she asked. She could open her eyes very wide, and now they looked as though they might roll out of her skull.

We all stood silent, terrified. Finally Heike, the brave one, said, "What happened, Madame?"

Madame thrust the wad of paper into Heike's hand and crossed her arms across her chest. Heike opened the lavender stationery, which fell apart in her hands, as Madame had ripped it into pieces.

Heike bent over and fished the stray scraps of paper from the ground. Holding up the disparate pieces in her hands, she began to read:

January 16

Dearest girls, Dearest Madame Tartakov:

I am so depressed I hardly can live any more. The courtesans' ball plays again and again in my mind, like new every time. I will find some other way to pay my owe to Madame. I promise it. If you care for my life you will please don't search for me.

I will miss all of you.

Zeynep

The room was in an uproar over the Turkish girl's note. There was some confusion as to whether this was a runaway note or a suicide note or both.

Madame marched up to Justine and tweaked her nose between forefinger and thumb. Justine yelped.

Madame said, "YOU ARE HER ROOMMATE! YOU KNEW!"

"No! I didn't!" cried Justine, whose nose was starting to bleed. "She said nothing to me. She didn't even pack most of her things. I couldn't know, Madame."

Madame was still seething but seemed to believe Justine. "FIX YOUR NOSEBLEED," she said, picking up a square box of Kleenex from the demilune table in the hallway and hurling it at Justine. It hit Justine squarely on her already put-upon nose.

"I'M GOING TO FIND HER," said Madame.

"Madame, please be careful how you handle this," said Heike, again the only person brave enough to speak up. "They do honor killings in Turkey. If you talk to her family about her, they will be obligated to track her down and murder her."

Madame's eyes surveyed us suspiciously. We all nodded to indicate our agreement with Heike, though we really weren't sure of the facts. Heike would later explain that Zeynep's family, as a member of the upper class, probably did not engage in this practice. But none of us found this comforting.

"WE WILL SEE," said Madame Tartakov, storming down the stairs and into her bedroom. She slammed the door and got on the phone, screaming at her interlocutor in Russian.

Justine, who had a Kleenex wad protruding from her nostril, began to cry.

Four days later, Zeynep moved back into the house on Sixty-second Street, and we learned how Madame handled those who did not pay their debts to her.

Madame had had very little trouble finding Zeynep's parents in Istanbul, based on information Zeynep had provided on her H1 work visa application. Without disclosing the precise nature of her relationship with Zeynep, Madame asked where she might find the girl. Unaware of anything amiss, Zeynep's parents innocently informed Madame that their daughter was stopping with a cousin in Chicago, and they provided the phone number.

Madame called the alarmed Zeynep. Our dear mistress explained that she was required by law to report to the Immigration and Naturalization Service that Zeynep had left her employ. Under the terms of Zeynep's visa, this would mean that she would have to leave the United States within ninety days or face deportation.

Clever woman, that Madame Tartakov. By sponsoring her girls for work visas, she killed three birds with one stone: the visas made her business appear legitimate; they gave her access to several contact numbers of the girls' friends and family; and they gave her something to hold over the girls when they threatened to leave. And it was all almost totally legal. She wouldn't have to get her hands dirty at all; the INS could be far more menacing than she.

Even so, Zeynep resisted. The phone call ended there.

The next day, Madame was ostensibly talking on two cell phones at once, holding one to each ear. She had Zeynep on one phone; on the other, she was speaking to a "friend of a friend," who happened to be standing on the doorstep of Zeynep's parents' house in Istanbul.

KEPT

"Zeynep," she said, "my business associate is now going to give a package to your family manservant, whose name is Ercan; right, Zeynep?"

The package contained video footage of Zeynep's degradation in the St. Estèphe Hotel room at the courtesans' ball. It was shot by a hidden Web camera, which had been placed in all the rooms.

"If you return to me," Madame told Zeynep, "my associate will not deliver package. He will tell your manservant that he is mistaken, has wrong address."

Zeynep acquiesced into one of Madame's phones; then, on the other phone, Madame instructed her associate to make the excuse and quit the house without leaving the package behind.

The next day, Zeynep was on a plane from Chicago to New York.

And here she was. Madame threw a small, joyless party to celebrate Zeynep's return. No one touched the cake.

Being very selfish, I was mildly comforted by Zeynep's story in one regard: as Madame Tartakov's U.S. citizen, I did not face deportation. As for blackmailing me with a tape, I was paired with a gay man at the courtesans' ball; there was not much she could do with footage of two people watching television. She had nothing on me. Or did she?

A VERY BRIEF WORK HISTORY

"I AM ENTERING the workforce," I announced one Sunday afternoon at Joshua's apartment. We had just had a late breakfast of Zabar's bagels and lox and were on the sofa, my head nestled in his lap as I languidly watched CNBC.

"I thought you had a job. As a translator," Joshua said absently, his eyes never straying from his book even as he stroked my hair. He was reading Lyotard's *Lessons on the Analytic of the Sublime.*

"As you witnessed, that isn't working out too well for me. No more freelancing. I want a real job."

"Great, I think it will be good for you. What brought this on all of a sudden? Trust fund running out?"

"Something like that. After years of telling me to be conspicuously idle, my father told me the other day to learn a trade; can you believe it? It's a bit late now, wouldn't you say? And now I'm royally screwed. I am completely unfit for work. I've never held a job for more than a year. Why can't I have a job like the ones my family has always had? One in which I get paid just because people like having me around. In which it is impossible to measure my achievements. In which I can lie around and look pretty."

"That leaves you with only one option," said Joshua. "Prostitution."

I coughed into Joshua's lap. "Sorry," I said, straightening myself up.

KEPT

"You have an Ivy League degree," said Joshua. "Surely that compensates for your family's woeful fall in stature." His eyes remained fixed on his book. I was so jealous of his books.

I said, "You, of all people, should know how little that's worth. What are you going to do with your philosophy Ph.D., do you suppose?"

"Teach."

"And what if you can't find a university that's interested in an expert on the sublime?"

"Then I'll do something else. Go to law school. Work on a salmon boat."

"If you were in Korea a century ago, and from a family like mine, your future would have been assured. You would have been the king's court philosopher."

"What makes you think everyone was so enlightened then? I don't know much about Korean history, but I'll bet the king was just as likely to chop off his advisers' heads as take their advice."

"Some kings, perhaps, but not all. My ancestor—" At the word *ancestor*, Joshua put the book over his face and pretended to snore. I pressed on. "My ancestor, King Sejong the Great, was a true philosopher-king. He commissioned the creation of the Korean alphabet. Someone like you would have been on that committee. I have a picture of him, even." I pulled a Korean one-thousand-won banknote out of my purse and showed it to him. "That's him."

"Gee, you look just like him," said Joshua.

"Obviously that's a stylized portrait. I wouldn't expect you to understand. He also invented the telescope."

"You'd be abhorrent if you weren't so damned ridiculous. Now, you're going to get angry at what I'm about to say, but I'll say it anyway. You're quite clever, Judith. That sort of cleverness doesn't come from a pure bloodline. That's got to be the result of some p-p-peasant blood mixed in there, somewhere."

"Or it could just be I'm descended from lots of really smart people. Anyway, I hate being clever. I really do. Intelligence in a woman, above a certain degree, is a waste. You need only look at my recent history for evidence of this."

"Your recent history?" Joshua's brow furrowed behind his book.

I've been putting my foot in it more and more of late. "What I mean is, my intelligence has rendered me unfit for normal work."

"You rendered *yourself* unfit for work because you said your breeding prohibited it. Don't you find these excuses exhausting? It would take far less effort just to suck up and deal."

"Can't you just support me? It's said that two can live as cheaply as one."

"Not when one of them is you. Anyway, on my stipend, even just one can't live as cheaply as one."

"What do I do?"

"Be a mensch."

"A 'mensch'? I though that meant, be a nice person. I *am* a nice person."

"No, you're not. In any case, its meaning is more general. Be a human being. Do what people do."

SO I DID what people did.

Joshua suggested I go to one of the headhunting agencies that advertised in *The New York Times*. I chose one that specialized in placing secretaries, as I stood the best chance of not arousing Madame's or Yevgeny's suspicions by taking a job that I could leave promptly at five P.M.

Jobs For All, as the headhunting agency was called, was a tiny, cramped office near Bryant Park. A pear-shaped woman greeted me from her desk; she was picking gum off the bottom of her shoe. "Hi, I'm Jessica Fusshuckster. 'Scuse my feet. I'll be your headhunter, or, should I say, headhuntrix." She laughed in a way that sounded like hiccuping. I handed her my résumé. She donned the glasses that were dangling from a chain round her neck and skimmed over the papers. "Okay, lemme see. What type of work are you looking for?"

"Something with as little responsibility as possible."

"Good, that's all I got. Okay. Your name is Judith Min-Hee Lee. What's Min-Hee?"

"It's my Korean name."

"Okay, do we need that on your résumé? Can we take it off and just have it be Judith Lee? Otherwise people will think you're a foreign national and they'll think you need an H1 work visa, and they're not going to even read further."

"I'm a U.S. citizen," I said.

"I know, dearie, but you know how it is."

At that moment, another headhuntrix slammed down her phone, leaped from her desk, and rang a large bell that hung in the middle of the office. It was a big gong-shaped bell, the kind used in boxing rings. Everyone in the office, six all told, applauded thunderously.

"Are they expecting us to fight?" I asked.

"No," said Mrs. Fusshuckster. "We ring the bell when we make a placement. Okay . . . ooh, look at all these languages. What do you mean when you say, 'French: Proficient.' That's a little vague. Could you take down a phone number in French?"

"A phone number? Of course."

"Well, then, you should have put 'French: Fluent.'"

"That's not fluency."

"Don't undersell yourself like that, dearie. It's not becoming. Now, your work experience begins with 'investment bank analyst.' I'll change that to 'secretary.' We don't want to price you out of the market. And what did you do as a *dame de compagnie*?"

"I read aloud to an old blind lady."

"Could she give a reference?"

"Probably not, because . . . she's . . . blind."

For some reason, Mrs. Fusshuckster accepted this explanation. She continued, "Never mind, then. But, honey, your hair. It's falling over your face. Pin it up or something.

"Okay, the other thing is you need to smile more. No one wants a little sourpuss as a colleague, now, do they? And let's see your handshake. Ewww, I feel like I'm touching a corpse. Let me show you what that feels like. See? Not too pleasant, is it? But not too firm, either. Grip like you're giving someone a hand job."

I put my hand over my mouth in surprise.

"No need to be so prissy, missy. And those shoes are sling-backs. No good."

"These are Bruno Maglis," I said.

"Are you going to a cocktail party? Heel and toe must be fully covered."

Am I doomed ever after to rely upon permutations of Madame Tartakov for my livelihood?

"Are you going to ask me to live in your house?" I asked.

"Huh? What's the matter with you? You think I'm Eileen Ford or something? Also, your lips are chapped. Use Blistex. And Visine."

MRS. FUSSHUCKSTER placed me as a personal assistant to Tamara Harris, the ad sales director of *Teengal*, the nation's top-selling magazine for teenage girls. "This is a plum job," Mrs. Fusshuckster had said. "If you do well there, the sky's the limit. You could go on to be personal secretary to the publisher herself."

TEENGAL MAGAZINE, WEEK OF FEBRUARY 15:

Tamara Harris was out on holiday when her supervisor had hired me. I met Tam, as she likes to be called, for the first time when I reported to work Monday morning. I had been sitting at my desk for half an hour when, at nine-fifteen, a hip-wiggling, generously endowed woman in a leather skirt started walking past my desk. She walked back and forth several times, each time stopping to stare and blink her long lashes at me with a vapid smile. Every time this apparition appeared, I smiled and nodded in return, wondering whether she was some village idiot.

Finally, on the fourth lap past my desk, she said, "You're not my new assistant, are you?" I answered that I guessed I probably was.

She extended her hand forcefully in greeting. We were terrified to behold each other. I had never before been in the presence of a genuine Southern belle. An angry god could not have brought about a bigger mismatch of boss and secretary, but Tam was clearly determined to make me her friend.

As I discovered over coffee in her office, Tam has one of the few American dialects that betray not only a person's origin but also her family's trade. If Daisy from *The Great Gatsby* had a voice that was "full of money," then it can also be said that Tamara Harris's voice is full of tobacco. By this, I do not mean that she is a smoker. She is not. She is, however, descended from seven generations of Carolina tobacco farmers whose income is handsomely guaranteed in that their entire crop is purchased annually by Philip Morris. She has lived in New York for just over a year, having previously worked in the *Teengal* Atlanta bureau.

She is quite charming but has a very dolled-up appearance, like Jodie Foster's child-prostitute character in *Taxi Driver*. The downy flecks on her lapel, which I had assumed to be dandruff, were actually bits of her face powder. I realized this on Tuesday, when she smiled at me artificially to thank me for coffee, and her face flaked off in a blizzard.

Tam is clearly very good at her job. She was born for sales; she is responsible for more than 25 percent of the magazine's new clients, including the much sought-after Jaguar account, though I don't see how midwestern teens are the target market for Jags. Tam said, "Brand loyalty starts in the cradle. Our audience is the only demographic that matters in the whole country. You might as well hang yourself when you get to be *my* age." I feel I can learn much from her.

Tam has a sign in her office that reads, SURPRISES ARE FOR BIRTHDAYS ONLY.

"What does that mean?" I asked her, indicating the sign.

"Isn't that great? I got it from a sales seminar I attended last spring. It means, don't surprise me. Got that, Judith? Don't surprise me."

I put up a sign on my own desk that read, NO MOLESTAR.

"You need to take that down," she said. "That's disgusting."

"It doesn't mean 'no molesting,' I said plaintively. It means 'no bothering.'"

"Well, of course people have to bother you, honey. What do you think a secretary is for, anyway?"

On Wednesday, she asked me, "Can you run these figures for me, honey? You know how to calculate a CPM?"

"What's a CPM?" I said.

"It's just a fancy word we like to use to show the advertisers how much bang they're getting for the buck. It stands for cost per thousand, but I don't know where the *M* comes in."

"It's Latin," I said. "M is one thousand in Latin."

"Well, aren't you a smart little French fry! I'll have to tell that to the clients. How do you pronounce that?"

"How do you pronounce what?"

"*M* in Latin. Is it 'emmm' or 'ummm'?"

Teengal forbids its sales staff to have computers. "Makes sense to me," Tam said. "A saleswoman's place is on the phone or on the road." But assistants like me do get computers. This is truly a poor management decision; I do not think they realize how much power this places in the hands of us underlings.

As a result of this Luddite anticomputer policy, Tam and I have the potential to form a genuine, old-fashioned boss-secretary bond to which I greatly look forward. One of my tasks is to take dictation. On Wednesday, Tam called me into her office to take down a letter to a prospective client of hers, a Mr. Cademartori. I said, "Isn't that the name of a cheese-producing company? I think it's near Lake Como." I felt confident in this, as Madame Tartakov had made me study cheeses.

"Lake Como? Is that in Korea?" Tam asked. She squinted at my scrawl. "Judith, I don't think this is what I said at all. 'Your Southerly Slattern, Tamara'?"

I need a few more months to test this theory, but I think that everyone's menstrual cycle in this office is not only synchronized but synchronized to coincide quite unfortunately with the closing week of each of the monthly issues. On Tuesday there was a lot of crying and slamming of doors.

I am learning a great deal by working in an all-female office environment. In my checkered but fascinating work history, I have learned that every office has a different idea of what it considers an acceptable way for employees to use their downtime. At my investment-banking "analyst" job last year, bosses looked the other way when employees spent the whole day on their personal stock portfolio. And on Friday afternoons, most of the office stopped working altogether to participate in the weekly food bets. It was a bizarre macho tradition endemic to investment banking. One week the office held a habanero-pepper-eating contest. Once it was a milk-drinking contest; the most anyone could drink without throwing up was six quarts.

Another week the traders on my floor planned an excursion to a Japanese restaurant for a blowfish-eating contest, to which I strenuously objected.

"Bullshit," said one of the traders. "You either live or you die. Big fucking deal."

"You are all amateurs," I said. "I happened to grow up in a city with blowfish restaurants at every corner, and I can tell you with the certainty of experience that somewhere between death and life lies a vast gray area known as three-day cramping diarrhea."

My censure served only to make the bankers more excited still; they extended the bets to include stakes on who would get the runs, and for how long.

At the bank, it was unthinkable that I should choose to do something else while the lads were engaged in these games. If I had brought my knitting to do on a Friday afternoon, for example, I would have been kicked to the curb, but if I'd been willing to drink six quarts of a known emetic, I'd have been queen for a day.

At *Teengal*, a different standard applies. Here, it is considered perfectly acceptable to spend a great deal of office time on personal grooming. Most of the girls take time during the workday, and not even during their lunch hour, to get their nails done, eyebrows shaped, and hair coiffed. When I walk past the various offices of the ad saleswomen, I often see them applying layers of lacquer to their hair or nails, or to whatever part of their body requires shining.

There was a scandal on Wednesday. Every February, the beauty department holds a sale to get rid of all the millions of free samples they received during the previous year. Cosmetic and fashion concerns will do anything to have their products recommended by *Teengal* editors, and they think nothing of sending a shearling stole or a jeweled wristwatch to the beauty department in the hope of an endorsement.

Whatever is left over after the beauty editors have had their pick is sold for charity. No item is priced at more than three dollars. To avoid a stampede, each girl is given a number at random to determine the time slot during which she will be allowed to enter the sample sale. Though each shopper is permitted to purchase only thirty dollars' worth of merchandise, that's still enough to guarantee that the best items will be gone after the first twenty people have passed through. I myself was number eighty-seven, but I still made out quite satisfactorily, with an Origins pedicure set containing a large bumpy soap, salt rub, and exfoliant; a loofah mitt; two Chanel lipsticks; a pair of space-age eyebrow tweezers that snaps the hair out using spring technology; a *Cosmopolitan* makeover computer program in which you scan your photo and try on different looks before applying them to your face; and a box of lavender bath beads.

But high corruption was afoot. When the saleswomen and their assistants went around one another's offices to display their purchases, a commotion surrounded Tam's desk.

"Where was this foot massager at the sample sale?" a saleswoman named Jocelyn asked Tam.

"I don't remember," said Tam.

"What was your number in the draw?"

"Thirty-seven."

"Well, mine was sixteen, and I don't remember seeing the foot massager. Or this four-ounce bottle of Shalimar. Or this Hermès scarf! I definitely would have remembered seeing a Hermès scarf!"

"They were all there," said Tam. "On the tables with all the other merchandise."

"You're chummy with the beauty editor, aren't you?"

"We're friends, yeah, is that a crime?"

"Did she give you a sneak tour of the sample sale before it started?"

"That is the foulest suggestion I ever heard in my life." Tam's voice was strident. She said, "Judith, come in here. Did I step away from my desk even once this morning?"

"No, ma'am," I lied. "Not even to use the toilet." Jocelyn narrowed her eyes at me and stormed away angrily.

Tam thanked me by slipping one of her purchases under my desk. It was a tube of body glitter.

The job is turning out far better than I had anticipated. I find myself with a great deal more free time than I deserve. Tam asked me on Thursday morning to rewind some *Teengal* promotional videotapes for her. I looked at them and said, "These are rewound already."

She said, "You can't tell just by looking."

I said, "The tape is all on the left reel, so that means they're all rewound."

She thrust the tapes into my solar plexus. "Just rewind them anyway," she said. While pretending to be rewinding the tapes I managed to sneak a cigarette break and get some gossip in with the office manager.

I am utterly grateful to have Tam as a boss. I spent all of Friday playing Tetris on the computer, while managing to convince her that I was compiling her entire client file into an elaborate database.

"This will help you to no end when I have completed it," I said. "You—or, I should say, I—will be able to look up any account by name, company, revenue, NYSE symbol, their purchasing history; anything you like."

I managed to shirk off numerous tasks by claiming to be hard at work on this database.

"When do you think you'll get it up and running?" Tam asked.

"Not for a while yet. There's a malfunction in the Perl coding I'm using, so I'm trying to convert everything over to Visual Basic."

"Okay, well, you know what's best, my little prodigy."

I was in a bind on Wednesday because Yevgeny wanted to meet me at four-thirty. I asked him to reschedule; he refused. I called Jung, mistress of ruses.

"Jude?" she said. "I can hardly hear you. Speak up."

"I'm at *Teengal*. I can't really talk louder than this. I need to get out of here early today to meet Yevgeny. What do I do?"

"Leave a decoy jacket on your chair, and an open can of soda by your desk. This deception has the additional benefit that it makes it unclear what time you arrive at the office the following morning. Go to the control panel on your computer and disable your screen saver, because it activates after a few minutes of inactivity and people will realize you've been away from your desk. These are rather primitive techniques, but from what you tell me of Tam, she should be totally snowed."

I followed her instructions, and also created a dummy page for the database, and password-protected the computer from curious browsing. I started using these techniques daily to arrange my early departure.

I also found a way to smoke without having to take the elevator down fifty flights and exit the building. There was a fire exit on the far side of the kitchen, and I could conceal my pack and lighter there, as well as hide the butts in an obliging potted plant.

TEENGAL MAGAZINE, WEEK OF MARCH 1:

On Thursday, the fire alarm went off and everyone had to evacuate the building. The publisher was hopping mad because everyone lost an hour and a half of productive time and we're right in the middle of the prom issue. Later, Tam called me into her office.

"Honey, did you butt out a lit cigarette into the plant on the fire escape?"

"Are you sure it was a cigarette? Maybe there was some combustive reaction between the competing spray cans."

"Honey, Jocelyn saw you sneakin' off to the fire escape with a pack of cigarettes."

I was incredulous. "Jocelyn? You'd believe Jocelyn, who tried to poach your foot massager?"

"Honey." She folded her arms and gave me the hairy eyeball.

"At any rate, topsoil doesn't catch fire."

"That's not a real plant, honey, it's all plastic. You did three thousand dollars' worth of damage to the fire escape."

"Shouldn't a fire escape be fireproof?"

"Honey."

"You're letting me go, aren't you?"

"I'm sorry. But, before you go, can you tell me where I can find that database you been working on? I want your replacement to finish it."

"Look under a file called Tetris."

"Tetris? Okay, honey."

"Tomorrow is my birthday," I said pitifully. I should have anticipated her response.

Pointing to the SURPRISES ARE FOR BIRTHDAYS ONLY sign in her office, she yelled, "Surprise!"

The following evening, Joshua took me out for my birthday dinner, which also turned out to be a consolation dinner. We went to a new restaurant owned by a French Vietnamese restaurateur; the wine cellar of his Paris restaurant was featured in *Wine Spectator* some months ago. I was terribly excited, though the meal would cost Joshua a third of his student stipend for the month.

As we ate, Joshua said, "How old are you today, Judith?"

I shrugged.

He said, "Always so secretive. You are Brünnhilde, surrounding yourself in a ring of fire to keep people out. I mean that literally, too, like the fire you started in your office."

I said, "Now do you see what I mean? Even when I try to do honest labor it doesn't work out for me."

Joshua said, "I'm not saying you deliberately started a fire, but your resentment at having to earn a living comes out in everything you do."

"What do I do now?"

"Quit smoking. Save your pennies."

"What does smoking have to do with anything, Yevgeny?"

Joshua put down his fork. "Yevgeny? Who's Yevgeny?"

Shit shit shit shit. "Yevgeny Onegin," I said. "The, uh, Tchaikovsky opera."

"Oh," said Joshua, brightening momentarily. "But no, what was that opera about again? I should know this; I practically memorized the *Oxford Companion to Opera*. Isn't Yevgeny Onegin some jaded aristocrat? That's right, he's debonair and wickedly charming but has no feelings, and he rejects the woman who's in love with him." His brow furrowed. "I remind you of *him*?"

Oh, well done, Judith. "Sorry, I must have it confused with another opera."

At that moment the restaurateur, whom I recognized from the photos in *Wine Spectator*, began making rounds at the tables, asking everyone whether they enjoyed their dinner. I began chatting with him animatedly in French, which made Joshua roll his eyes.

The large-ish woman at the table next to me observed my French banter with interest. She wore a pink blazer, too small for her, and in the back it had ridden up high on her neck, almost like a hood. It gave her a slightly sinister appearance. I had rather assumed she was impressed with me, until she opened her mouth.

"Can you ask the waiter in Vietnamese whether they take credit cards here?" she said.

"He's not a waiter; he's the owner. I don't speak Vietnamese," I said, confused.

"But what were you doing just now?"

"That's French," I said incredulously.

"French?" She had a wide-eyed look of extreme surprise and some embarrassment. As a remedy for losing face, she simply repeated her mistake. "It sounded like Vietnamese." She turned to her husband. "Didn't that sound like Vietnamese?"

"All educated people speak French," Joshua said. The woman's lips fluttered. Her husband glared at me and Joshua. They got up and left. How surprised I was at Joshua's sudden hauteur. How I loved Joshua at that moment.

"I'm a bad influence on you," I said. "The Joshua I met in front of Thor's bathroom would never have said anything like that."

"Oh, no, please don't cry," he said, reaching across the table and stroking my face, knocking over the salt shaker in the process.

"Do you see what I'm up against?" I said. "Why did my parents go through all the expense and bother to make me accomplished? Fucking French lessons and piano lessons and drawing lessons and tennis lessons and no one appreciates it."

"*I* appreciate it," he said. "It wasn't in vain. You're the most fascinating woman I've ever met. Otherwise I wouldn't put up with all your *chazerei*." His words made me weep harder.

"Let's go home," said Joshua, gesturing for the check. "This place sucks. Too many tourists."

"First throw salt over your left shoulder," I said. "You spilled."

"I didn't know you were so superstitious. I think we'll be all right without it," he said.

Joshua really should have listened to me about the salt.

17

MAURICE HALL

"JUDE? Is that you?"

It was April Fools' Day, and I was standing at the lox counter at Zabar's. The speaker was a fellow lox customer, a short, devilishly handsome man with George Stephanopoulos hair, who I realized was none other than Boswell, Heike's gay client.

"Boswell!" We kissed on both cheeks.

One of the lox cutters shouted, "Number 105."

An elderly man in a walker croaked, "I'm 105. I'm 105."

I said to the man, "You're C105, I'm B105. That's me they're calling. Don't pretend you don't hear me, old man. You're crazy if you think I'm going to yield. You're not up for a long, long time." I shoved my way up to the counter, producing my ticket.

"Feh!" said C105, waving his hand contemptuously at me and shuffling to the side with his walker.

"Eastern Nova, half a pound, paper-thin, please, and from the middle of the fish," I said to Harry, the most skilled of the lox cutters.

"You got it," he said.

"Sorry about that," I said to Boswell.

"Not at all. A lox spot, once lost, is never recovered. How've you been? How's the discreet bourgeoisie treating you these days?"

"Funny you should ask. I have a favor to ask of you. It's bourgeois, and I want you to be discreet."

. . .

"YOU'RE SOMETHING of a fag hag, aren't you?" Boswell asked the following Wednesday over drinks in some wood-paneled midtown club building.

I shrugged and said, "I wouldn't go that far; I just find homophobia to be the pinnacle of poor taste." I didn't see the point of this; I thought we were there to discuss the possibility of his finding me a job.

"So everything just boils down to bad manners? You really are an aesthete. Do you know much about gays in Britain during the early twentieth century?"

I replied that I did not.

"This was the world of Oscar Wilde, the underworld that E. M. Forster wrote about in secret. These gay, upper-class Englishmen would seduce scruffy cockney sailors and lounge around with them, the beautiful dirty youths not understanding a word of the conversation, in all likelihood. I see this type of class commingling happen often even now. Believe me, it's far more common in the gay community than among breeders. I mean, heterosexuals, in your parlance."

I wondered where this was leading.

"You are wondering where this is leading," he said. "We've been looking for someone like you for a long time," he said.

"Who's 'we'? I hope you're not running some pimp service for gay men, because I don't think I'd be very convincing as a male prostitute."

"No, nothing like that. Do you know what this building is that we're sitting in? In the 1930s it was a Mafia social club, and now it is New York's premier exclusive club for homosexual men. A-listers only. It's scarcely different from the Metropolitan Club or Harmony Club, except we're gay. We conduct business here, we socialize, we play cards and billiards, we drink fabulous port. Some very powerful men belong to this club. Some very important decisions have been made behind its doors. And we need a *salonnière*."

"A what?"

"A *salonnière*. It must be a woman. By tradition it is always a woman. Someone to arrange things. Someone to set up introductions where necessary, to keep the member list exclusive, to make sure things are running smoothly. You wouldn't be serving drinks or cleaning in any capacity. No filing, no typing, no answering phones. You'd be adulated. Like Madame Charpentier. You know who that is, don't you?"

"Sure," I lied.

"She ran the most illustrious of literary salons in Paris, attended by the likes of Émile Zola and Guy de Maupassant. So? Would you be interested?"

I said, "Having recently heard definitively that I have been denied membership to the Young Crotonia Club, I find your offer irresistible. But, not to look a gift horse in the mouth, why me?"

"Do you know how a racial minority is like a homosexual? We are otherworldly creatures who wear the raiment of ordinary mortals. Disguise becomes our second nature. As a result, we develop richer interior lives."

"I don't want a richer interior life."

"Bit late for that, darling."

"What now? You need my CV? I'll have to revise it. Again."

"No need. You'll have to meet Chester, the manager," Boswell said, "but it's really just a formality. He will do as he's told. So, my dear, welcome to Maurice Hall."

I REPORTED to work the following Monday. I was greeted by Chester, a trim man wearing white gloves and a morning coat. It was he who explained to me that the name of the club was a pun, Maurice Hall being the protagonist of *Maurice*, E. M. Forster's novel about a well-born closeted Edwardian homosexual.

Chester squinted at me. "You're wearing too much eyeliner," he said.

"And you're not wearing nearly enough," I said.

"I can see why Boswell likes you. Okay, I'm supposed to show you the ropes. I'm the weekday manager; you report to me. You greet the guests as they come in."

"Do I stand by the door?"

"No, what do you think this is, a Japanese department store? I just mean, when you spot them, wherever you happen to be, you greet them with a 'Hello, Mr. So-and-so.' You'll have to learn everyone's names. Before we get to that part, though, please sign this nondisclosure agreement, though really it's just a formality. Boswell tells me that your day job, or night job, as it were, requires a good deal of discretion as well."

I read it over. "This says I can't even disclose that I signed a nondisclosure agreement."

Chester nodded. "A self-referential NDA. It's the latest thing. Postmodernism." He handed me a folder. "Here is a printout of our membership face book. Commit it to memory. If you take this out of the building or make any copies, you will be summarily dismissed. It is printed in unphotocopiable blue ink, in any case."

I looked over the list. "Oh, my God, you have Famous Beat Poet as a member? I thought he was dead. Or living in Boston."

"Same thing," said Chester.

"Former Mayor of New York City is gay? I just thought that was a rumor."

"It remains a rumor. He doesn't seem to have any sexual preference either way. A monk, practically. We have actual monks, too."

"And cardinals. And right-wing politicians. And editors of the *National Review*. Why don't you allow women, though? Lesbians, at least?"

"Lesbians don't have any money," he said.

"Is that legal? To have a club that excludes women?"

"By New York State law, any club with under four hundred members can make such exclusions. One of the authors of that decision was in fact also a member of this club, I think."

"How does a club like this stay solvent with under four hundred members? The operating costs must be enormous."

"Endowment."

"Well, even with your impressive client list, I don't see why this manner of expense is necessary to hide one's sexual preference. In New York, no less."

"It isn't just that. Over half of our members are openly gay, in fact. This club has purposes that far outweigh the evasion of homophobia."

"Like what?"

"You shall soon see. Not all at once."

I MET JOSHUA at his apartment later that evening, in high spirits. I eagerly told him what I was allowed to tell of the day's events. He was not as supportive as I had hoped, saying, "Are you that addicted to elitism? Why is it that when you finally decide to work with an oppressed minority, it can't be in the context of helping them in a humanitarian way. No-o-o, it has to be at a private club where they exercise exclusion for the sake of exclusion."

I hated it when he condescended so. I said, "What do you think academia is, Professor Spinoza?"

"MR. ROCHESTER? Mr. Rochester?" I said, hoping I was guessing correctly. It was teatime, my first official hour as *salonnière*. "I'm sorry, sir. We don't allow the use of mobile phones in this room. Perhaps you'd care to step into one of the private booths?"

"Oh, sorry, I forgot," said Mr. Rochester, a worn-looking man. He was chatting with a hotshot type with very shiny hair and shiny shoes; Mr. Robberbaron, I believe. Robberbaron handed Rochester a computer memory stick, saying, "Here's an op-ed I was hoping you could run sometime this week. Before the IPO, which is on Friday."

Mr. Rochester put the stick in his breast pocket. "Done," he said.

"I want them to go down in flames," said Robberbaron.

"This will help, certainly," said Rochester, patting his chest where the memory stick nested. "As for that other thing, Poitou can help you with that."

"Is he here now?" asked Robberbaron. Rochester shrugged.

Robberbaron snapped his fingers at me.

"Yes, Mr. Robberbaron?" I said.

"Miss Judith? Do I have that right? Do you happen to know whether Mr. Poitou is present?"

"I believe he is not, Mr. Robberbaron. The markets only just closed five minutes ago."

"Can you have him sent here, please?"

"Most certainly."

I picked up the house phone, and looked up Poitou's number in the face book. New York Stock Exchange, board member.

"Mr. Poitou?"

"Speaking."

"The curfew tolls the knell of parting day."

Silence.

"Mr. Poitou? The curfew tolls the knell—"

"I can be there in twenty minutes. That's the best I can do."

"Very good, sir."

I walked over to Rochester and Robberbaron. "I've taken care of it, Messieurs."

I helped myself to a plate of nibbles, though I wasn't sure that was appropriate. There were three choices for everything. Sandwiches: walnut and crème fraîche, watercress, fig and bacon. Molds: salmon terrine, asparagus in tomato aspic, pâté de foie gras. Vegetables: ratatouille, *courgettes farcies,* haricots verts in an emulsion of black-eyed peas. Desserts: poached pears, strawberries and cream, rhubarb tortes. Wines: Emilio Lustau Manzanilla Papirusa, nonvintage; 1985 N. Joly Savennières Clos de la Coulée de Serrant; 1979 Bollinger. Water: Perrier, Badoit, San Pellegrino.

Chester beckoned me over to the reception desk. "I'm bored, come talk to me," he said. "How's it going?"

"You are fortunate in your kitchen staff," I said. "Oh, are we allowed to partake? Good. Do they do high tea every day?"

"This isn't high tea. High tea means strictly that it's served to seated persons at a table, not buffet-style."

"Even with a spread like that? I didn't know that."

"We're rather by-the-book here in some ways. Makes up for the complete lack of regulation in others. Although, in the old days, they wouldn't have served alcohol at tea, high tea or otherwise. It is a deplorable lapse in tradition."

"But at least they actually make proper tea."

"You know what the secret is? Well, it's not a real secret, obviously, or I wouldn't tell you. Each type of tea blend is assigned a different verse from Psalms. The person who makes the tea recites the appropriate verse, and when he's done, he knows the tea's finished steeping. Not before and not after."

"Which tea gets 'The Lord Is My Shepherd'?"

At that point, two men, both alike in dignity, walked in wearing identical camel-hair coats. I stood up. "Good evening, Dr. Pazzi and Mr. Nierenschlimm." They nodded in silent greeting and sauntered to the tea room.

Chester said, "Do you know about those two? Nierenschlimm needed a kidney. Since he's so old, he was pretty low on the priority list to receive donor kidneys. He met in here with Pazzi, and had a transplant within forty-eight hours."

"How did Pazzi arrange that?"

"Illegal kidney broker, most likely. Some poor schmuck went under the knife under God knows what ghastly conditions so that ancient man could live to see Wagner's *Ring Cycle* in Bayreuth, Germany. They only put on the production every seven years, and he has tickets for the staging five years from now."

"You're being facetious."

"A little. But highly privileged people feel they have the inalienable right to have their dying wish granted."

At that moment, Boswell walked in. We air-kissed. "Just checking up on my girl," he said, twirling his ivory-handled umbrella. "A little bird tells me you've done well so far. I think you've found your true calling. Congratulations to you, my dear."

"Oh, I heard congratulations are in order for you as well," I said ironically. He and Heike were getting married so Heike could get a green card.

Boswell said, "Thanks, dearest. How do you think we'll fare in the INS interview? Can I pass as a breeder?"

"Only if you stop using words like *breeder*," I said, winking.

"Rah-ther," Boswell said. "Good gravy, are they still serving wine at tea? How atrocious."

THE FOLLOWING FRIDAY, when I entered Maurice Hall, Chester was frantic. Without saying hello, he held my hand as a doctor would when informing someone that a loved one was dead. "Judith," he said earnestly. "Do you play the piano?"

"Ay, sir, but very ill."

"Well, it'll have to do. Tonight is Symposium night and the flute girl isn't coming in. She has a sudden audition or something." Chester rolled his eyes. "You'll have to be flute girl tonight."

"Piano. You said piano."

"We call it flute girl here. Can you be ready in an hour?"

"You meant today? Now? But I can only play one piece without sheet music or preparation. The *Pathétique* Sonata, by Beethoven."

Chester scrunched up his nose. "A bit robust, but it'll have to do. Put this on." He handed me a Balducci's bag.

I went into the men's loo—Maurice Hall had no ladies' equivalent, in fact—and pulled out the contents of the bag: a toga.

I emerged from the loo clad in the toga, though I wasn't sure I was wearing it correctly. "Where's my laurel?" I asked.

"Women don't wear laurels," he said. "Only Symposium members."

"Really? I was just being facetious."

"Well, I'm being serious. Hurry up. Practice a few minutes if you can, then don't stop playing. You have to be playing already when the members walk in."

Twenty minutes later, I was no better a musician than when I had started. I clanged out my foul tune while a dozen or so members walked in, clad in togas and laurels. I registered little else, as I was concentrating on my stiff fingers and the tapping noise my highly uncomfortable shoes were making against the brass piano pedals.

Finally Mr. Robberbaron announced, "The Symposium shall commence. As is traditional, the flute girl will now be dismissed. Ahem. The flute girl will now be dismissed."

"Oh!" I leaped from the piano bench. "Excuse me, gentlemen," I said, retiring from the room and closing the double doors behind me.

I scurried over to Chester. "Is that an orgy in there?"

Chester shook his head. "I wish. Tearfully boring, mostly. You can eavesdrop if you like, but don't reenter the room or they'll kill you. You were quite wrong about your playing, by the way. It was really lovely."

The double doors did not contain sound very well, so I was able to hear rather clearly without having to put my ear to the door.

Mr. Robberbaron spoke. "As is traditional, our orator will recite from the funeral speech delivered by Pericles of Athens, as recorded by Thucydides."

Dr. Pazzi cleared his throat. " 'Our natural bravery springs from our way of life, not from laws. We are lovers of the beautiful and we cultivate the arts without loss of manliness. We all join in debate about the affairs of the city. For heroes have their whole earth as their tomb.' "

The group rapped their knuckles against their chairs in applause.

Mr. Robberbaron said, "It is Mr. Meno's turn to open our discussion. Please take the floor."

Mr. Meno said, "According to Aristotle, how many species of angels are there? The first to answer correctly will receive fifty thousand dollars from me. All wrong answers, on the other hand, will be penalized, first at one thousand dollars, then a sum to grow progressively larger."

Mr. Robberbaron said, "The chair recognizes Dr. Pazzi."

Dr. Pazzi said, "In that case, the correct answer is thus: there are no species of angels, because only entities that have an essence can be divided into species."

Applause filled the room.

I whispered to Chester, "What is with all this wanking? Is that a real bet?"

Chester shrugged. "Probably. This kind of high-stakes pissing contest is quite common in Symposium. It was frowned upon in the old days, but, you know."

"Decline of civilization?" I asked mockingly.

"Yes. Since the Enlightenment."

"Oww!" I collapsed to the floor.

"I was just kidding. I have nothing against the Enlightenment," said Chester defensively.

"It's my stomach," I said. "Take me home."

Boswell, who had heard my wailing, pulled the door slightly ajar and stuck his head out. "What's happening?" he asked.

"Flute girl down!" yelled Chester, wrapping me up in a blanket.

18

Yevgeny in the Bath

IT WAS CLEAR that I would have to deal immediately with my intestinal condition.

About a week after I passed out at Maurice Hall, I met with Yevgeny at a room in the St. Estèphe. We had commerce, and I put a lot more effort into it than usual, in anticipation of the favor I was about to ask of him.

Afterward, Yevgeny drew up a bath for himself. I put on a hotel robe and sat on the closed toilet. I took a deep breath, then began my pitch.

"Yevgeny, you know how my stomach has been hurting recently?"

He poured some bath beads into the water. "What? No. Your stomach?"

"Yes," I said incredulously. "How could you not know what I'm referring to? Don't you remember that time at the Plaza when I had to go home early because I was doubled over in pain?"

His eyes darted up as he struggled to recall. "Well, what about it?"

"Well, it turns out that it's because of the clips that were used to tie my tubes. They say the problem will probably go away if I untie them, which is great, because I never really wanted to tie them in the first place." I was worried now. If he were angered by my request, he might get me into trouble with Madame Tartakov.

"Tie what? Untie what?" he said, testing the water temperature with his fingers.

"You're kidding, right? My fallopian tubes."

He covered his mouth sheepishly. "I'm sorry, what are those again? They're part of the female plumbing, right?"

I was a bit confused. "You really don't know, do you? Madame Tartakov made all the girls get their tubes tied—it's a procedure of stopping the ovum . . . " He looked baffled. "It's a means of permanent birth control," I said.

"Ewwww," he said, genuinely disgusted. "Like a hysterectomy?" He leaned toward the bath and began mixing the water with his forearm.

"Sort of, only reversible. You really didn't know?"

"Absolutely not. That's utterly barbaric. Is that even legal? I would never have been a party to something like that."

I almost wept with relief. "I knew you couldn't have had anything to do with that," I said. "So you'll lend me the money?"

"What money?"

"I have fifteen hundred dollars in savings, and three thousand dollars more from my father, and I only need seven or eight thousand more for the surgery."

He squinted at the bottle of bath salts, then held it under my nose, asking, "Is this patchouli oil?"

"Are you listening to me?" I asked, breaking into a panic sweat.

"Yes. You want eight thousand dollars. You've overshot. How could you have only fifteen hundred dollars saved?" He stepped into the bathwater and opened a different bottle of bath salts. "I've been paying fuckloads to Madame Tartakov, and even if she's giving you shit wages, which I'm sure she is, you should still have more than fifteen hundred dollars."

"Most of my share goes directly to paying off my debts to Madame Tartakov," I said, dipping my hand into the bathwater and swirling it around nervously.

Yevgeny said, "Don't touch the water, please? You've got sticky fingers."

I removed my hand and dried it on the bath mat. "Sorry. Anyway,

Madame Tartakov made sort of a loan-shark arrangement for me. And I'm not really good at saving. I only really started when I realized I needed the surgery."

"You're asking me for a lot of money."

"But it's not that much for someone like you. I spend a lot more than that in a single month on clothes and such, using your credit cards."

"This is different," he said, exfoliating his kneecap with a loofah. "I'm stretched as it is. I'm already spending the maximum amount possible without requiring my wife's cosignatures."

"This hotel room must have been five hundred dollars, right? We'll just go to less posh hotels, and I won't put another penny on your store cards."

"I'm sorry," he said. "Can't you take out a bank loan?"

I shook my head. "My credit is very poor."

"The fact that I have money is not in itself a reason why I should give any to you," he said. "I thought you understood these things, Jude. There will always be people richer than you and people poorer than you; that doesn't mean that everyone has to pass money down the chain. Because then the poor would become rich and the rich would become poor, and you'd be no better off than you were before. You forget yourself, Contessa."

I then lost all shame. I got down on my knees, placed my elbows on the rim of the tub, and begged, my bathrobe falling down my shoulders. "I'm not asking for money in order to achieve economic parity," I said, tears streaming down my face. "I can't stand the pain anymore. I had to go to the emergency room at one point. Please."

"I'm really sorry about your situation, Jude, but I can be of no assistance. It's not just the expense. I can't let myself be taken advantage of by a common prostitute. First it's the surgery, then where does it end?"

"I'm not a common *anything*. Yevgeny, you and I are united by the belief that what we are courses through our blood, remember? That blue-bloodedness is something you are, not something that you do. We are the same; we understand each other."

"You and I, the same?" he said. Droplets of bathwater hung from his eyelashes, giving him a harmless appearance that belied his cruel tone. "What if you remove the clips and then get pregnant? Do you think I'd allow a child of mine with a freakish cleft toenail to see the light of day? I'd hunt you down and scrape it out myself with a coathanger, if necessary."

I was about to lose my lunch. My innards rumbled. I clutched my belly.

"Oh, please, that's enough," said Yevgeny, shampooing his hair.

I leaned over the bathtub and grabbed on to the rim to balance myself.

He said, "Please don't touch the bathwater," just as I began to vomit into the tub, with him still in it. Buckets and buckets of vomit. Yevgeny screamed.

How very Jean-Paul Marat, I thought, pleased with myself. I wiped the barf driblets from my mouth using the bundle of clothes he had placed, neatly folded, on the bathroom stool.

19

WALPURGISNACHT

Wo Es war, soll Ich werden.

Where Id was, there shall Ego be.

—SIGMUND FREUD

AFTER the hurling episode, it seemed likely that I had fallen out of favor with Yevgeny. Yet this offered me no solace, as it would be just a matter of time before Madame would begin to pair me with other unsavory types until my debt to her was paid. And in the interim between Yevgeny and the new client, Madame would be charging me for room and board at a secret, extortionate rate that was being added to my tab.

I apologized profusely to Yevgeny for my outburst. To Madame Tartakov I was as alacritous as ever. But secretly, I conspired to get out of the game.

Joshua was the last bastion of integrity—or was it mere sanctimony? I called him and asked him to accompany me to Zadie's annual costume party to celebrate Walpurgisnacht, the eve of May Day, when the witches come out and do their final mischief before their summer holiday.

I would have to tell him everything, and see whether he would still have me. I would test the boundaries of his goodness.

· · ·

JOSHUA picked me up from my house and we headed to Zadie's loft in the West Village. She was dressed as her namesake from *The Book of One Thousand and One Nights,* wearing some belly-dancing outfit she'd picked up on a trip to Turkey years ago. Her man, Natalie, was dressed, unconvincingly, as Che Guevara. His mustache looked like some kind of furry slug.

"Very original," I said. "But do you really think that Che Guevara would have worn a Che Guevara T-shirt?"

"Hi, you guys!" Zadie shrieked at me and Joshua. "Come inside. My navel ring is getting cold. What are you supposed to be? Oh, *Lord of the Rings!*"

Joshua said, "No, I'm Diogenes," gesturing at his toga and his lantern. "I'm supposed to be looking for an honest man in Athens and then I fail to find any. I'm sorry, I'm not good at this costume thing."

"No, you look great!" Zadie squealed. "And Jude! Whoa, who are you?"

"Holly Golightly," I said.

"Huh? Is that someone I should know?" Zadie said. "Oh, duh! Right, the call girl from *Breakfast at Tiffany's.*"

I was kind of annoyed that she didn't recognize me as Holly; I'd streaked my hair, and accoutred myself with an onyx cigarette holder, pearls, and a tiara and even a real Givenchy dress.

"Sorry, sweets," Zadie said. "I thought you were supposed to be Miss Scarlet."

"Who the fuck is Miss Scarlet?" I asked.

"She's the, uh, Asian character from the board game Clue, the one with the cigarette holder."

Key and Jung were at the party, too; I recognized them instantly because they were the only guests out of costume. "Hello, *Tante, Oncle,*" I said. "You know, Zadie should stop allowing you to attend these costume parties if you're not going to dress up."

Key, clearly high, said, "Holly Golightly. We all know what happened to her, right? Where she was, there shall you be. German: *Wo sie war, sollst du werden.* French: *Où elle était, y deviens tu.* Latin: *Quo ea fuit* . . . Shit . . . I can't remember. Hey, Thor? How do you conjugate *ero?*"

"Excuse me," said Joshua, who had little patience for this. "Judith, you want some of this orange-and-black punch?" He walked away without getting my answer.

I hit Key on the arm. "What's the matter with you? Thank God Joshua's too innocent to divine your meaning."

I went to go find Joshua, who was with Zadie. She was showing him her navel ring. Scheming hussy! Fickle fake lesbian!

Zadie whispered in my ear, "He is besotted with you." I felt guilty.

I said, "Joshua, can we talk in the stairwell? Behind the fire exit? I want to tell you about something."

"Woo-hoo!" said Zadie. "You can always use my bed, you know."

"Uh-oh," Joshua said. He held my hand worriedly; I released it to get out my cigarettes. I led him out Zadie's front door and through the fire door in the hallway, a cigarette dangling from my lips. The filter was so drenched with my nervous spittle that I had trouble inhaling through it.

We sat on the steps of the stairwell between floors four and five, he two steps higher than myself, among cigarette butts and broken beer bottles. I could feel the vibrations of Zadie's party music through the steps. "There's something I should have told you long ago," I said. "But I hope you'll understand why I couldn't."

"This sounds worrisome," said Joshua, nervously hugging his knees.

"Far worse than you could ever have imagined. You may have wondered why I have no visible source of income, aside from the translation work, which as you noted is very infrequent . . . " At that moment, I fell forward and collapsed over the steps.

"Should I call an ambulance?" said Josh. He knelt over me and wiped the beads of sweat from my brow.

"No. Just hand me the pills from my bag." He complied swiftly. I swallowed one without water. "It'll pass; it always does. Just stay with me a minute."

"Where would I go, silly girl?" he said, continuing to dab my forehead with his sleeve. When the pain subsided, he said, "Is there anything you can do about gallstones?"

I said, "Well, this is part of what I wanted to tell you. I don't have gallstones, and my appendix is fine. That scar on my belly is from getting my fallopian tubes clipped. It's the clips that are putting pressure on my intestines and causing this pain."

"Why did you lie?"

"I was embarrassed."

"Why'd you have to have your tubes clipped?" asked Joshua, confused. "Were you . . . did you have a cyst?"

"No, it's not that sort of problem. I didn't have to do it at all. I'm just an idiot."

"Isn't there anything you can do?" asked Joshua. "Can you remove the clips?"

"Yes, but I can't afford it." I started to cry. "I'm such a bad person. You don't know the first thing about me." Was I feeling sincere contrition, physical pain, or was this all playacting? Do you always become what you pretend to be? I thought of the Yeats line Joshua once quoted to me: "How can we know the dancer from the dance?"

"Shhh," he said. "How much do you need?"

"For what?"

"To untie . . . to remove the clips from your fallopian tubes."

"Eight thousand," I wailed.

Joshua bit his lip. "I'll get it for you," he said.

"No, Spinoza. How?"

"I can take out a student loan. I'll just have to teach an extra class over the summer; it's not a big deal."

"I can't let you do that," I said. "You who have so little."

"I want to do this," he said. "Please let me do this, Jude."

He was dead earnest. "All right," I said. I nestled my head in his lap. "I'll pay you back."

I just couldn't tell him about my being a courtesan. It would have seemed almost rude at that moment, a slap in the face, after his unbelievably generous offer. More pertinently, I was also in a great deal of pain.

Joshua said, "You know, I often fantasize about your death."

"Pardon?"

"It's the logical extension of romantic desire. It's a common literary trope. As in Wordsworth's poem—

What fond and wayward thoughts will slide
Into a lover's head!
'O Mercy!' to myself I cried,
'If Lucy should be dead!'

I smiled, teeth clenched with agony, and said, "In your fantasies, how did my death come about? A murder-suicide, after you catch me with another lover?" The compulsion to confess grew stronger, but I was finding it difficult to breathe.

"No," he replied. "I imagined you sort of like this, except in my fantasy you are a consumptive like Mimí in *La Bohème*, coughing up blood and passing away limply in my arms."

"You know I hate bohemians," I said. At that moment, something in my head seemed to spiral downward, and all was black. I had fainted from the pain.

THE RELUCTANT SHIKSA

Wir kannten nicht sein unerhörtes Haupt,
darin die Augenäpfel reiften. Aber ...

. . . .

... da ist keine Stelle, die dich nicht sieht.
Du musst dein Leben ändern.

We could not know his fantastic head,
where eyes like apples ripened. Yet ...

. . . .

there's not one spot that doesn't see you.
You must change your life.

    —RAINER MARIA RILKE, "Archaischer Torso Apollos"
      (Archaic Torso of Apollo)

I HAVE BEEN etherized upon a table—twice. Once to have my tubes tied, once again to untie them.

In the weeks following Zadie's Walpurgisnacht party, Joshua's loan came through, and I booked an appointment to have the clips removed from my fallopian tubes. It was a fairly quick procedure, easier to undo than to do, apparently. There was still no verdict as to whether I would have trouble becoming pregnant in the future, but at least the irritable bowel syndrome would probably subside, or so I was told.

Yevgeny sent flowers to the hospital but did not visit.

Jung, the very girl who had enticed me into this wretched life, could not be bothered to visit either. My only visitors were Joshua, Heike, Boswell, and Chester from Maurice Hall.

Chester had sat by my hospital bedside and said in a Cary Grant voice, "Ju-dy, Ju-dy, Ju-dy. Boy, you look really different without makeup."

"Asshole," I said.

"I mean, you look really young. You're really just a kid. I had no idea. You shouldn't be doing, you know, your day job. Can't you forget all that other stuff and come work at Maurice Hall full-time?"

I shook my head no, eyes hot with tears.

"Oh, come on, don't cry. We'll sort this out when you're all better, okay?"

I FINISHED my convalescence at Madame's house. I told everyone I had pinkeye and wore an eye patch to perpetuate the story that bought me a great deal of privacy, though of course Heike knew the truth. During this time I read and read and read, buying books I thought Joshua would want me to read. Like those of Benedict de Spinoza, the seventeenth-century Jewish philosopher who, like his latter-day namesake, forsook his faith in favor of proper reason. On the same shelf I spotted *The Guide for the Perplexed,* by Maimonides, the medieval Spanish Jewish mystic. When I saw the title, I thought, *That's for me,* and bought it.

SEVERAL WEEKS had passed since the surgery; I healed nicely. I resumed work at Maurice Hall, coming in two or three days a week. My hours were flexible, so I was able to avoid arousing Madame Tartakov's suspicion. And the company was good; the club members would solicit my occasional opinion on such matters as the merits of allowing Armani to exhibit at the Guggenheim, or whether it was acceptable for opera productions to use microphones onstage. There was usually a lull between tea and supper, during which Chester and I would play backgammon, and on occasion he would steal away for a nap while I manned the front desk.

It was during one of the latter periods, when I was alone in the club's anteroom, that Yevgeny entered the building.

I had not seen him in weeks. He looked preened as always, wearing a paisley silk scarf. I froze on the spot, then said, "How did you find me?"

I could not decipher his expression. He smiled the sort of crooked smile that people have when they are feeling gassy, and said, "Why are you here?"

"Why are you following me?" I asked.

"I wasn't following you. Why are you here?" he repeated.

"Are you a member?"

"No. I thought you had pinkeye."

Chester, who apparently had been roused from his nap, shouted from the back room, "This conversation is lacking in irony."

"Shut up, Chester," I shouted.

"Do you work here, Jude?" asked Yevgeny, trying to peer into the office. I leaned over and shut the office door.

"No, I'm just filling in for a friend," I said, tremulously. "You here to see somebody?"

"Who's on the premises now?"

"I am not at liberty to disclose that," I said, trying to sound officious and failing.

"Aren't you going to offer to take my coat, or are you going to vomit all over it?" Yevgeny goaded.

I said, "You might as well tell me why you are here; as you see, I am the troll guarding the bridge at the moment, and you've no chance of getting farther without making yourself quite plain."

Yevgeny looked thoughtful and cocked his head toward the front door, signaling for me to step outside. I nodded, shouting to Chester through the office door that I would return shortly.

We stood on the front steps of Maurice Hall. The wind whipped through his locks, making him look more than ever like a portrait of Bacchus. He said, "I'm here to discuss my membership application."

"Oh, come *on*," I said. "Do you know what manner of club this is?"

"Of course."

"I happen to know that you're not gay."

"What are you going to do, out me as a hetero?"

"It's not just that you're a hetero, although that strikes me as reason enough for you not to join a gay salon. It's also that you deeply resent gay men for supposedly having created some sort of classical-music cabal for the sole purpose of thwarting your musical career. Or, are you in fact here to rectify that somehow?"

Yevgeny put his hands in his coat pockets. "You were always the smart one, Judith. I went around town asking, 'Whom do I have to blow in this town to get an audition for the Metropolitan Opera orchestra pit?' and I was directed here, to meet with a certain Mr.—"

I said disgustedly, "That's quite enough. This isn't that kind of club." I wasn't sure whether he was serious.

Yevgeny said, "Really, Jude? Because I have a hard time believing that you could be connected with any institution that did *not* somehow involve an exchange of sex for favors."

I was too busy cooking up a scheme to be wounded by his barb. I said, "Perhaps we can exchange favors of a different sort. Neither of us particularly wants much to do with the other at this point. If you continue to keep up appearances, however, and pay Tartakov her fee, I will agree to help you with membership at Maurice Hall, or at least get you in touch with the right people here."

He shifted his weight from one foot to the other. "Intriguing," he said.

I added hastily, "Of course, these things take time. I have only just started working here, and have to earn their trust."

He thought for a moment and said, "I'll give you three months, during which time I'll cover my fee to that Tartakov woman."

"That's not enough time," I said coolly.

"I'll make it worth your while. If you succeed, I'll cover the rest of your debt to Madame. Well, in installments."

I didn't believe him. "But regardless of the outcome of my efforts, three months' payment to Madame. In advance."

He looked hesitant. "Won't Tartakov be suspicious if she gets it all at once?"

"Pay me. I'll wire it to her or something."

"Done," he said, pulling an eye-popping stack of bills out of his wallet, which made me realize two things: that he had come to Maurice Hall specifically seeking to make this transaction with me, and that I could have held out for a good deal more money. Bargaining wasn't part of my upbringing.

IN EARLY JULY, I found myself sitting in the smoking room of John F. Kennedy Airport, where I was awaiting Joshua's flight back from a fellowship interview in Germany. The assembly of people were decidedly not like me: middle-aged Japanese businessmen, craggy David Carradine types, big-haired Texas broads. No glamour girls; indeed, no girls even close to my age who didn't have goth makeup and eyebrow piercings. "Can I bum one of those?" I asked a man holding Dunhill Lights.

The Dunhill smoker was a corpulent, rusty-haired man with earlocks and a skullcap. He nodded and slid the box across the armrest with his chubby fingers.

"Are you flying to Seoul?" he asked.

"No, I'm picking someone up who's on the Munich flight," I said.

"But you're Korean?" he asked. "Thought so. I go to Korea four, five times a year." He smiled proudly. "That's where I'm headed now. I'm actually the rabbinical inspector for several food-manufacturing plants in Korea. One of them makes the aspartame for a famous diet soft drink. I make sure that process and ingredients are in compliance with the laws of kashruth. I do beef inspections also." His eyes crinkled into a smile. "Are you perplexed?" He gestured at the Maimonides book I was reading, *Guide for the Perplexed*.

I blushed. "Oh. I suppose I am."

"I see this," he said. "Have you considered converting to Judaism?"

"Should I?" I asked.

He said, "I can't answer that. But think about what Rambam—that's Maimonides—says. In Christianity, man got the gift of reason only after he sinned and was expelled from the Garden of Eden. In Judaism, man has always had reason, from the moment he was created, and that's why God saw fit to punish him in the first place. In other words, the fact that you have reason makes you responsible for your own decisions. You don't have to sin first in order to have knowledge."

I was taken aback by the man's frankness. "Can I have another cigarette?" I asked, reaching for his pack.

"Ach, no!" he said, lurching back. "Sorry, I'm not allowed to touch you. I'll slide the box over, and then, when you've taken a cigarette, slide it back."

THAT EVENING, back at Joshua's, he graded student papers from his least favorite class, Philosophy and Literature. He was commenting bewilderedly as he read his students' work, saying things like, "This is so bad that I wish more people would plagiarize."

Meanwhile, I knitted and watched *Little House on the Prairie* reruns on television. I am completely fascinated by this show. In this particular episode, Pa Ingalls was asking his daughters to stay home from school to help out on the farm.

Joshua lifted his head from a student paper entitled "Paradise by the Dashboard Light: Blindness As Metaphor in Milton's Later Works."

He said, "Michael Landon, né Eugene Orowitz, was not born a

goy; he was made a goy, or perhaps had it thrust upon him. He had an Irish mother and Jewish father, like me."

The rabbi's words had been turning in my head all day. I mean, you have to be deeply impressed by someone whose convictions are so strong that he's willing to walk around a place like Seoul with ear-locks.

I hesitated a long time before sitting up and asking Joshua, "Do you think I would be happier if I were Jewish?"

Joshua was expressionless. "Happier? Do I seem particularly happy to you?"

"Yes . . . no."

"Please don't tell me you're considering converting to Kabbalah?" he said.

"No, just common-garden Judaism." I was squirming in my seat.

"I don't see why you thought that would impress me, since, as you know, I'm not really into the whole Jewish thing."

"I need an experience that will transform me completely."

"Try Catholicism first. It's bloody; you'd like that."

"I want something more secular," I said, realizing a minor flaw in my plan.

"I don't think you can convert to secular Judaism. Why not become Buddhist?"

"Why, because I'm Asian?" At the mere suggestion that the conversation was going to take this turn, I was poised like a cobra to strike.

"No, of course not. A lot of Jews become Buddhist anyway; JuBus, they're called, or maybe it's BuJus. So really, it's almost like converting to secular Judaism."

"Korean aristocrats don't become Buddhist," I said testily. "That's a peasant's religion. Your suggestion offends my sensibilities."

"If it's not okay to be Buddhist, then why is it okay to become Jewish?"

I scrambled for an answer. "A Korean Jew is a noncategory. And therefore not wrong, particularly."

"You're not fooling anyone," he said, moving the stack of student papers from his lap to the coffee table so he would have more bodily freedom to express his consternation. "You can't hide. In this country, you'll never really be off the charts. You're perceived as Asian, first and foremost."

"I know; it's one of the many drawbacks to the absence of a traditional class system."

"Now, maybe this is an unfair assumption," said Joshua in a condescending tone that signaled an unpleasant escalation, "but it has occurred to me that you use elitism to cushion yourself against having to deal with race. And that now you intend to use religion to do the same thing."

I patted his hand with ironic tenderness. "I don't 'use' elitism, dearest. I *am* elite. Toward what do these accusations tend?"

"You're always rooting for the wrong minority," he said. "You're going to be upset with me for saying this, but don't your own people need you more? Why do you continually want to glom onto someone else's problems?"

"I'm sure I don't know what you mean by 'my own people.'"

Joshua sighed and said, "I just want to know what you are hoping to achieve by converting to Judaism. I know all about this. You should hear the stories my mother tells about her conversion, and it'd be even more horrendous for you. Jews aren't really interested in converts unless they're blond, in which case they can feel like they've exacted revenge against the goyim. It's like that H. G. Wells story *The Time Machine*. The world of the future is ruled by these beautiful, fair-haired, vapid people called the Eloi, while the ugly Morlocks, who are the engine behind their civilization, live underground. But once in a while, the Morlocks kidnap an Eloi. The Jews are like the Morlocks. They like the idea of enslaving blonds."

I said, "I think even Thor would be offended by that."

Joshua said, " 'Everyone hates the Jews,' as the Tom Lehrer song goes. Why should I be an exception? And Tom Lehrer went to Harvard, so he must be right."

"I don't think that's funny," I said.

"I would expect you to know the difference between funny and ironic. Why would you want to be a member of a group whose identity is based on exclusion? Who would never accept you as their own unless you carry the gene for Tay-Sachs disease?"

"You're quite wrong," I said. "If I actually go through the conversion, my race won't matter to them. It's like how the French feel about people who speak French. They feel we're all brethren."

"You Francophiles are so susceptible to brainwashing. The Francophone solidarity is one of the biggest myths about France; remind me to lend you a book I have on the subject."

I rolled my eyes to indicate my level of interest in his suggested reading list.

Joshua had on that arrogant "debate face" I did not like. He stood up and paced like the university lecturer that he aspired to be. "Let's see if I understand this. You think the Jewish identity is so-o-o-o powerful that it will subsume your Asianness."

I said, "And why is that inaccurate? You are living proof, Spinoza, of the consuming power of the Jewish identity. You yourself are only half-Jewish by birth, not religiously observant, and a self-hating Jew to boot, and yet you are wholly Jewish in your self-identification, all of which confirms that you can be more Jewish in the breach than in the observance."

"Our situations are not the same, Judith."

"You're the one who says that a man's name is his destiny," I said. "And Judith means 'Jewess.' So it's in the cards."

"Let me ask you something, Jude: is this about trying to be white?"

"No," I said. "It's about *not* being a goy."

"And how do you define *goy*?"

"Everyone who's not exactly like me."

. . .

IT'S TIME-CONSUMING to change one's life. By the ides of July, I was not only working several evenings a week at Maurice Hall, I was also exclusively dating Joshua, which strangely took up more time than dating two men at once; and I had commenced tutorials with Rabbi Lipman.

I met with the rabbi in his offices at Temple Ohavei Shalom, a Conservative synagogue on the Upper West Side. Joshua, who was unsupportive of my conversion, had nonetheless given me one piece of advice: try a Conservative congregation, because Orthodox was too hot and Reform was too cold, and "Conservative Judaism is the one that Goldilocks liked."

The rabbi wore glasses held together with a Band-Aid around the temple and frame, and had a long, hoary beard that held dozens of bread crumbs as its prisoners. He said, "You mind if I eat while we talk? Want some? No? You sure? So, who's the boy?"

"The boy?"

"Most times people convert because of a loved one. Is there a young man?"

"Um, what's the right answer?"

"There isn't one, really, to be perfectly honest," he said. 'No' is a problem; 'yes' is also a problem. You know, I'm supposed to turn away a prospective convert three times before accepting him. Or her. So for the moment, all answers are wrong. All wrong."

He balled up the aluminum foil from his sandwich. "All right. Today I'll give you a list of books and other items I want you to buy. If you're still interested, come again and we'll talk."

I went to Park Side Judaica and picked up the moron's guides to Judaism on the rabbi's list, as well as a mezuzah, a Shabbat candle set, a kiddush cup, a prayer shawl (not required for women, but recommended nonetheless), a menorah, and cupboard tags labeled "milchig" and "fleishig" (dairy and meat).

I took the items to the register. "Oh, a convert kit," said the salesman. "Would be easier if they just sold it as a set."

. . .

THE FOLLOWING Saturday morning, I went to Shabbat services at
Ohavei Shalom. After it concluded, an elderly woman put her prayer
book in my lap, then the others in her pew followed suit as they left
the room, until I was weighed down with dozens of books. One of
these women would later confide to me that they had all thought I was
a Shabbas goy, one of the gentiles whom some synagogues hire to
switch off lights and perform other tasks forbidden to Jews on the
Sabbath. At the time, I put the books away on the shelf—what else
could I do?—and joined the others downstairs for kiddush.

Following the blessing of the wine, there was some sort of social
hour. A jovial-looking man approached me, slurping whiskey out of
a paper cup. "Wanna hear a joke? Okay. So this Jewish couple is tour-
ing through China, and it's their dream to meet some of these leg-
endary Chinese Jews, the lost tribe. So finally they visit this village
where the Chinese Jews supposedly live, and there they are, in the
flesh, wearing yarmulkes and everything! So the couple is ecstatic and
they introduce themselves as American Jews, and say how happy they
are to meet their Asian counterparts, yada yada yada. When the couple leaves, two of the Chinese Jews scratch their heads, and one of
them says to the other, 'That's funny, those two didn't look Jewish.'"

"I don't get it," I said.

"What's not to get?" he said, walking away in exasperation.

The following Saturday at kiddush, a youngish, serious-looking
man bearing a vague resemblance to Joshua came up to me. "I hear
you're considering converting," he said. "I'm generally not opposed
to such things, but people in your situation often lack a real understanding of what the Jewish identity is. A person can convert, but it
doesn't mean that they have a personal stake in the perils and persecution facing Jewry. And that's part and parcel of being Jewish. I
don't care what other people say. You can't just dehistoricize the Jewish experience and take Hitler out of the picture. Although"—he bit

his lip contemplatively—"although, I guess Hitler would have killed you, too."

I recalled that Natalie, Zadie's companion, had once told me the same thing. Strange bedfellows. I said, "Oh, believe me, I'd have been among the first to be put on the train. You have no idea. In fact, I'd have been there way before you, hogging up all the good hay."

"That's not amusing in the slightest," he said. "You should be ashamed."

I later mentioned this conversation to Joshua. He covered his eyes with his hands. "I told you this was a bad idea."

A MONTH after our initial visit, I met again with Rabbi Lipman in his office to give a progress report of sorts. I told him about the Hitler remark, and he apologized profusely. "A troubled lad, that one. Jews are no better than anyone else in that regard; I'll be the first to tell you that. Many people make the mistake of thinking they can escape stupidity in a house of worship. But we're not worse than anyone else either, I hope. So please don't stop coming to synagogue. Going to synagogue is like lifting weights. You can't really reap any benefit unless you do it regularly."

Then I told him about my other reservations about Judaism.

"Per your suggestion, Rabbi, I tried to keep kosher experimentally, to see whether it was a life I could tolerate, and I have to say, I'm not so sure how I'm doing giving up pork. I mean, it's not something I ever ate very much of, but just a few days after starting to keep kosher, I had a deprivation dream, that I was at a deli in Bologna and there were these giant Italian sausages hanging from the rafters."

The rabbi lowered his eyes and said, "Forgive me, but I don't think this was a food dream you were having, young lady. I did not just say that, by the way."

I giggled and then continued. "That actually brings me to my biggest reservation of all. I'm also a little bit concerned about the laws concerning the, uh, uncleanliness of women . . . once a month. I mean, not only can they not have, uh, relations during that time, but they're considered untouchable; they can't even enter the synagogue. That seems very . . . retrograde."

The rabbi shrugged exaggeratedly, raising his upturned palms in the air. "That's sort of something we're not really emphasizing these days. You have to understand, though, this is Moses talking, and they were very important to him, these family purity laws."

"But Moses had several wives," I said, "so it was no skin off his ass. Sorry, Rabbi, I mean, off his nose. He could rotate between them. While one of the wives was having her, uh, menses, Moses could just be with another one."

The rabbi scratched his beard thoughtfully. "I don't think so," he said. "I mean, women living together, their periods tend to synchronize, right? So they'd all be menstruating at the same time." He shook his finger at me. "I did not just say that, by the way."

21

JOSHUA'S MOTHER

I WAS NOT looking forward to meeting Joshua's mother. Though Joshua had assured me she was a lovely and big-hearted woman, I had heard him talk on the phone with her several times, and his end of the conversation usually didn't sound too promising to me. While on the phone with her, he would always maul bits of paper that happened to be lying around, and writhe as if he had to go to the bathroom.

Before you meet your boyfriend's mother, you can glean information about her by taking inventory of the items around the boy's house. This tells you not only what the mother deemed fit to give him but also what her son felt obligated to keep. Joshua had a cupboard full of chipped china, a VCR whose rewind function was broken, and a makeup mirror framed with fifty lightbulbs.

"Spinoza, why does your mother think you want a makeup mirror?"

"She gave it to me, that's all. I don't use it, obviously. But if she comes here and notices it's gone, she'll be offended."

"Why, does she aspire for you to become a drag queen?"

"I don't think she'd mind."

"And what about the chipped plates? Aren't you insulted that she just dumps her shittiest stuff on you?"

"Lay off it, okay? You don't even talk to *your* mother."

"Well, that's because in my family, when people insult us, we correspond through august epistles. We don't come back for more abuse. I think my way is more normal."

Mrs. Spinoza had been born into a reasonably affluent, patrician Irish Catholic family from Newport, the kind of family that had worshipped Kennedy in previous generations but was on the cusp of turning Republican. She had been cut off from her family when she converted from Catholicism to Judaism to marry Joshua's father. Just to be on the safe side, however, she attended synagogue on Friday night and Mass on Sunday morning; she observed both Lent and Passover. I grudgingly admitted this showed some strength of character on her part, but Joshua assured me that it signified no such thing. "She does it out of condescension," he had said. "To remind my father that she was marrying downward."

"But don't you think that's an important thing I have in common with her?"

"What, that you're slumming by being with me?"

"No, idiot, that I'm considering converting to Judaism."

"Trust me; she won't be impressed."

I SUPPOSE it's because of watching too much television that I am ceaselessly astonished to discover that children and their parents often look alike. I had rather assumed that Joshua's features came from his father, but when Mrs. Spinoza entered the restaurant, I saw that I was wrong. She even shared her son's habit of wearing an all-brown outfit, though on her it looked good. She was tall, like her son, but she bore her height regally, whereas Joshua slouched. The primary dissimilarity lay in the eyes; Joshua's were paranoid, hers were hard and confident.

The only thing marring her otherwise muted appearance was a large antique pendant, a round cut of amber that had grown cloudy over the years. It gave me the shivers. It looked like a cataract, like the blind eye of a Stygian witch.

"Judith!" she said, pulling me toward her into a proper two-cheek

Y. EUNY HONG

kiss, which surprised me; her son, once upon a time, did not even know how to help me into my coat. We took our seats, Mrs. Spinoza and I silently surveying each other.

"My goodness, napkin rings?" she said, pulling out the napkin and placing it on her lap. "Don't people know anything? Proper restaurants aren't supposed to use napkin rings, you know."

I said, "Because a napkin ring is meant to signal that the napkin has been used previously and has not been washed." I smiled demurely.

She raised her eyebrows admiringly. "Yes, quite right. Your friend knows her etiquette, Joshua. Too bad you don't." Unlike her stuttering son, she had a steady, cultivated voice.

"Yes," said Joshua. "I'm a philistine sitting in an Ascot box."

Mrs. Spinoza and I laughed, united by Joshua's implied flattery. This was going far better than I had previously suspected. Why had Joshua jettisoned this genteel side of his upbringing?

She said, "Judith, Joshua tells me you read a great deal."

"Sometimes," I said, prepared to be intimidated by the prospect of discussing literature with this great scholar's mother.

She asked, "Have you read *Tuesdays with Morrie*?"

I chortled appreciatively.

"What's so funny?" she asked.

"I thought you were being ironic. Aren't you?" I laughed again.

Mrs. Spinoza said, "Why would you assume such a thing?"

Losing nerve, I said, "Just . . . it's just incongruous. I mean, you look so much like your son that I was taken aback at the difference in your tastes. Oh, please just ignore me." I laughed a third time, though now it was out of nervousness.

Mrs. Spinoza stared at me and said, "Why do you keep laughing, dear? Do you need some water?"

I looked to Joshua for succor. He was busy removing the hydrangea centerpiece from our table and placing it on a neighboring table.

"He's afraid of plants," Mrs. Spinoza said in a false whisper that was audible to all. "Ever since he was little. Whenever my husband and I had a big fight, one of our plants would die, so Joshua became convinced they were sentient." My jaw dropped in delight and disbelief.

"So that's why he never gives me flowers," I said. Mrs. Spinoza and I had a little chuckle. Joshua wouldn't look at either of us. Mrs. Spinoza smiled widely, weirdly. Her lipstick feathered, exposing every wrinkle in her lips that her makeup couldn't reach. That smile, that picket-fence alternation of painted and nude flesh around her mouth, would stay plastered on her face for the duration of the luncheon.

Speaking in a slow, steady voice, she said, "Never given you flowers? How odd. He's given flowers to girls before. In fact, guess who I spoke to on the phone the other day, Josh."

"Huh? What?" said Joshua, who was tearing his paper napkin into bits and twisting the pieces into little strings.

"Sandy Snell. That little bundle of energy you introduced me to when I visited you up at school last year. Remember we went to her sculpture exhibit, Josh? I signed up to be on her mailing list and we've been keeping in touch." She was ostensibly talking to her son but she was looking at me. I sat serenely, something you learn to do very well when Madame Tartakov raps you on your knuckles every time you slouch.

But Mrs. Spinoza wouldn't let me just ignore her. "Such a dynamo. So talented. Judith, have you ever met Sandy?"

I responded no at the same time that Joshua responded yes. I looked at him quizzically.

"You met her, Jude. At the Hungarian coffee shop near Columbia," he said. "Brown ponytail, overalls. You referred to her as a Bolshevik."

"Really?" said Mrs. Spinoza, deep creases forming at the sides of her mouth as she put on her biggest grin. "Joshua's great-grandfather, on his father's side, was an actual Bolshevik."

I was caught off guard by this disclosure. "I'm so sorry, Mrs. Spinoza. Of course I didn't quite mean . . ."

"Of course you didn't. I can see why someone like you might find Sandy a bit silly, because she's so passionate. Don't you find her *passionate*, Joshua?"

Joshua interrupted, dropping the napkin he was mangling. "Since when are you talking to Sandy, Mother? She never mentioned anything to me."

"Just the past few months," said Mrs. Spinoza. "We're friends. A woman can be friends with her son's lady friends, can't she?" She turned toward me, grin transfixed. "Don't you agree, Judith?"

I should have counted to ten. Instead, I said, "The way I was raised, one doesn't use the term 'friend' so casually. A friend is strictly someone you know well, and not a work colleague, not an acquaintance, not someone whose mailing list you're on, and definitely not someone from a different generation. It would be disrespectful for someone my age to refer to someone your age as a 'friend.' And vice versa."

Joshua covered his eyes with his hands and moaned.

Mrs. Spinoza was a good deal cooler than her son. She took a long drink of water, leaving a lipstick stain on the rim of her glass. She said, "There's a Korean greengrocer near my house. The display is gorgeous; it looks like a garden. Tell me—I read this thing in *The New Yorker*, I think it was—is there any truth to the rumor that the Korean immigrants get up and running so quickly because they're funded by the Korean mafia?"

"JUDE, stop screaming," said Joshua. "Those people in the elevator are probably calling the cops."

We had just entered Joshua's apartment, having returned from a most disastrous lunch with his mother. I swung around my handbag and hit him on the head with it.

I said, "If you were never romantically involved with that Communist, then why would you attend her art exhibit with your *mother*?"

Before Joshua could muster a response, the phone rang. Joshua picked up the receiver with entirely too much alacrity. "Hello-o-o . . .

Well, maybe because you just dug in your claws the moment we sat down. . . . I don't want to talk about it right now. . . . She is here, but that's not the reason. . . . She is, but that's not why. . . . What children? Rejected in what way? . . . That's really original, Mother. . . . Well, that won't be necessary, as no one's getting married. Mom, I have to pee. Good-bye."

I stood there, narrowing my eyes at him. "Your mom insults me and the way you defend me is by saying 'I have to pee?' That's not very gallant."

"Jude, Jude, please. I had to say something to shut her up. What precipitated that statement is that she had said that if I married you, she would sit shivah. That means she would mourn for me as if I were dead. Oh, and she threatened to commit suicide."

"Am I meritorious of all that? Sitting shivah and committing suicide? I hope she realizes she has to accomplish those two tasks in a particular order. That ignorant, racist, tacky, racist, immigrant, racist cow."

"She is not a racist; stop saying that."

"That's the problem with a liberal education," I said. "The accusation that she might be racist is ten times more offensive to you than her saying racist things."

Joshua said, "It's not just what *she* said. Was it really necessary to bring up the Irish potato famine when her *pommes soufflées* appetizer arrived?"

"Just making conversation," I said. "Same as she."

"Let me just ask you one thing, Jude. Would you have had it in for her so bad if she hadn't assumed you were connected with the Korean greengrocer trade?"

"With *any* trade. I know I've said this before, Joshua, but this time I mean it. Good-bye. I doubt very much that we will meet again."

"We may have to meet again, if you're still in my closet the next time I try to get out my coat."

I had opened the wrong door.

22

SITTING SHIVAH

NOT A WEEK after I had stormed dramatically into Joshua's closet, I received a phone call from Rabbi Lipman.

"Uh, Judith, I think you'd better come see me."

A familiar feeling overtook me, that of getting called into the principal's office at school. I was certain someone had complained to him that I was smoking outside the synagogue on Shabbat. Probably that lady with the weird patchwork-quilted hat who claimed she was the synagogue's "chairwoman of ritual" and kept harassing me about what I was doing wrong.

I arrived at Rabbi Lipman's office; as usual, he was eating. This time it was soup out of a plastic tub, which he was dripping all over his desk.

"Uh, Judith. Mind if I eat? Something rather worrisome has come up."

"I know what it is and I'm very sorry. But don't you think it's a far worse violation of Shabbat to meddle and peach . . . er, snitch on me to the rabbi?"

"That's one way of looking at it," he said, looking very concerned. "I have to say nothing quite like this has happened before."

"Not true," I said. "At least two other people routinely sneak out during the Prayer for the Dead to smoke."

The rabbi knitted his eyebrows. "Now who's snitching?" he said.

"But I don't think we're talking about the same thing at all. I received a strange phone call from the mother of your boyfriend, Joshua."

I felt genuine terror. "You can't be serious. What did she want?"

"Well, it took me a long time to get that out of her myself. At first she asked about our fund-raising, our membership, that kind of thing. Then she mentioned you. She asked what I thought of your conversion process."

"How did she even find out what synagogue I was going to?"

"Her son, no doubt."

"I can't believe he would tell her something like that."

"Judging from the way she talks, I doubt Joshua knew he was revealing anything. She probably ferreted it out of him without really knowing what she was looking for."

I nodded. "What did you tell her?"

"I told her the truth, that you were bright and everyone likes you, for the most part; everyone who matters, anyway. That you made a very good impression on me and on the congregation. That I wish some of the others would take a page from your book. That we hardly have any members under thirty anymore, converts or otherwise, and I felt privileged you chose our synagogue."

I was too stunned to be moved by the rabbi's words.

"It gets worse, I'm sorry to say. Mrs. Spinoza tells me, 'I am thinking of sitting shivah for my son. What do you think of that, Rabbi?' She asked very plainly, as if she were genuinely seeking my advice on *halacha*, on Jewish law. But of course she was trying to get at you through someone you respected as an authority figure, namely, myself."

"What did you say?"

"I said, 'Well, Mrs. Spinoza, as rabbi I cannot condone anyone sitting shivah for someone who isn't actually dead. But if you do choose to sit shivah for your son, I'm sure he'll be fine.'"

"I appreciate your telling me this, Rabbi." I began to put on my coat.

"I'm not quite done yet. Now here's where I become Mr. Buttinsky. I don't know this boy, and I know I am being very selfish in saying this, but I don't think the Jewish community should have to lose you just because of this nut-job lady. How are things now between you and this boy? Is it serious? Why hasn't he been coming around to synagogue with you?"

"I don't know," I said. "We're sort of on the outs at the moment."

"I'll take that to mean that it's not too serious, so maybe for the moment you want to keep it that way. I have seen this many times, and the mother usually wins in the end. That stuff you see with the son defying his parents and running off with the girl, and not talking to his parents for years? Like in *Love Story*? That's goyishe stuff. Doesn't happen with our people. Have you read Sholem Aleichem's short stories *Tevye and His Daughters*? They became the basis for *Fiddler on the Roof*. I put it on your recommended reading list."

"I didn't get to it," I said sheepishly.

"In one of the stories, Tevye's daughter Chava marries a Russian, leading Tevye to disown her. In the Hollywood version, Havilah chooses true love over family. In the original story, Havilah leaves the Russian and comes back to her family with her tail between her legs, begging forgiveness. That's how we do things."

"I think you may be underestimating Joshua," I said.

"Oh, I'm sure he will come to your defense, and tell his mother what she can do with her threats. But over time, he will become like someone who's had their liver removed, and an arm and a leg, to boot. He will become like the living dead. He will live only half a life."

I said, "Are you trying to protect me from Joshua's mother, or Joshua from me?"

"How can you say that after all I've just told you?"

"Because all of this *chazerei* would go away if I just stepped out of the picture. If I had never met Joshua."

"No, she is who she is, this mother of his. It all comes out in the end. The truth about people always comes out."

WHY BASTARD? WHEREFORE BASE?

Why bastard? Wherefore base?

        —*WILLIAM SHAKESPEARE*, King Lear, *act I, scene 2*

JUNG WOULD KNOW what to do about Joshua's mother. She may be a total degenerate, but she's never steered me wrong with boyfriend advice.

She had invited me to come over one evening for supper. I wanted to talk to her alone, before Key arrived, so I got there early and made a dash for the elevator. The doorman said, "Whoa, whoa, whoa, young lady."

"Don't you recognize me?" I said. "Got another drug delivery for my uncle?"

The doorman looked down at his ledger and waved me in silently. When Jung let me into the apartment, I saw that her look was agitated. Key sat on the sofa in a foul mood, so much so that Jung suggested he do a line or two of coke. When he refused, Jung and I knew we had something to worry about.

Jung sat with her arms folded stiffly, cradling an elbow in each hand. She said, "Jude, I do think Joshua's very nice to you, and my initial impression of him has improved. But you can't date him any-more."

"Snob," I said. "I was wondering when the other shoe would fall, when I would get this long harangue from you."

"Forget all of that. His mother rang up me, Key, Thor, and Zadie today."

I blanched. Key muttered something under his breath that sounded contemptuous.

Jung said, "She could find Thor easily because their families are now connected through marriage. As for the rest of us, she apparently culled bits of information Joshua mentioned to her in conversation. She's got that immigrant resourcefulness, that one. She found me at my place of work, and Zadie through a gallery that last displayed her work over three years ago. Then the Spinoza woman called the Har-vard alumni office to find Key. When the office wouldn't release his contact information, she called the undergraduate photography jour-nal for which Key used to write, and got the current editor—some idiot sophomore—to look up my brother on the alumni mailing list. She's very charming, Judith, singing your praises but clearly trying to get some kind of dirt out of us, or at least an ally."

I felt nauseated.

"I think she's just a telephone compulsive," said Key disgustedly.

Jung said, "You were too vulnerable with Joshua, anyway. Con-verting to Judaism just for a boy; honestly."

"I haven't decided about that yet, and it isn't for Joshua's sake any-way," I said.

Key burst out, "Who are you to comment on people's choice of mate, Jung?" I thought Key might be coming to my defense, but I was soon disabused of this illusion. He muttered, "I cannot even begin to express my disgust with Emerson."

Jung asked her brother, "How could you object to someone you've never met?"

"He's not one of us," Key said. "He's a pasty, smelly white guy."

I chortled loudly and said, "This conversation is ridiculous. Emerson may be pasty and smelly, but he is most assuredly not wh—" Jung silenced me with a look.

Jung replied, "Civilization advances by cross-breeding. Otherwise the species dies out." She was susceptible to platitudes in times of stress.

"I have always found that difficult to believe," said Key. "Ever notice that half-black, half-white children are often mottled? Do you consider that an improvement on either race?"

"No one here is *African-American*," she corrected. Over time, she was becoming less and less like her brother. But she was still, apparently, a compulsive liar. What could she have to gain from the concealment of Emerson's ethnicity?

Jung added, "You're the one who married the underage French girl."

"Yes, and I learned my lesson. Why do you think I left her?"

"Because I made you." Her eyes misted; she looked off to the side.

Key picked up a butter knife that lay on the table and clutched it tensely in his fist. "Exactly. And now I need you to do the same for me. Where do you find these people, Jung, in front of the men's toilet at Port Authority? That other fellow you were tooling around with a few years back. He was *color-blind*, for Christ's sake!"

Jung let out a loud huff, half-smiling with incredulity. "So what? Unless you were planning to use him as an interior decorator, I don't see why this would affect you."

"God fuck it, Jung, seven different schools and you managed to avoid taking science at any of them? Color-blindness is a genetic defect, Jung. It's passed on through the Y chromosome. Genetic defect. You can't introduce things like that into our family! Once it's in our bloodline, it's there forever, forever, forever." He slammed his fist on the table, still tightly clutching the butter knife.

I looked back and forth between the two, afraid to move. Jung closed her eyes briefly, then opened them and said, "What has that to do with us now, Key? That was Lance. This is Emerson. Emerson is not color-blind."

"Fair enough," said Key. "Let's say you accept Emerson's proposal." This was the first I'd heard that the boyfriend had proposed officially. At that moment I noticed Jung sported a new ring, a tasteful classic-cut solitaire with a platinum band.

Key continued, "You know what will happen when you have kids? The huge Caucasian babies will shatter your pelvic bone as they exit your body. You'll probably need a cesarean."

"Lots of women get cesareans. They don't die," said Jung.

"It's not just mortality you have to be concerned about. One person's life is nothing. You have to think about the baby, you selfish cow. By breeding with a white man, you know what you would be introducing to the gene pool? Cancer. Down syndrome. Pores that exude the smell of rotting meat. Freckles. We don't have these things in our family. You know, it says in the Bible, one drop of piss in a huge bucket of water is still piss."

"Oh, really," Jung said. She folded her arms across her chest.

Key said, "I once had to take a school trip in the fourth grade, to an orphanage outside of Seoul. There were, like, six half-white kids there, and they were all massively retarded."

I attempted to get a word in edgewise, but when siblings fight, they block out the rest of the world.

Jung said, "Emerson is (a) Korean; and (b) a member of our class, and distantly friendly with our mother's family. Perhaps you can imagine why I chose not to disclose this fact earlier. He has a pedigree superior to our own. Mother's family will undoubtedly sanction the match."

"Will his family sanction it?" asked Key, snarling. "You're illegitimate."

"There's no shame in that. The only thing I have to be ashamed of is you. That's why you've never met Emerson." Key was turning pale. Jung continued, her voice escalating, "I will be married and free from you. I finally can have something for myself, and I don't want you to get at him. I don't want you to chase him away. Because we can't be like the Egyptian royalty, Key, keeping everything in the family, generation after generation of sisters and brothers fucking."

"Jung," said Key quietly, shaking his head in my direction. They had forgotten I was there. Until I saw their deer-in-the-headlights blanched expressions, it hadn't occurred to me that the Egyptian reference was anything other than a distant analogy.

24

JOSHUA'S FIRST PRESENT

WHEN I LEFT Jung's apartment and returned to Madame Tartakov's, Justine said, "There was a phone message for you. Someone named Thor. He said he wanted to talk to you, most urgently."

"I'm not in the mood to talk to Thor," I said. No doubt he was in on this filthy secret, and Key had put it upon him to calm me down or give me some alternative spin to the story. "I'm taking a Seconal and then going to bed. Tell the other girls not to disturb me, okay?"

I drifted off to sleep. The Seconal was supposed to help reduce the number of dreams, but I dreamed fitfully, that Jung and Key were Geb and Nut, Egyptian gods of the earth and sky, siblings who were also lovers. I was awakened by Justine throwing cold water on my face.

"Ow!" I yelled, ready to slap her.

"Judith, I'm so sorry, but you were in such a deep sleep. There's someone at the door for you, very handsome. He says he has to talk to you, right now. He seems a bit agitated."

"Okay, tell him to give me a minute." I lay in bed, trying to gather the strength to rise. I hadn't seen Joshua since the day we had lunch with his mother. Presumably he was here to apologize.

I sloppily applied some mascara, put on my slippers and a bur- gundy La Perla lingerie set, and draped a yellow silk robe over it, tying the belt but leaving my undergarments fully exposed. I headed down the stairs. The door was open halfway, blocking my view of my ardent young visitor. "You can come in, Spinoza," I said. "At least to the foyer. Madame's away at a dance competition."

When I arrived at the landing, I pulled the door open all the way, and screamed.

I was standing face-to-face with Thor. He was red-faced and dripping with sweat, and reeked of booze.

I gasped, frantically attempting to cover myself.

But he did not look lascivious; he did not notice I was half-naked. I had never seen him look so slovenly. The wind was blowing through his heavily gelled hair, making it stand on end. He wore an old goosedown vest with five years' worth of ski-lift tickets attached to the front zipper. He looked nervous, his hand shaking as he held out a letter taped to a brown-paper parcel. I took the items from him, confused. "From Joshua," he said, stepping backward with uncharacteristic awkwardness. "I'm so sorry." He kissed me chastely on the cheek, turned, and walked briskly away.

I opened the letter.

August 18

Dear Judith,

I apologize for this craven manner of communication; I know that I should be telling you this in person rather than sending an emissary. But at the moment, I find it more important to protect myself from further abuse than to appear—to use one of your favorite words—gallant.

Hypocrisy runs through your veins. You always thought that I was too caught up in theory and not practice. But all along it was you who espoused etiquette without the slightest trace of underlying kindness.

Yesterday evening, Thor invited me to meet him at a champagne lounge in Tribeca with his nimrod banking friends. As you can imagine, this would not have been my first choice either of company or of pastime, but Thor is now related to me through marriage, and I try occasionally to make nice with him. Several hours into the evening, just as I was about to excuse myself from the locker-room talk, a tall, familiar-looking woman walked past us. She headed for another table and sat alone. I recognized her as being Heike, your roommate.

I have two points of reference with Heike: one, I met her at your doorstep the night I helped you with the German translation; two, as it happens, she is, or was, a student at Columbia, though in a different department from me. She was in my ethics class two years ago. Last night, however, she was peculiarly adamant in her denial of ever having met me in either context.

Thor's friends assumed I was on the make with Heike, so they dragged me and Heike to sit with them, making grotesque hooting noises. As Heike approached our table she looked aghast, her eyes transfixed on one of Thor's colleagues who had been sitting with us, someone called Jeremy.

I gasped: Jeremy, mergers and acquisitions, who heckled me during the charades game at the courtesans' ball.

Now, this cad Jeremy seemed to think Heike looked familiar, too. He started sniggering, and asked me, "So, young scholar, you are a new client of Madame Tartakov, I presume? How still waters do run deep." Confusedly, I informed him that I spoke enough languages not to require the services of a translator (perhaps in your reticulum of fibs you have forgotten that you told me that Tartakov ran a translation service), and that I knew Heike through her roommate, Judith Lee. At that point, Jeremy's snigger evolved into a chilling, diabolical cackle.

Heike made a call from her cell phone and left abruptly, without meeting whomever it was she was waiting for. Her charade, her denial of ever having met me, does her credit as a friend to you, even if she is a poor liar. So you see, it's not just Americans who refuse to tattle; you were wrong about that.

Then Jeremy said, "Judith Lee? As the poet says: 'Alas, I knew her well. She hath borne me upon her back a hundred time.'"

You can only imagine what Jeremy proceeded to tell me. Mind

you, Judith, I have never harbored the illusion that you were a girl unacquainted with the world, but never could I have imagined the depravity Jeremy described. I defended your honor (such as it is!). I was going to jab a fork in his trachea. He laughed. It was Thor who pulled me out of that bar and took me home in a cab. He sat up with me all night, plying me with whiskey. He didn't know your secret either, it seems. Thor was as shocked as I was, but he defended you to the end, which will no doubt surprise you.

All the pieces started to come together. On several occasions you called me Yevgeny by mistake—it's rather a strange name to be called in error more than once. Jeremy confirmed that he did indeed know a Yevgeny who was a client of that Tartakov, of that modern-day Fagin.

You unspeakable hypocrite. To allow yourself to be bought by men is the very pinnacle of the bourgeois, which you claim to detest so. As for your tubal ligation, the reversal for which I paid, I can only assume that Tartakov is to blame. I do not begrudge you the money; you required the procedure to ease your pain, for which I was glad to be of service. I never expected the money to be paid back, in any case.

Thor suspects the twins put you up to it. I quite agree. What a family. After your patronizing me about your lineage; what a family.

It is with the deepest regret that I must tell you that I can have nothing more to do with you; nothing, but nothing. That you are vain, spoiled, and bigoted, I could tolerate, even indulge. That you are a liar, a strumpet, and a prostitute (I do not feel the latter two words are redundant, as you cuckolded me in the one instance and sold your body for money in the second), I cannot countenance.

Regretfully,
Joshua Patrick Spinoza

P.S. This letter is accompanied by a parcel.
Don't get too excited.

With shaking hands I tore open the brown paper to reveal the first and only gift I had ever received from him. He had returned my opera glasses.

I went upstairs to pack; I couldn't see what I was putting in my suitcase. I heard Heike clomping up the stairs. "Oh, no," she said breathlessly, bursting into our room. "Why didn't you call me first? Didn't you see my note? After Joshua recognized me at the lounge, I tried calling you a half dozen times at the house. Oh, Judith, why don't you have a cell phone?"

I said, "I told you, I couldn't get one. Bad credit."

Heike said, "I came home yesterday and waited for you in the room for hours, then I had to go and meet Boswell. I left you this note." She pulled off a paper that she had taped to the headboard of my bed. Heike read aloud, " 'Extremely urgent. He knows. Speak to no one before first speaking to me. Heike.'"

I wailed, "All right, you left a note, your ass is covered; are you happy now?"

Heike took me into her expansive Teutonic arms and covered my head with maternal kisses as I wept. She whispered, *"Schätzchen, Schätzchen,"* into my ear.

25

DARK NIGHT OF THE SOUL

JOSHUA had apparently subscribed to caller ID, for the ostensible purpose of screening my calls. I tried calling him from the house phone several times, but kept getting his answering machine. Suspicious, I asked Heike to call Joshua from her phone, and I could hear him pick up and say "Hello?" even though I had failed to reach him seconds earlier. Heike hung up on him.

I had never been overly energetic, but now my life force was drained away.

After Heike fell asleep one night, I pulled out my very best stationery and began to write.

August 20

Dearest Joshua,
    No matter how much you despise me, this can be nothing to the deep hatred I feel for myself—

That wouldn't do. I drew a big scribble through the page, and started again with a new sheet. I recalled that weird thing Joshua had said to me before we first made love, about how he fancied himself as Faust, teaching Helen to rhyme in sync with him. If literary allusions and big words were what he wanted, that's what he deserved.

Dearest Joshua,

Upon our initial meeting, you gave the impression of being a heurist, a sophist. Your *Weltanschauung* does not permit for nuance and thus falls apart utterly in the face of human frailty. What good is your philosophy if it does not enable you to live in the world? The falcon cannot hear the falconer, the center cannot hold—

Strike that. New page.

Dearest Joshua,

In most literature on the subject of vice (e.g., *Moll Flanders; Madame Bovary*), the fallen one descends gradually, by falling upon hard times while coming under the influence of charismatic and corrupt individuals. Realizing that you would not find this explanation satisfactory, I will attempt to provide a more reflective response.

It has perhaps not escaped your notice that I am ill-suited for the struggle of life. I was raised to be polite but not considerate; conversant but not informed; charming but not likable.

Even as I mocked you for what I perceived as a lack of real-life experience, it should be apparent to you that you are far more capable than I am of living in the world. I was gathering experiences, but with no purpose, as a relief from boredom and from the responsibilities of adult life.

I was raised with a sense of entitlement, as you well know; indeed, this is what you despise most about me. I come from the sort of family where one can say, with a straight face, "Do you know who I am?" "Do you know who my father is?" and such. Yet I chose to live in America, which is ample proof that I did not wholly adopt this attitude; for a time, in fact, I found such attitudes repugnant. But I find that in the end you cannot escape who you are—I was raised with the need to be treated as though I were different from other people. As repulsive as you find this notion, it has helped me to survive countless setbacks and the idiocies of the modern world (e.g., as you pointed out, racism in America, a subject I do not enjoy discussing) with relative grace.

When my aunt Jung first proposed the idea of courtesanship to me, I admit that my initial revulsion did not last long. The arrangement appealed to my sense of vanity, and to my immediate financial woes. And Madame Tartakov, like all good dictators, created a mythology that made it easy for us girls to rationalize our choice to live this life. She told us, for example, that we were all to wear garter belts because that was the secret to Aphrodite's allure.

I am alarmed at the ease with which I became convinced that this was the only profession that made use of all my talents. Being a courtesan allowed me to hone these feminine arts that you find so alluring.

I am not a writer, as you are; my witticisms die, like fruit flies, shortly after being hatched. They arise most easily in the company of men, in the spirit of coquettishness. Outside of the demimonde, there would have been no forum for my wit that you so admire.

As you know, however, I did make a half-assed effort to be a good person. Finding religion, for example. But I was so deeply convinced of my inherent goodness that in the end it became my ruin. I felt my nature was so untouchable that it could not be changed regardless of contact with the outside world.

With you I experienced something I never had before: a partnership wherein I did not have the upper hand. You did not attempt to conquer me. You did not objectify me. This was a language I did not understand.

Why did I become a courtesan? I did it, in the end, because my vanity prevailed over my principles, just as your male pride prevailed over yours. I mean, does someone wishing to be taken seriously really use the word "cuckolded"?

With sincere regret,
Judith Min-Hee Lee

One night I got home to find Heike twisted up in her sheets and clearly hungover. "Phone calls," she said, pulling the dress she wore the previous day over her face to block out the rising sun. "You got a bunch of phone messages while you were out. Madame was annoyed."

"Josh?" I asked, wishing I could sound less eager.

"No, your aunt. Jung."

"Oh. Well, she can call till the cows come home."

Heike pulled the dress away from her face slightly, to look at me. "What's wrong?"

I sighed. There were so many things to be upset about that I didn't want to talk about them all at once. "My uncle Key violated his own sister, probably since childhood, I've come to realize. No wonder he never really had a girlfriend. I kind of thought he might be gay or something, but now I realize he thought every other girl was just impure, beneath him. He didn't want to commingle his bloodline with anyone else."

Heike listened; she was good at that. Then she said, with that same anthropological detachment that caused her to become a courtesan just for a doctoral thesis, "I think that is really incredibly cool. It's a common literary trope that a man and woman meet as strangers, become lovers, and later discover that they are long-lost siblings. Even before they knew they were related, they felt some uncanny connection. Like Siegmund and Sieglinde in Wagner's *Der Ring des Nibelungen—The Ring Cycle*. Your family is like a living mythology."

"Why is it that when someone has done something truly awful, people say the gods have done it also?"

Heike said, "Incidentally, I doubt very much that Key slept with his sister in the interests of closing the bloodline. If you're right about their doing it from childhood, and I think you probably are, it was probably motivated by something else. Pure animal lust, for example. Let me ask you something: did they have separate wet nurses?"

NOT WANTING TO spend my nights alone, I asked for more shifts at Maurice Hall; I now worked there six evenings a week. It was proving fruitful. They didn't really need *salonnière* services full-time, so Chester increased my responsibilities by having me check the ledgers. I had learned bookkeeping and Microsoft Excel during my brief investment-banking secretarial career, and Chester was surprised by how easily I took to my new responsibilities. Having to concentrate on a somewhat repetitive task forced some of my concerns to the background, and I now understood why Joshua thought a regular job would be good for my character. I was just so saddened that he was not around to witness my transformation.

Incidentally, I discovered during my nights at Maurice Hall that Yevgeny was right about one thing: several of the Metropolitan Opera's top patrons and former concertmasters were members of the club. Even so, I was not willing to help out Yevgeny, that knave of hearts. On the other hand, I had a demonstrated history of succumbing to desperation. Who could say how long my newly found moral resolve would hold out?

WHEN A WEEK PASSED and my mood had not improved, Heike dragged me on one of my free nights to a nightclub in Greenpoint, Brooklyn, that played the kind of Euro club music she liked. It was tucked away behind the rear entrance of an emergency room, which proved to be a propitious location.

I'm not sure how this happened, but at some point I found myself snogging a Polish boy from the neighborhood, who for some reason was wearing a windbreaker in the middle of a club. He was probably no more than eighteen, and he had arrived with another man, whom he claimed was not his lover, but then the Pole asked me to enter into a ménage à trois with them, in the bathroom.

I said, "Loos are for waste elimination, only."

"Then just come home with me."

"No."

He grabbed my hand and thrust it into his pants.

"Okay, let's get this over with," I listlessly agreed.

He said, "I'm too drunk to drive now so I'm going to the bar to get a Coke first, okay?"

"Good idea," I said, thinking nothing of the danger of getting into a car with (a) a stranger; and (b) someone who has admitted to being too drunk to drive. I found Heike and told her that I would be leaving the club without her.

"Good. That was the whole point," she said.

I waited for fifteen minutes and, assuming I was being stood up, went over to the bar to get a drink. There I found him clutching his head in his hands. He told me, "I seem to have stabbed my eyeball with my lit cigarette."

"How did you manage that? Are you a spastic?"

"Take me to the hospital."

I guided the half-blind Pole to the emergency room across the street. At this point, I had seen most of the ERs in the greater New York area.

An attending nurse took the Pole immediately to the doctor without doing his paperwork. Then the triage nurse asked me, "What's your friend's name?"

"I have no idea," I said.

She scowled. "I suppose it would be a waste of time to ask you whether you have his insurance information."

"Your supposition is correct."

I stretched out on the orange plastic chairs in the waiting room and napped. An hour later, the Pole emerged with an eye patch, explaining to me that the doctor had had to use a metal brush to scrape the burned ash out of his eyeball.

It was seven A.M. "Can you give me cab fare?" he said. I threw a twenty on the ground and left the building. My humiliation was complete.

Or so I thought until I reached the curb and realized that I had just given that Polish cyclops the last of my cash. I walked home, my heels wobbling over the pavement.

When I arrived home, it was nine-thirty in the morning. Heike was sitting on the sofa; when she saw me, she leaped to her feet.

"You should be asleep," I said, tiredly removing my shoes.

"I'm so sorry," she said. "You need to pack."

"Why, are you kicking me out?" I asked, disorientedly. It was difficult to carry on a conversation over the din of the nightclub still pounding in my head.

Heike said, "Your mother called here late last night. She got the number from Jung, which I think explains why Jung was trying to call you so frenetically."

I was horrified. "I'm doomed. Madame didn't tell my mother anything, did she?"

"Judith, stop being so self-absorbed and listen to me. Your mother wants you to come home. To Korea, she means. Your cousin, the one with the cancer, is in his last stages. She and your father want you to say your good-byes to him. She wants you to fly out immediately."

"Oh." I stood a minute, taking in what she had said. I was trying to force myself to be sad about my dying cousin, but Heike was right; I am selfish.

I asked, "Did . . . am I going to be in trouble with Madame Tartakov if I go to Seoul?"

"Not now that she knows how to reach your mother. She said your mother sounded so frustrated at the difficulty in finding your number, and so incoherent, that it was clearly not a ruse. Madame told me to express her condolences. And a reminder that you still owe her money, the interest of which will accrue at the usual rate as long as you are gone. Heike sighed. "Judith, Judith. How could such a young person without a gambling problem or drug addiction get into so much debt? This is not a small thing now; it's taken over your life."

I nodded pitifully and quoted Mr. Micawber of *David Copperfield*: " 'Annual income twenty pounds, annual expenditure nineteen and six, result happiness. Annual income twenty pounds, annual expenditure twenty pounds ought and six, result misery. The blossom is blighted, the leaf is withered, the god of day goes down upon the dreary scene, and—and in short you are for ever floored. As I am!' "

Deathbed Confessional

I CALLED MY MOTHER on the house phone. She spoke coldly of logistics, as if we were kidnappers arranging a ransom drop-off: she would book a flight for me on her card, send the car to the airport in Seoul to pick me up, the driver would hold up a sign, and so forth. She then proceeded to rattle off the highlights of the social calendar for which my presence was requested.

"What should I do first, Mother, visit my cousin, or see a gallery exhibit in which three of your closest friends demonstrate how they overcame menopause through pottery class?"

"What? Don't be obnoxious. And, oh, how much do you weigh these days, anyway? There was a thing on TV last night about Maria Callas. Did you know she swallowed a tapeworm to lose weight?"

"I'll look into it before I get there."

I WAS A BIT SURPRISED that Madame was letting me go, though I suppose it helped a little that I tried not to make my discontent known. Of course it occurred to me that I might be able to take this opportunity to escape from Madame Tartakov. But the idea of stepping into an unknown future, wherein I would have to remain overseas or change my name, seemed unappealing.

Not to mention that her parting words frightened me.

"Bon voyage," she said in an unfriendly tone. "By the way, I hear interesting rumor. You know Struwwelpeter Industries GmbH? Oh, I forgot, yes, you do know, because you translate document for their illegal IPO."

So Joshua was right about the document after all.

"They are now under investigation for securities fraud. They think there was, what word they used—a leak. They trying now to find out who is the rat. I have some influence with someone there, can maybe convince them that it wasn't you."

"Of course it wasn't me," I said, not entirely certain how worried I should be. "I wasn't aware of anything illegal, and even if I were, I don't give a rat's—I mean, I don't give a flying fig."

"You, maybe not," she said, her eyes glistening. "But maybe someone else is giving flying fig. Like your gentleman friend."

The breath evacuated from my body. I wasn't sure how she had found out about Joshua's involvement in the translation, but there was no point in protesting. The best thing I could do to protect him right now was to dissociate myself from him. "He's not my gentleman friend anymore," I said, with badly feigned nonchalance. "You might as well leave him out of this."

"Be that perhaps," she said. "In any case, if this gets out, there's very little I could do to protect your friend. Crooked businessmen are dangerous, crazy people. Who knows what jumping to conclusions they will do? By the way, your mother is a *lovely woman*."

It was a vague threat on her part, not carefully thought out. But as I had witnessed with the Zeynep situation, Madame was capable of turning an idiotic, half-baked plan for vengeance into something really scary, if she made half an effort.

Changing her angry expression to one of smarmy charm, she said, "But listen to me, what am I saying! None of this necessary at all. Because you will stay working for me until your debt to me paid in full. Like I say to Zeynep, I am not hard-to-figure-out kind of woman. I just want money. Is this seems fair?"

"More than fair," I said, with a voice of cowardice and obeisance that made me despise myself.

• • •

I FLEW from New York to Seoul, carrying two cartons of Mild Sevens that I couldn't even smoke on the plane.

The nicotine withdrawal made me miss Joshua. I met him, after all, at that party of Jung's while he was exiting the toilet and I was concealing a cigarette. The enduring triptych of addiction, waste elimination, and love.

"You look very pensive," said the man sitting next to me. He was sipping cheap cognac and had bloodshot eyes. I truncated the conversation by putting the airline headset over my ears, tuning in to a channel that played Italian pop songs. "Ba-ba-ba-ba-bambina," the current tune went. Four minibottles of scotch plus two Benadryls later, I was almost comfortable.

I ENTERED THE Incheon International Airport arrivals hall and peered out joylessly at the crowd, finally spotting a squat man in a cheap suit and ugly tie. He waved; it was Driver Cho, as we called my father's chauffeur. Whom I hate. When I was little he always used to get me in trouble with my parents, once telling them that he saw me stomping out a cigarette as he pulled up to pick me up from school. We bowed perfunctorily and he relieved me of my baggage trolley. I followed him silently to the car and we drove off.

"Where are my parents?" I asked from the backseat.

"They didn't think there would be enough room for them to come along, what with your luggage, miss. But they are of course very excited to see you." He kept staring at me disturbingly in the rearview mirror. "You're in your father's seat," he said. "You shouldn't be sitting on the right. Slide over to the left."

"My father's not even here," I said. This was a familiar argument, one I used to have with the driver constantly: the seat diagonal from the driver is the privileged seat and too good for me, even if I was the only passenger. "If it was so important to him to determine the car seating assignment, he could have come to pick me up."

I harrumphed and leaned my head back, pretending to sleep.

When I got home, the driver opened the door for me and handed me a key. "They asked me to give you the house key and to tell you to let yourself in quietly. They're asleep."

I grunted in thanks, declining his help with the luggage. I took my bags up the lift, let myself into the flat, and climbed straight into the cold, dusty bed in what used to be my bedroom.

I AWOKE at six-thirty A.M. to the sound of my mother rapping on my chamber door. Late rising and jet lag are signs of poor character in the Lee house.

I let out a slow, guttural moan.

I lay in bed a few minutes, threw on some clothes, put my hair in a ponytail, and walked out of my room to the sitting room, blinking at the two blurry figures on the sofa. "Hi," I mumbled in English.

"Who taught you to talk that way?" snapped my father, as if I'd just been cussing up a storm.

I gave the Korean morning greeting in long form, and bowed disorientedly.

"Ungh," my father grunted, eyes fixed on the television.

"How was the flight?" my mother asked, sipping coffee. "We've already had breakfast, but there should be something left."

"No, thanks. I had a bit of traveler's complaint last night, actually," I said.

My mother said, "Do you mean diarrhea? But you don't look any thinner."

I found her insensitivity vaguely reassuring in its familiarity.

"Did you have *plans* this morning?" she asked.

How passive-aggressive of her. I said, "I have a rendezvous at the discotheque."

"I don't think that anyone who would agree to meet you in a discotheque in the morning could be very reputable."

I'd forgotten how literal she was. I said, "I'm in Korea for one reason alone; what do you mean, do I have plans? I'm going to go view the body, of course. I mean, the invalid? Min-Joon? Are you coming with me?" I was having trouble focusing; I needed a cigarette, badly.

"We saw your cousin yesterday," said my mother. "We sent home the driver, though. You can go out and flag a taxi, right? Take some money out of my purse." In spite of having chided me for the informality of my greeting, they were neglecting to say hello or good-bye; they were captivated by their television talk show, on which the subject of discussion was differing male-female attitudes as to how long a person should spend in the shower.

COUSIN MIN-JOON was the only male scion on my father's side, and therefore the only Lee family heir. Key didn't count, as he was a bastard. When Min-Joon died, he would end the family line. The Lees are nevermore to have further entries in the family archives, which record only the male lineage. Posterity will see a notation in the Lee annals after my father's and my uncle's names, indicating that this particular branch of the family is closed for business.

The family misfortunes were compounded by Min-Joon's second wife, his soon-to-be widow, who had hit the mother lode. Min-Joon's father, my uncle, had long ago transferred the land holdings to Min-Joon's name, partly for tax purposes and partly because he found that this practice brought him good luck: the lands in his son's name rose in value, while the lands in his daughter's name remained stagnant. But once again the allegory of the farmer and the horse apply: good and bad luck are part of the same double-edged sword. Min-Joon's wife now held the deed to the Lee family cemetery. Personal wills are not always legally binding in Korea, so my cousin could do nothing before his death to prevent the disappearance of the lands that had been in the Lee family for generations.

I took a taxi to the hospital, following my mother's directions, and was led into a pleasant-seeming ward, sweet-smelling and prettily decorated, which left me completely unprepared for how awful my cousin looked. By the time the cancer was diagnosed, it was too far gone to bother with chemotherapy, so Min-Joon still had a full head of his trademark wavy hair. Other than that, he was utterly unrecognizable. He looked like one of those X-rays of a fetal chick while it is still crouching inside the egg. It was revolting. Disgust is a very selfish creature; it does not allow for sentiment or compassion.

"I wish I had gotten to know you better," he said, smiling weakly. "You're the only one of the cousins who's come to visit me. What a wretched family."

I nodded politely.

"Do you mind if I rest? I know you just got here, but I'm not having a good day. I hope you'll understand. But I do want to tell you something. This family is hiding something. I know about it, but I don't think I'm supposed to know." His breathing turned to faint whistling, as though his narrow body had shrunk into a hollow reed.

"Quiet," I said. "You should sleep; I'll go now."

"The secret lies in the archives," he said. "You're a clever girl, you'll find it. Though really it's in plain view, as most family secrets are."

TRUTHFULLY, I was glad my obligatory appearance at the hospital was over and done with. I could sleep in a bit, formulate a plan for paying off Madame's debt, and be a child in my parents' house once again, which, all things considered, might not be so odious after all.

And I thought I just might try to see what Min-Joon was talking about having to do with the archives.

But not yet. I spent two days being neither asleep nor awake, vegetating on the sofa with my parents in the sitting room.

This was the most time I'd spent with them in a decade. I could barely hide my shock at how old they suddenly seemed. They found the room temperature too cold when I found it uncomfortably warm, they had taken to eating dinner very early in the day, and apparently they had moved all their investments from the aggressive, speculative variety to safer, low-yield securities. "It is no longer important at my age to increase my wealth," my father said, a statement that I found utterly depressing.

I suppose I am at an age when people start to witness a role reversal between themselves and their parents. Now it is *I* who must chastise them for watching entirely too much television. It is I who must gently suggest that they throw out their innumerable pens that have no ink, as otherwise it creates a great inconvenience for those who are trying to take down phone messages. And the same parents who once forbade me to yawn or sigh have now taken to farting with impunity.

Yet there was something very tender about all of this. I was witnessing my parents at play. My father, whom I had always found terrifying and stern and the worst cultural snob I had ever met, was now addicted to Jim Carrey movies. My parents received a delivery of a half dozen such videos from the video store, and their arrival seemed to galvanize my dozing father, who eagerly popped one into the VCR. We were halfway through before my mother said with odium, "We've seen this one already." My father insisted on finishing it anyway.

My father rented so many movies, in fact, that he seemed to have come to an arrangement with the video store. He compulsively refused to return videos. Having no other choice, therefore, the video store got into the habit of coming around to our house to collect their videos—not their normal practice by any means, but it was either that or never see their tapes again. Somehow my father managed to trick them into bringing him a new crop of videos on each of these visits, so that what had begun as a way of dealing with delinquency had now become my father's exclusive video delivery service. He got on the phone and they came in a matter of minutes; I saw them do it. And they didn't even charge him late fees; perhaps because he was quite possibly their best customer.

I admit it: I was impressed. Even in this tiny way, he was making the mountain come to Mohammed. It was exactly what I had been taught to do, only he did it with so much more finesse.

I grew up with the firm impression that my parents had an unparalleled and intimidating classical-music library, but now I noticed that it included the soundtrack to the movie *Titanic* and at least three previous *losers* of the Eurovision Song Contest.

And my father seemed to have acquired a large collection of joke books from around the world, with such titles as *The Big Book of New Zealand Jokes*. His explanation was that he needed material for speech making. But when I flipped through the books, I saw that he had dog-eared only the smutty jokes.

We watched television the whole goddamn day, with only the most cursory of conversations passing between us. My father nodded off to sleep for a few minutes, eventually rousing during an advert for underarm deodorant.

"Oh, sorry; did I drift off?" he slurred contentedly, his eyelids still heavy. "Television is like a lullaby, have you noticed?"

My mother then said, "I forgot something! I have something for you, Judith." She leaped from her rocking chair and walked into her room, gesturing for me to follow her. She opened her closet and started to open and close different boxes. A present? What manner of present?

"I've been saving these for you since menopause," she said, showing me a large box containing hundreds of unopened maxipads. "I don't need these anymore. Why don't you take them?"

Some of the pads were as big as diapers.

"Thanks," I said, taking the maxipads from her.

I HAD ALWAYS THOUGHT that my parents couldn't stand the sight of each other, that they were staying together only to avoid the social stigma of divorce. I saw now that, though they were constantly making cutting remarks at each other, they had a sense of togetherness that was enviable, a kind of bond that is lacking in modern couples. In the West, there is a popular belief that an ideal couple is one who, even if they were not shagging, would have been friends anyway. My parents, meanwhile, share no hobbies in common, and each still thinks that the other is some bizarre creature, and yet for this very reason they have retained a sense of wonderment about the opposite sex.

My mother, in particular, seemed a great deal calmer than she was when I was little. The volume of her speaking voice had reduced by at least ten decibels. Let us not mince words: she had greatly improved without me around.

THREE DAYS after my visit to Min-Joon, I was awakened by the sound of my mother shuffling into my room. She was holding a cordless phone, which she wordlessly placed next to me on the pillow.

"What did I do?" I asked groggily.

"Jung is on the phone for you," she said, leaving my room and returning to the blaring television in the sitting room.

I walked over to the door and shut it, then returned to bed with the phone resting near my ear. "What is it, Jung?" I asked uncomfortably. We had not spoken since the day I learned of her deep and abiding admiration for pharaonic matrimonial traditions.

"So how is everything over there?" she asked with a tone of everydayness that irked me.

"Oh, it's fabulous," I said. "Why am I here by myself, Jung? When are you guys going to show up? It's not fair."

" 'Not fair'? That's not really very tactful, is it? As it happens, we are unavoidably detained."

"You can't use your illegitimacy as an excuse to pick and choose your responsibilities to my family." It was the first time in my life I had ever berated her.

"Key and I weren't raised in the same house, Judith. You do realize that." I was taken aback by the abrupt segue and briefly held the phone away from my ear at the mention of Key's name. Jung continued, "We weren't really very familial toward each other. Not like brother and sister. And he protected me from our family. For two very messed-up people, that kind of feeling of mutual salvation was very

easily conflated with amorous feelings. It's really much more common than you might think. When I was at school in Lausanne, lots of
the girls slept with their brothers, although admittedly it was usually
stepbrothers and half-brothers."

"I don't need to hear this," I said.

Jung's slickness disappeared. She screamed, "LISTEN! JUDE,
LISTEN!!"

I had never heard her raise her voice like that. I fell silent.

Catching her breath, she continued, "Neither Key nor I ever felt
comfortable without the other. We would try to date other people, but
we would always come back to each other. Until I met Emerson. At
which point, I tried to extricate myself from Key, and you saw how
furious he was. He's not taking it well at all. I haven't seen him in a
few weeks, and that's the longest we've been out of touch since moving to New York."

"How long has this been going on?" I asked numbly. "Since you
were kids?"

Jung mumbled.

"You're going to have to speak up," I said crossly.

"Since we were fourteen. He came to visit me at Lausanne, having
snuck away from a school skiing trip. We hadn't seen each other in
such a long time. All of my friends were fawning over him and saying how charming he was, and I was so jealous. That's when it
started."

"You're repulsive."

"I wouldn't expect an outsider to understand."

"An outsider?" I was incredulous. "Blood purity must be some
sort of cult for you, if you and your brother think of your own niece
as an outsider."

"Jude, you sleep with men for money."

"So it's better to sleep with your brother for free?"

"I don't disparage the things you do; as you recall, it was my idea
to set you up with that life. I ask only that you extend me the same
courtesy. Both our acts are victimless."

"You can't exculpate yourself from blame by making a moral equivalency argument," I said officiously.

"What a crashing bore you are, Jude. You should like Joshua now," she said.

"I consider that a great compliment," I said, hanging up the phone.

I called her right back. "Since you brought it up, have you—have you heard from Joshua?" I asked.

"No," she said. "I imagine you're dead to him now." She hung up.

I rummaged through my parents' liquor cabinet; all they had was some open, suspiciously frothy Chivas Regal. Forget it, then; I would have to go to bed with all my wits about me. How peculiar it felt.

27

ROUND-EYED GIRL

I HAD NOT FORGOTTEN Min-Joon's words about the family secret. I asked my father whether he had ever been to the family archives.

"No," he replied. "Why?"

"I thought I'd have a look."

"I don't think you should bother," my father said opaquely. "Your name isn't in it, you know. Girls' names are not recorded. Besides which, our immediate family line ends with me and my brother."

"Just the same, do you know how to get there?"

"No idea."

Well, I certainly wasn't going to press my dying cousin. I spent the morning calling around different civic-records offices until I found someone who was able to give me a street address for the archives.

I napped, resolving to steal away the next morning to visit the archives. But I was sidetracked by a surprise from my mother.

She awoke me the following morning; not once since arriving had I been allowed to sleep past seven A.M. She said, "I have another present for you. We're going to a medical clinic."

"My present is an early flu shot?" I asked.

"You'll see," she said.

I have said that my family is contemptuous of the medical profession, but doctors have rather grown on me. They can help you change your life.

For the third time in under a year, I was to undergo a completely elective surgical procedure with the promise that it would better my life—in May of last year to tie my tubes, then in May of this year to untie them, and now this.

My mother and I took a cab to a medical clinic in the ritzy Apku-jung neighborhood of Seoul. The waiting area had white leather sofas and white coffee tables, and ficus trees planted in white pots. The smell of green tea wafted through the air, but not real green tea; rather, the scented-candle kind of green tea that you can buy at the L'Occitane store.

The receptionist handed me a medical questionnaire. I laughed when I saw that many of the questions were identical to those I had been asked before getting my tubes tied. My mother saw what I was writing, then clamped her hand on the clipboard, removed the page, and crumpled it into a ball. "Start over with a new sheet," she said. "There's no reason to write down all those antidepressants you're taking."

"But don't they need to know?" I asked. "What if there's some kind of interaction with the anesthesia?"

"I have friends who come to this clinic," she said. "What if the doctor tells them you're on antidepressants? Then what? What will I tell them?"

"Why would he tell your friends? Isn't there a doctor-patient confidentiality code?"

"I don't think they really observe that. You know how it is here. The doctor went to the same university as your father; that means we're all in the same circle."

"Same department? Same year? Same golf course?" I asked.

"It doesn't matter," my mother said. "In Korea you find out things about people even if you don't really want to know. That's just how it is. Sometimes you act as if you never lived here."

"So what if your friends find out? If they make fun of you for having a daughter on antidepressants, you can make fun of them for injecting their nerves with the contents of a dented soup can."

"That's not how Botox is done. Please just start over and leave out the antidepressants. If there's any drug interaction, I will take full responsibility."

My mother and I were led into the office of a short, baby-faced man in his forties, bearing a supercilious expression. This was Dr. Kim. He had that stiff, coarse Korean hair that, when untamed, looks like a pompadour.

"Why are you smiling?" he asked sternly. He continued, "Turn to face me." He picked up a metal instrument that looked like a very thin letter opener and pressed it into my eyelid, saying, "This is where we would make the stitches."

"Will there be knives?" I asked timorously.

He addressed my mother instead of me. "No, fortunately, your daughter doesn't have fatty eyelids, so it won't be necessary to make incisions or suck out the fat. We can do this with a few stitches to each eye, so the healing process won't take more than a week."

I was at the clinic to undergo double-eyelid surgery, by which an Asian eyelid is made to look Caucasian by means of either an incision to the eyelids, stitching, or both. It is by far the most popular cosmetic surgical procedure in Korea.

One by one I saw friends and acquaintances succumbing to this surgery. John Park, a Korean-American guy I knew at Yale, flew to Seoul over spring break our sophomore year just to have his eyes done. Upon his return to school, he wore shades for a week while the wounds healed. When he stopped wearing them, he made up a spectacular lie to explain the transformation in his appearance: he claimed that he had had a cyst removed from one eyelid, requiring a fold to conceal the scar. Then, the doctor allegedly told John that he *might as well* get the other eye done, too, for symmetry's sake.

Had John lived in Korea, the cover story would have been unnecessary. When it comes to this procedure, no one asks and no one tells. Someone might have flat eyelids one day and folded eyelids the next, and it's just understood you don't say anything. Here in Apkujung, it is not uncommon to find thirty plastic surgeons in a single city block.

How easy this all was. They led me to the surgery room on the spot, dressed me in a paper gown, and put me on a slab.

I gasped loudly as I saw an enormous needle approaching my eyelid. Dr. Kim flipped my eyelids inside out and injected anesthesia into the pink underside of each eye. I felt a warm liquid dripping down my eyes: anesthesia, tears, and blood.

"You absolutely must stop weeping," said Dr. Kim.

"Stop," I said.

"You won't feel anything in a few minutes," he said.

"I said STOP!" I screamed at the top of my lungs, that seismic scream that always made those around me tremble from head to toe. The doctor and his two assistants looked at me, stunned.

I sat up abruptly, pulling off my paper hospital gown, which was drenched with blood spots that were already turning brown. "Where are my clothes?" I said, reducing my volume only very slightly. "My clothes!" I repeated. One of the nurses pointed at the curtained booth where I had changed. Another nurse scrambled to pick up the medical instruments I had knocked over.

My mother burst into the doorway just in time to see me tearing across the room wearing only my underwear.

"What is going on here?" she screamed.

"Maybe you'd better reflect on this a bit more," said the doctor, peeling off his gloves.

"I think we'd better," my mother said. "I'm terribly sorry, Doctor. Please do forgive me."

The doctor's face bore a "Fine, more golf for me" expression.

I grabbed my clothes from the changing room and hastily put them on. My mother squared away the payment for the surgery, signed some papers, and got some ice bags for my eyes.

The cab ride home was silent at first; I lay with my head back, holding the ice bag over my eyes. Finally, she said, "You were perfectly happy going along with this idea until you felt pain. Why do you always quit things at the first sign of discomfort? Beauty is pain."

I was angry that she had turned this into a question of my mettle.

"Everyone else has to be treated with the greatest of diplomacy and restraint; you were begging the doctor's forgiveness for embarrassing *him*, but when it comes to your own daughter, you have no problem telling me outright how unattractive you think I am. Not just telling me, but making me get cut up for it."

"This wasn't my idea. It was yours. You've been begging for us to let you get eyelid surgery since you were a teenager. We didn't want you to mutilate yourself, remember?"

"That never happened," I said, though the waver in my voice signaled to me that I was wrong before I was fully conscious of it. "And even if it did, I don't want this anymore. I've gotten into enough trouble trying to prove that I was pretty."

There was a long pause. Then my mother said, "What makes you so certain that I think you're unattractive?"

"For one thing, a lifetime of your being so obsessed with my weight that you rejoice at the prospect that I might have the runs or worms. For another—why have you been sending me all the photo albums containing my pictures? Except you can't bear to look at them? What did the note say? Oh, yes, 'I don't want these here.'"

"You think you know everything, don't you? So clever. But you're wrong. During the Korean War, my family lost every photograph ever taken of us. I have told you this before. And recently, there have been some worrisome talks in this country about another war coming soon. If there is one, I don't think I could recover from losing all my photos for the second time in my life. They're the most important thing I own in the world."

Now, why did she have to go and say a thing like that? My eyes, still concealed by the ice bag, stung with my tears.

"Would you like a piece of candy?" asked my mother.

"No. Thanks."

She fished one out of her purse and unwrapped it for me. She put a plum sourball in my mouth and I felt her finger on my lip. Previously, the only time she had ever touched my face was to check my forehead temperature. Perhaps it is not surprising that I develop chronic low-grade fevers in times of excitement or stress.

Her purse contained panacea for anything that ailed.

We were two emotional retards in a cab, channeling our love through a sodding Hermès handbag.

DORMOUSE

THE FOLLOWING MORNING, my eyes looked like two plums, just from the trauma of getting locally anesthetized. I lay on my parents' sofa for most of the day, keeping an ice bag over my eyes. My father made general grunts of disgust when he caught a glimpse of my purple distended eyelids, and locked himself in his study.

The following day, I resolved to visit the family archives. After an afternoon nap. I drifted off to sleep, then was awakened by my mother calling out my name.

"Huh? What?" I asked, absently rubbing my eyes. Then I remembered how much pain I was in, and howled.

"Don't move," she said. "Judith, do you suppose you could stay here another week or so?"

"I'd really rather not," I said, thinking about Madame Tartakov.

"I mean, is your plane ticket open for the date of return?"

"I think so," I said. Her voice sounded strange. I slid the lukewarm ice bag off my eyes.

She continued, "I ask because I think it might be a good idea for you to stay."

"You said that already, Mother."

"There is to be a . . . funeral."

So Min-Joon had passed already. "Oh, shit," I said. That's what I said: Oh, shit. "I guess it's a good thing I came when I did," I added.

My mother was silent, got a bit shifty-eyed, and said, "Jung will be coming over, of course, with the body."

I was now deeply confused. "Why would she need to do that?" I asked.

My mother said, "Well, it wouldn't be traveling in the cabin, of course. The coffin would come in the cargo hold."

"How can Jung and Min-Joon be in the same plane at the same time? Min-Joon's . . . body is here, whereas Jung is in New York."

"I didn't mean Min-Joon," said my mother, speaking rapidly and stumbling over her words. "I meant Key. Your uncle Keyoung is dead."

KEY, IT SEEMS, was doing laughing-gas shots with Thor two nights earlier. They had bought whipped-cream canisters and released the nitrous into balloons, and inhaled the gas from the balloons. Key got a sudden embolism; Thor called an ambulance, but Key was dead on arrival at the hospital. This boy who had snorted untold lethal substances with nary a scratch died with a balloon stuck in his mouth.

Jung's parents were handling the tragedy with typical Lee sangfroid. They were traveling, and rang me up from Bali to ask whether I would meet Jung at the airport and help out with the grisly logistics—helping to clear the coffin for entry, if necessary, and arranging for its transport.

I waited anxiously at the Incheon Airport arrivals terminal, downing coffee, biting my nails to the quick. I barely recognized Jung as she emerged—she was stripped bare of her gaudy jewelry and wore a tatty Wellesley sweatshirt and glasses. She smiled at me tentatively, with pain and fatigue behind her eyes. I ran to her; we embraced for a long time. For the first time I could remember, she did not smell of perfume.

My eyes welled up with tears. Jung waved her hand dismissively and said, "I took care of the coffin transport; it's going directly to the funeral. Oh, wait a second, he might have been held up in customs."

"We have to pay customs on a *cadaver?*" I choked. Bad choice of words. I immediately clamped my hand over my mouth lest some other idiocy leak out.

"No, no, dummy," said Jung, trying to be jovial through her puffy, bloodshot eyes. "I didn't come alone. Thor was going to come, but he chickened out, thinking that my parents wouldn't be able to stand the sight of him. He was probably right about their reaction, even though you and I both know how . . . reckless Key was." She cleared her throat nervously. "So Thor paid for a proxy to go instead."

"Judith?" called a familiar baritone voice.

I was dumbstruck. It was Joshua. He was standing behind the cordon inside the arrivals gate, blocking the other passengers from exiting. I stood dumbly, then ran toward him, then stopped cold in my tracks. Just because he was here didn't mean he was delighted to see me. Besides which, it would have seemed indulgent to focus on anyone other than Jung at the moment. Joshua collected himself and walked toward me and Jung.

"Hi," Joshua and I said to each other meekly.

"*Je vais m'évanouir,*"* I whispered to Jung.

"French is not a code," said Joshua, looking at the ground. He looked up at me and cleared his throat, looking as though he was about to say something.

Jung pissed all over the moment. She said, "Who's here to collect us, Jude, my pissant chauffeur or yours?"

Flustered, I led the two of them to Jung's family chauffeur.

I fervently hoped Joshua and I would be seated together in the back, but he said, "You two have a lot to discuss," and took the shotgun seat with cold, unreadable gallantry.

We rode in silence. Joshua looked out the right-side window for the entire ride. I stared at his sloping yet masculine shoulder, at the back of his neck. I reached over to tuck in a Gap shirt tag that was sticking out. As my finger touched the base of his neck, I felt a

*"I'm dizzy."

warmth rush through my body. Joshua lurched forward at my touch.

"Sorry," I said, devastated. I tried to catch a glimpse of his face in the side-view mirror, but was unable to.

It was just as I had feared. I was irretrievable, too filthy to clap eyes on.

Our first stop was at the Seoul Intercontinental Hotel. "My mother's family put Joshua up here," said Jung. I bristled; their hospitality seemed inappropriate somehow, as though they were claiming him. Jung said, "I'll help him check in. You can stay in the car." I opened my mouth to protest that I should be the one seeing Joshua off, but I remained still, waiting in the car with the driver, who kept giving me inquisitive looks.

Jung returned to the car with too much bounce and bravado for my taste, considering that she had just lost her brother. I knew her better than I did anyone else in the world, yet I could never tell when she was miserable; no matter what happened, she continued her flirtation with the cosmos at large.

She dropped me off at my apartment and squeezed my hand. "Thank you for coming, Judith. I appreciate it." We waved good night and I entered my parents' unlit apartment. My parents had already gone to bed.

KEY HAD at one point expressed a wish to be buried with my side of the family. No one objected.

My family drove up in silence to the Lee family cemetery, which holds the remains of seven generations of Lees. Joshua was to ride up in Jung's family car. No one but Jung knew of my history with Joshua, and everyone was under the assumption that Joshua was a close friend of Thor's and that he therefore was the sole responsibility of Jung's family. I was thinking about how strange it was that Joshua's first introduction to Korea would be a funeral.

It was the first cool day after the summer. My family was dealing with death in their usual heartless way. "Where's that nincompoop caretaker?" one of my uncles tut-tutted. "There's a foxhole or something over here; he should have smoked out the animals and covered up the hole. Not to mention that the grounds are overrun with weeds."

"He's drunk again, I'll bet," said my father. "Can somebody go collect him, please? Judith, will you go get him? And bring this American friend of Jung's; he seems at a loss as to what to do with himself here. The caretaker lives in that hovel down the rocky side of the hill, close to the highway."

I walked over to Joshua, who was wringing his hands. Without making eye contact, I said, "Make yourself useful," and tilted my head in the direction of the caretaker's house. We climbed down the hill. Joshua went ahead of me to hold back branches as I walked down. I slipped anyway.

Joshua said, "I would have thought that you'd have something up your sleeve a bit subtler than this damsel-in-distress thing." He took my hand to steady my footing.

"What's that supposed to mean?" I asked. He abruptly released my hand. "It was very good of you to come," I said awkwardly. "So are we friends now?"

"Of course we're friends," he said. I was crushed.

We came to the hovel, where the caretaker's wife squatted in the yard as if she were taking a dump. Upon closer inspection, it seemed she was just scooping water into a vat. When she spotted Joshua and me, she bowed quickly and ran to the house in terror, screaming for her husband.

The caretaker emerged in a sweaty undershirt. I told him, "I'm Chairman Lee's daughter."

He bowed furiously and said, "I'm so sorry, I'm so sorry that I don't know what to do with myself."

"Collect the necessary items," I said. He bowed again and went into the house. Joshua seemed impressed. I explained that the man's obeisance arose from the fact that our family allowed his family to be buried on our land.

The caretaker emerged with three teacups. "Sorry, my wife is locating the funerary items. It'll be just a minute. Please, have some tea. I'll need some myself, at any rate. It's a long walk over that hill."

I explained to Josh what was happening. It was strange to be speaking to Joshua solely in my capacity as a translator; we had barely spoken since his arrival in Seoul.

Joshua took my lead in accepting the caretaker's tea, which was actually some stewed persimmon juice with pine nuts floating in it.

The caretaker said, "I do a lot more work here than you realize, I'll have you know. When one of the Lees dies, I measure out and dig the grave, and I ensure delivery of the enormous obelisk of a head-stone. Your cousin's headstone had a misprint; did you know that? I had to lug it back to the stonecutter."

"We are of course very grateful," I said.

The caretaker slurped his tea noisily. He said, "What's his name, the sick one, Min-Joon? Is he close to the end? I need to plan."

"Perhaps," I said, impatiently. "Can we go, though?"

The three of us—Joshua, the caretaker, and I—headed back up toward the family cemetery, with several rests in between. "I'm not in such fabulous health, you know," the caretaker kept repeating. I translated the preceding conversation for the bewildered Josh.

Joshua put his hand tentatively on my upper arm; it might as well have been down my pants, such a tingling did I feel. "I may not get a chance to speak to you again today," he said. "I think it would be most appropriate if I remained invisible. But I need to talk to you: can you come by my hotel tomorrow? I mean, if you think your parents wouldn't be offended by your leaving the house."

"I'll be there," I said, my heart leaping like a gazelle. Even if he were just to reject me all over again, I didn't care. I just needed to be with him.

We arrived at the top of the hill. My relatives looked vain and insouciant and were dressed very smartly; they could just as easily have been attending a wedding as a funeral.

The rituals for funerals are similar to those for ancestor worship. One of my uncles read a prepared statement, incense was lit, wine was poured. The men bowed twice, the women four times. Each family member performed this ritual in succession, in descending order of seniority.

I had been avoiding Jung for the duration of the funeral; now it was our turn to bow. We drew close together and she leaned against me. The force of her being had departed, and she was unrecognizable: soft, frail, limp. I held her body to mine, puppeteering her movements.

As we bowed, her lip quivered, and she screamed so loudly that the birds overhead in the trees flew away.

She pried my hand away from her waist and dropped to a crouching position on the ground. She used her hands to scoop handfuls of dirt and shove them into her mouth. I couldn't stop her; she swallowed three handfuls before finally lurching forward and vomiting muddy liquid. I stood her up; her face and eyes were red from the exertion of expelling, and her teeth were blackened with mud. I wiped her face with my coat sleeve.

She released herself from me once more and knelt on the ground. Before anyone could figure out what she was doing, she picked up a sharp rock from the earth and dug it hard into her wrist, dragging it forcefully down the length of her inner arm, along her vein. Not the way the girls in my college dorm room used to it, which was to make tiny ineffectual gashes across the wrist. As I have said, Jung never does things by halves.

I screamed. Joshua reacted before anyone else did, quickly taking off his tie and making a tourniquet for Jung's arm. Some elderly relative of mine, some second cousin whose name I never knew, politely pressed his hand on Joshua's shoulder, signaling that this was a family matter. Joshua obediently rose and retreated.

"It wasn't sharp enough, wasn't sharp enough," said my second cousin in a booming voice, trying to feign calmness. "It broke the skin, but not the vein. It's as if she did it with a fingernail. And she doesn't need this." He untied Joshua's necktie from Jung's upper arm and held it out to Joshua, who took the tie and then retreated once more, this time standing by my side. He was scared.

"But she's really bleeding a lot," I said, indignant tears streaming down my face. Why had he removed the tourniquet, except to punish his niece for creating a scene?

"She'll scar, that's for sure," my second cousin said. "But really, nothing happened."

29

SORRY

THE FOLLOWING MORNING I went to Joshua's room at the Seoul Intercontinental. I knocked at the door; he opened it, and I caught my breath. I leaned over to embrace him, but he stepped backward, almost hiding behind the door.

"At least show some gravitas," he said. "We were just at a funeral." He wouldn't look at me. And indeed, what else could I expect from someone who has based his entire academic career on moral inflexibility?

I sat on the bed, then leaped up abruptly, realizing that Joshua might perceive any such gesture as a tawdry overture worthy of a strumpet. I awkwardly pulled out the desk chair and sat there instead. His back to me, Joshua opened the hotel minibar and mixed me a strange cocktail; he couldn't mix drinks to save his life, another difference between him and Yevgeny, one that seemed to matter very little now. I took it from him and sipped it. It tasted of apple juice, Midori, Absolut Citron, Jim Beam . . .

I said awkwardly, "How did you arrange things with your students?"

He said, "I got another grad student to take over my classes. I told the department head I had a family emergency. And Thor, of course, covered my expenses."

"That was very kind of you," I said. "You didn't have to go through all the trouble."

"You've been through a lot," he said. "I'm so sorry. For your woes."

"It's worse than you think," I said. I had such a bad conscience about concealing so many things from him that I now told him everything about Jung and Key's intimate relationship. He already had such a low opinion of me, I reasoned, that he couldn't possibly be perturbed by further lunacy from my family.

He was silent and solemn. Then he said, "I like to take a rational approach to these things."

I laughed reflexively at his familiar opening. "Sorry," I said. "I'm just nervous."

Joshua frowned at my levity and continued, "Maybe incest is just narcissism, and anyone who has loved is guilty of narcissism. Like in the Mozart opera *The Magic Flute*. Papageno can only love Papagena because she is the mirror image of himself."

"That's my favorite metaphor. Did I tell you that?"

"No, I came up with it *all by myself*," Joshua mocked. "It's not as if the opera was in your secret possession all this time. *Now* who's being narcissistic?"

I said, "We both are, though; isn't that your point? That you think I'm the female copy of you?"

"No," he said firmly. "You are not the female copy of me."

I had anticipated some resistance, but nonetheless his words knocked the wind out of me. "Of course not, how presumptuous of me," I said bitterly. I looked down at the writing desk, staring abjectly at the room-service menu, eyes welling up with tears before I even realized how sad I was.

Crying, done properly, requires concentration and solitude. I was getting so wrapped up in the act that when Joshua finally spoke, it was an unwelcome interruption. "You have looked into the abyss," he said.

"I never understand a word you're saying," I said.

"Understanding is not that important," the philosopher said.

He held my head to him, stroking my hair, and we clutched at each other, he standing, I sitting.

I said, "I'm sorry, Spinoza."

He leaned toward me and gently pawed the tears from my face. For as long as I have known him, he has had to tidy me up.

We talked all day and into part of the night, nestling on the bed. "That was some letter you sent," Joshua said, entwining his fingers with mine. "Very literary. All you needed was a reference to the 'rosy-fingered dawn' and you'd have the entire Western canon."

I moaned with embarrassment. "I wish I had never sent that," I said. "Please burn it."

Joshua said, "I certainly will not; it's going into the scrapbook. Though I hope you will burn mine, the one I had Thor bring you. It was pretty sanctimonious. And, on the subject of contrition . . . I know my mother called your rabbi and the twins and your friends. That's beneath contempt. I can't even apologize."

I shrugged.

"Can I ask what Rabbi Lipman's response was?" he said.

"He told her that no rabbi would condone the mourning of a child who isn't dead."

"Very sensible."

"He told her that if she still decided to sit shivah for you, that you'd probably get over it."

"I certainly would."

"He also said that I should get out of this while I still have the chance."

He paused to reflect. "You probably should."

"Are all Kantians so tenaciously rational? So heartless?"

"Sorry. It's serious, I know. I have always taken the path of least resistance in my dealings with people like my mother, caving when I should be firm."

"I could never hold anything against you again, not after what I've done," I said.

"We don't have to talk about this if you don't want to," said Joshua nervously.

I shook my head. "Too late for that." I bowed my head in shame.

Joshua sighed and said, "I don't want you to feel for the rest of your life that you're in moral debt to me. But can you just . . . help me to understand why?"

I proceeded to tell him about my debt to Madame Tartakov.

"But there was more, I assume? Something appealing you found in this life?"

I nodded.

Joshua said, "The truth is, I will probably never want to know everything. For the moment, we have to try to figure out how to get you out of this. I've reached my debt maximum already, helping you with the . . . surgery."

"I'm so sorry I didn't tell you then. I wanted to."

Joshua sighed. "I know, Judith. You probably tried to tell me dozens of times in your own way, like the time you invited me to have dinner at your Upper East Side bordello. Later, after I found out what was really going on, I retroactively pieced all the evidence together. Madame Tartakov had Fabergé eggs and Steuben glass; yet they were surrounded by ratty furniture and peeling wallpaper. What else could that disparity mean, except that most of those trinkets were gifts from men."

I smiled crookedly. "Since when are you so knowledgeable about the demimonde?"

"After my . . . discovery of what you did for a living, I read up on courtesan literature."

I said, "This whole time I suspected that you were an ivory tower, a high-handed moralist. But I must have been wrong, because you have forgiven something most people wouldn't."

Joshua smiled modestly. "Philosophy isn't just for mental m-masturbation, you know; I wouldn't do it if I weren't wholly convinced of its practical value in helping us lead richer lives. Philosophy, I'm referring to, not masturbation."

30

DEBT REPAYMENT SCHEMES

JOSHUA AND I discussed ways to get me out of debt.

He said with his usual levelheadedness, "Call Heike to get a sense of the limits of Madame Tartakov's patience. Once we know how much time you have to stall, we'll take it from there."

So I called Heike from Joshua's hotel room. "You'd better come back in a week, I'd say," she said.

"Yevgeny agreed to continue to pay her fees through the end of the month; can't she sit tight until then?"

"I wouldn't count on it. Madame is on a rampage. She's threatening to sell off your clothes."

"To whom, the Salvation Army?"

"No, Encore."

"I said, 'To whom, the Salvation—'"

"*Nein, Blödchen*.* Encore is the name of the store," said Heike. "A high-end secondhand shop. It's one of the stores that buy up clothing from the Park Avenue society types, from the Paris and Nicky Hiltons of the world, who constantly wear fabulous gowns in which they can only be seen once. These women send their dresses, in near-mint condition, to these specialty shops that buy them for a quarter of the original prices. Don't worry, though, Madame wasn't serious about selling your clothes. She can't have you coming back to work with an empty wardrobe."

*"No, stupid" (diminutive).

"A quarter of the price? That's actually . . . a lot. I could get seven hundred dollars for one of my Chanel suits."

"No, it has to be really looking like new to fetch that kind of price. You always have weird stains on your garments. Something you and Joshua have in common, now that I think of it. Too bad you didn't do more shopping. If it is clothes from the current season, they give you even more, sometimes a third of the retail price."

"Thank you, Heike, you have saved me from perdition."

"If you say so. Listen, hurry back, okay?"

When I got off the phone with Heike, I said to Josh, "I'm going to need to make some more phone calls. Can you give me a little privacy?"

"This is *my* hotel room."

"So go to the gym. Please. Love of my heart." He sighed, put on a coat, and walked out the door.

I called Zadie.

"Juuude!" she said, her voice full of liquor. "Where are you? Are you in New York?"

"Uh, no, Zadie, I'm in Korea. So is Jung," I said very slowly and loudly. "You know that Key is dead, Zadie?"

"Oh, shit! Thor told me. Sorry, I forgot."

I sighed. "Never mind about that. Zadie, how do you feel about doing some shopping with Thor? I'm going to FedEx you some store credit cards. I want you to go on a big splurge, and take Thor with you to pass as Yevgeny Slivovitz. If a well-dressed, swaggering man like Thor presents them with a card, they won't have the audacity to do a signature check. Buy as much as you can, but be inconspicuous at the same time. I mean, don't buy five wedding dresses, for example. Try to be consistent in the sizes that you buy to make it seem like you're legitimately shopping for yourselves. Zadie, are you getting all this?"

"Huh? You wanna talk to Thor?" said Zadie.

"Not really," I said.

Zadie said, "He's here. Thor, it's Jude."

"Uh, hello, Jude," said Thor, considerably more sober than Zadie. "I'm really more sorry than I can say. About Key."

"I believe you, Thor, but let's have this conversation when you don't have Depeche Mode blasting in the background, okay?" I repeated my shopping instructions to him.

"Sounds like a good plan, Judith, but can you give me a notion of how much you've put on these cards for the last six months or so? I can't go outside the standard deviation from your normal spending habits, or it will raise red flags and they'll block the purchase automatically and call him."

"How do you know so much about credit-card fraud?" I asked.

Thor said, "That's what happens when you cross an investment banker with a former juvenile delinquent. Bet you never thought I'd be of use to anyone, huh?" His unwavering bravado was heartening.

TWO DAYS AFTER the funeral, my parents felt they had mourned enough for a bastard and they asked me to invite Joshua over for lunch; it was the very first time they had made such an offer. I didn't explain to them my relationship with Joshua; I never explicitly admitted to having boyfriends. It was not a deception; it was one of the unspoken rules of the house.

My parents largely ignored Joshua, and we all sat uncomfortably through the lulls until my father asked Joshua whether he was a Spaniard. I glared at my father, who was impervious to such subtle signals.

"No, I'm Jewish," said Joshua. "Half-Jewish."

My parents' eyes widened; Joshua had suddenly become fascinating to them. "You are? Why didn't you tell us, Judith? No, I would definitely have remembered if you had told us. What tribe are you?" My parents, despite their long *séjour* in the West, held the older Koreans' attitude toward Jews: that they were an ancient and almost mythological race, a race that Homer might have invented, and were endowed with supernatural protection from extinction. "How did they survive when the Phoenicians didn't?" they asked.

"I'm going to show Joshua around the building, okay?" I said, taking him out the door. We went down the elevator and I sucked heavily on a cigarette.

"Sorry about that," I said. "My parents, I mean. Sorry."

"Hmm. I can't be upset by comments that are so totally from outer space. No one's ever compared me to a Phoenician before. Your parents seem totally normal to me. You had me prepared for two m-monsters."

"I am grateful to your mother for lowering the standard for what you consider to be normal parental behavior."

He said thoughtfully, "You know what your father reminds me of? A lion with a thorn in its paw. You should talk to him more."

I harrumphed.

He said, "Don't you think your parents know you smoke?"

"Those two thickies up there? No, of course not. Well, I almost got caught once in high school. One time when Jung was over, my mother pulled her aside and showed her a mug she had found in my room, which I had been using as an ashtray. My mother asked whether Jung knew anything about it, and Jung said, 'Judith's keeping them for a friend.'"

"Why would you be keeping extinguished cigarette butts for a friend?" Joshua asked. "I doubt your mother bought that story."

"Jung and I used to look out for each other like that," I said sadly.

"Jude, I'm cold. Can we go inside?"

"I'm not done with the cigarette. Tell you what, we'll go into the basement. It's haunted. When I was twelve, a boy hanged himself down there. He had failed the entrance exam to enter Seoul National University."

"No, thanks," said Joshua. "Why did he do that?"

"His life was really over, from his point of view. I guess that's why the current president wants to get rid of the university."

"Well, that's not a proper solution," Joshua said, which surprised me. "You know, I wouldn't go so far as to say that I've come around to this classism thing of yours. That will never happen. But I do understand why your family wants to protect its way of life. They have a dignity about them. It would be a great loss if there were no more people like that left in the world."

"Thanks," I said, rather moved.

AFTER JOSHUA LEFT, I expected some kind of parental interrogation about Joshua, but my father's only comment was, "He's not very secular."

I said, "He's definitely not religious."

"I meant, he's not very tied to the mundane. He is monastic. Rather like our own ancestors. He will suffer."

I nodded. When my father's not trying too hard to demonstrate how insightful he is, his observations are usually spot-on.

31

The Cut-Rate Oracle

Owing to various distractions, some much more serious than others, I had not yet succeeded in visiting the family archives.

I called Joshua at his hotel. "Listen, I know I promised I'd take you sightseeing, my love, but can we put it off till tomorrow? I have to go to the archives."

"The vaunted Lee family archives?" said Joshua, with only the slightest tinge of condescension. "Can I come?"

"No."

"Please?"

"No, I'm sorry, Joshua."

"Why, are you worried about what you might find?" he asked.

"I'll call you later," I said crossly.

I took a taxi to the archives. The journey took much longer than it should have, because house numbers in Seoul are nonsequential, reflecting the overlapping gerrymandering systems throughout the ages.

I arrived at an astonishingly ugly yellow brick building. The archives were on the third floor, stacked between a barber shop and a billiard parlor. The hallway bathroom door was ajar, exposing a squatting toilet covered with dirty wet shoeprints. The French call this a Turkish toilet, but I had always assumed these were invented in

Korea. The stairwell smelled of mothballs, that trusty Third World air freshener. Such a dilapidated building was a rarity in Seoul these days.

I came to a door with stick-on lettering that read, FAMILY ARCHIVES, CHUN-JU LEE. Chun-ju Lee is the name of my particular clan, which hails from the western region of Chun-Ju.

I pressed the buzzer, which was cracked down the middle and blackened with fingerprints. A slight, elderly man answered the door, his hair slicked back into greasy silvery strings; he sported a circular Band-Aid between his eyes that made him look like a cut-rate oracle.

Yellowing doilies covered every surface throughout the office. A small potted ivy grew in the corner, whose vines had been Scotch-taped to the wall in a swirly pattern.

"Welcome," the archivist mumbled. "Why are you here?"

I asked, "Can you tell me how I can start looking at the ancestral charts that contain my immediate family?"

He disappeared and returned an eternity later, shuffling toward me with two file boxes. Nothing was computerized. The curator said, "This particular set only goes back to the 1700s. If you need to go further than that, please let me know." He creaked slowly into an armchair to watch a Korean variety show on television, in which two men were beating each other senseless with Styrofoam clubs.

I opened the boxes and was somewhat disappointed to find that instead of rice paper scrolls or parchment, all the documents had been photocopied onto normal sheets of paper.

The papers were parts of my family tree. It took me an hour to assemble just a dozen sheets. I surveyed my dynasty.

When I came upon my great-grandfather Chul-Soo's name, I noticed a strange notation accompanied by a seal, dated 1889.

"Sir," I asked the man nodding off before the television set, "can you please tell me what this seal by my great-grandfather's name means?"

He shuffled over. "Here, see?" I said, pointing at the seal. My stomach was churning—why?

"I'm looking, I'm looking." He examined the papers for a while, then smiled cryptically and said, "Did you know or not?"

"Did I know what?"

"Your great-grandfather wasn't a Lee. He was adopted."

Feeling dizzy, I sat down and said, "Do you have any documentation of this?"

He walked off, opened and shut several drawers, groaning vociferously at the pain of having to bend over, then brought over another file box and flipped through it.

"A letter," he said. "It looks as though there's a letter. Can you read Chinese?"

"Not very well. No. Can you translate it for me?"

He sighed. "I'd really rather not. I'll make you a copy, though."

"You're not going to make a note of this finding of yours in the archives, are you? I mean, I certainly don't give a toss, but I wouldn't want to upset other members of my family."

The man started peeling a clementine orange. "No, I'm not going to record that your ancestor's a fraud. The silence of history is part of what he paid for, as I said, so I'm ethically bound to comply. On the other hand, I'm certainly not going to destroy the evidence. Don't put those papers away; people always file them in the wrong order and then they can never be found again. Let me do it." He handed me a copy of the letter.

I thanked the archivist and left. On my way out of the building I got a big, hearty whiff of the Turkish toilet, enough to nauseate me for the whole ride home.

WHEN I ARRIVED at my parents' house, they were watching an incredibly loud, violent television movie. My mother said tiredly, "Your friend Zadie called. She left her number."

I walked over to the bar and pulled out my parents' ancient curdy Chivas Regal. "I'm getting rid of this," I said to my parents.

They grunted, eyes glued to the television set.

After drinking several gloopy whiskey shots, I rang up Zadie, mis-dialing several times. "Hi, Zadie? You rang? You better have good news because I'm having a shitty day. You sell the clothes? How much did you get?"

Zadie said weakly, "We really tried, Jude. We went to the stores for which you had credit cards, and up to that point there was no prob-lem, actually. We didn't raise any eyebrows; I guess those kinds of stores really do see customers haul off that much stuff regularly. And we kept to a respectable spending limit that Thor calculated so the stores wouldn't get a computer alert to call the credit department, though Yevgeny will hit the roof when he gets the monthly statement. We spent, all told, over seventy-four thousand dollars."

I sighed. "For which you got . . . anything close to half that amount? My debt, last I checked with Madame, is seventy-five thou-sand dollars, maybe more."

"We took the clothes to those secondhand stores on your list. Your friend was right; some of their stuff was really nice, Jude. You and I should shop there sometime. The shopkeepers were delighted to take the items off our hands, but you didn't warn us that they will only pay for a certain amount on the spot. The rest we left behind to be sold on consignment—I mean, you only get paid when the garment gets sold. Thirty days after, actually."

I froze. "Not cash on the barrel?"

"No. Apparently they only did that for Jackie O, because it was the only way she could raise large amounts of cash when she was with Aristotle Onassis. He wouldn't give her any money, just credit cards. Did you know that about Jackie O?"

"No, I didn't," I said. "Can we focus, please? How much ready cash do you have right at this moment?" I covered my eyes with my hands.

"Only nine thousand dollars."

I cursed for five minutes straight. "This whole thing was for noth-ing. I just wasted your time."

"Sorry!" said Zadie. "But some good did come out of it. Speaking of which, I didn't actually sell everything. We're keeping this ring we got. Is that okay?"

"A ring?"

"An engagement ring. It's just a little one. It's very tasteful, even if the manner of its acquisition was not."

"Whose engagement ring?"

Zadie sighed. "You really are depressed, aren't you? Think! Think!" Over the phone, I could hear her snapping her fingers rapidly in a "look lively" fashion.

"No," I said. "You and Thor? Just like that?"

"Just like that," she said buoyantly. "Spur of the moment. When we were on the command shopping spree, Thor saw a little sapphire ring at Bendel and said, 'Look, Zadie, we could get engaged for free and exact revenge on this Yevgeny person at the same time.' And I agreed. So? Aren't you going to say anything?"

"You could do worse, Zadie," I said. "You could do worse."

"UN-FUCKING BELIEVABLE," Joshua said later that day, when I told him Thor and Zadie's dubiously good news. "I knew nothing about it, I swear. They must have been bonking on the sly for ages. What a match. It's practically incest." At the mention of that word, his face looked pinched. "Sorry, I didn't mean . . ."

"No, no, you're right," I said, almost insulted that Joshua felt he had to tiptoe around me. "Our little group all paired off, I guess is what you meant. That's the kind of thing that happens when you don't vary your social circle. A misogynist homophobe who refers to Arabs as towel heads ends up with a feminist lesbian Lebanese."

Joshua said, "Let's remember to make them godparents to our children. That would really get Thor's goat. To have to be godparent to a Jewish child." He blushed as he realized he was talking about our mutual children. I pretended to ignore it, but my heart sang. Would our children be Kantians, I wondered.

Suddenly Joshua squinted at me and said, "Are you wearing purple eye shadow?"

I explained to him the bit about the aborted ethnicity reassignment surgery.

"What a fucking present," said Joshua. "That's like when my cousin got a nose job for her sixteenth birthday. Only a Jewish or Korean mother would think that plastic surgery is an appropriate gift for her daughter."

EZRA OF THE PENINSULA

I KNEW what I wanted to do with the nine thousand dollars Zadie had squirreled away for me. But Joshua wouldn't hear of it.

"But it's not enough to help me, anyway," I protested. "You can use it to repay your student loan, or at least the portion you took out for my surgery. Don't tell me you're refusing it because it was gotten by ill means."

Joshua shook his head. "I told you in my letter, I never expected that money to be paid back."

IT WAS DAY FIVE of our *séjour* in Korea. I was scheduled to meet up with Ezra Dwight. Joshua, who had met Ezra briefly at Jung's dinner party, was less than delighted, but Ezra was the only person I could think of outside of my own family who could read enough Chinese to translate my great-grandfather's letter.

Joshua and I met with Ezra at the NATO Café, tucked away in the basement of an otherwise grim commercial building. It was a favorite hangout of mine and Ezra's, as it had big comfy sofas and the staff was really good about letting us choose the CDs we wanted them to play. Coffee was eight dollars and severely watered down, but they let us stay as long as we wanted. Especially now that Ezra was famous.

Ezra was reading a Korean newspaper when we walked in. He was dressed like a Yakuza, in a pin-striped black suit, black shirt, and black tie. He waved at me and Joshua and folded up his newspaper. Joshua had a dodgy look as we were choosing seats; he didn't want either of us to sit next to Ezra. Joshua resolved the situation indelicately, by putting our coats and bags on the armchair next to Ezra, so that no one could sit there.

Embarrassed, I started fishing around in my purse. I said, "Okay, Ezra, here's the letter. It's to do with my great-grandfather's alleged adoption. How's your Chinese these days? Can you do this?"

Ezra looked it over studiously and pursed his lips. "I'll take this home and work on it, okay? I've forgotten a lot of Chinese, but presumably not as much as you." He opened his briefcase and put the letter in it.

Joshua said, "For someone who supposedly speaks so many languages, Jude, you sure are having to use translators a lot. Remember that illegal German stock offering memo I helped you with? Whatever happened with that, by the way?"

"Later. Later," I said, baring clenched teeth at him.

Ezra, as usual, didn't notice. He peered at Joshua over awful pink-tinted sunglasses and said, "And you, Jesse, how do you find Seoul?"

"The name's Joshua," Joshua said. "A bit congested. But a good deal nicer than Judith had warned. It must have been interesting growing up here. Jude showed me her anti-Communist posters. I couldn't have imagined that an elementary school would prove such an ideological battleground."

Ezra said, "Well, actually, Joshua, I think there's something to be said for coming to school every day believing sincerely that the future of humanity depends on your fervent participation. Koreans aren't jaded like Westerners are." He punctuated his words with a bored wave of the hand.

Joshua cleared his throat and shifted in his chair.

Ezra interjected, "Anyone for a game of cards? Do you have any?"

"No, we don't," I said.

Ezra said, "No worries. I'll take care of it." He snapped his fingers and the waiter came running, and Ezra passed him some money and asked him to run out and buy us a deck of cards.

Joshua was incredulous. "You fancy yourself Lawrence of Arabia, but really you are Kurtz from *Heart of Darkness*," he said to Ezra, plucking our coats from the seat next to Ezra and storming out of the NATO Café. I mouthed "Sorry" to Ezra. Thick-skinned as ever, he shrugged and made the "I'll call you" sign by extending his thumb and pinkie from his fist and waving it next to his ear.

Joshua and I took a cab back to his hotel. When we got to his room, I turned on the television. Joshua said, "Ezra is a complete poseur. This 'No one knows Asia like I know Asia' thing."

"But he did live in Korea his whole life."

"Sure, as a foreigner. As a white male. As the descendant of an old trading family that apparently cofounded one of Korea's first universities. As a TV star, who in America would not even get a role playing the role of the Wall in a Catskills production of *A Midsummer Night's Dream*. I've seen the way people on the street look at him, as if that prick is some kind of glorious cherub. He's enjoyed that gawking admiration his whole life, and now it's part of his character. No wonder he couldn't hack it in the States."

"That's funny, because he thinks I'm the one who couldn't hack it in Korea. He and I are the same."

"No way. Don't you dare compare yourself to him. It's normal for an Asian person to live in America. It is not normal for a white person to want to live in Asia."

"Very enlightened, Spinoza."

"In his case, it's true. He lives here to be given special treatment. You had that option, with your family's background, but you didn't take it. That's admirable, but there's one thing I still don't understand. You came into this world with the blessing of knowing where you come from, with every ancestor documented through the ages. And yet you're completely unmoored. History is supposed to give one solidity, but not in your case."

"If you're trying to say my unhappiness is by my own hand,

fine, I agree with you. But at least I fared better than poor Jung."

Joshua was downcast for a moment before saying, "I hate to say this, but it's probably a good thing Key is dead. Otherwise they'd have had to carry on this affair their whole lives, through marriages and children and grandchildren."

I began to cry.

"It's okay," he said. "He can't hurt her now."

"I miss her," I said. "And I miss him. The Dormouse is dead."

33

THE WET NURSE

EZRA CALLED the next day.

"I'm sorry about Joshua's behavior yesterday," I said.

"Huh? What? I thought we were hitting it off."

"Whatever. Did you take a stab at the letter?"

"Yes, and Jude, you are not going to believe what it says."

*"Je vous écoute,"** I said, trying to sound nonchalant.

"Okay. An official scribe signed and sealed the letter, but it was a wet nurse who dictated it to him."

"A fucking wet nurse? Of what pertinence is that?"

"Of extreme pertinence. She's your great-grandmother. My oh my, Jude, you're descended from a teat-for-hire. And an illiterate one at that, if she had to hire a scribe. The letter says something like the following:

Greetings to All Concerned Parties:

I am writing this letter, by the aid of a scribe and in the presence of two witnesses, to reveal a secret. Previously, this disclosure would have deprived me of the material comfort that has bought my silence all these years. As it happens, however, the issuers of this bribe have defaulted in their final largesse, so the truth can little hurt me now.

*"I'm listening."

254

Master and Mistress Lee, my liege and lady who retained me years ago as a wet nurse to their son, Lee Chul-Soo, have these fifteen years paid me to conceal the following: I am not their boy's wet nurse. I am his mother.

Now, it is well known that Chul-Soo is not the natural-born son of my lord and lady; they have in fact just legally adopted him, claiming him to be the orphaned son of a distant cousin. This adoption has been sealed by the royal magistrate, as is necessary in cases where a large legacy is involved. But this adoption is void, as Chul-Soo is not well-born, but the son of an illiterate farmhand and a wet nurse.

My husband and I were descended from agricultural laborers who have been in the Lee fiefdom for generations. We were born as *ssang nom*, of the lowest social class.

I was married off at sixteen. In the fullness of time, I became large with child, and gave birth to a son. Then Mistress Lee, the wife of our lord and master, gave birth shortly after I did, to a sickly, colicky, wan little boy. She asked me, peremptorily, to become wet nurse to her child. I did not have a choice in the matter; my husband's livelihood depended on our master's and mistress's good humor.

Mistress Lee moved me out of my own house and into the main house, so that I could feed only her baby and not my own. Fortunately, my son, Chul-Soo, was robust and jolly and grew strong even on milk from goats and cows, administered by my own mother. Mistress Lee's boy, meanwhile, grew weaker and cried more with each passing day. He seemed only to imbibe the ill feeling and resentment I passed on to him through my milk.

Mistress Lee slapped me whenever her boy cried. "What have you been eating?" she would ask. She had the cook put me on a strict diet. She locked me in a room and had bowls of dates brought to me, and she would not release me until I had eaten them all. This was all meant to provide the optimal nutrition for a strong, virile boy. But he died suddenly in his sleep at six months.

Madame Lee blamed me for the death of her son and claimed mine for herself. For relinquishing my son, and for my silence, I have heretofore been amply paid. But if another installment is not made forthwith, I will release this missive to the royal magistrate, who will have no choice but to nullify Chul-Soo's adoption. This will strip him of his title and legacy. Though he is the child of my womb, I am willing to risk this in order that right be done by me.

If, on the other hand, my demands are met, all will be better off: Master and Mistress Lee can protect their legacy through their son, my descendants will live as nobles, and no one will be the wiser. Posterity will forgive me for my venality.

Signed: [Seal] Witnesses: [Seal] [Seal]
The nineteenth day of the sixth month, 1889

"So," said Ezra, "Are you impressed? By my translation skills, I mean?"

I sighed. "Heike was right," I said, recalling her thesis on wet nurses and how they destroyed aristocratic families.

"Who's Heike? Is she cute?"

I thanked Ezra and hung up.

My ancestor was a wet nurse, one who tearlessly sold her baby. No wonder we're such assholes.

I had no way of coping with this discovery. If I had been more like Joshua, I would have appealed to the wisdom of great literary masterpieces. But all the literature on the subject of mistaken parentage—*Lorna Doone, Tom Jones, Tess of the d'Urbervilles*—involve children born into the lower classes who later learn that they are actually of noble birth. There is very little guidance on the reverse scenario, in which an uppity girl raised as a blue blood discovers that she is descended from an illiterate wet nurse. To what text do I turn for guidance? What homilies can offer me solace now?

. . .

JOSHUA'S REACTION to the news of my ancestry was predictable in its stoicism, but surprising in its content: "I never once doubted your stories about your background, but I always suspected that *you* doubted them."

"Good for you," I said.

"Sorry," said Joshua. "I guess this must be upsetting for you, huh? But it's actually kind of cool, don't you think? Your ancestors had pluck. I always told you that you were too smart not to have some peasant stock in you."

I could not be so blasé. I would never get back those years spent under that suffocating cloud of gloom that hovered over our family, arising from the resignation that we could never again achieve the glory that, as it turned out, we never had to begin with.

When I told my mother of my findings in the family archives, her response was strangely flippant. "Don't tell your father," she said with the slightest traces of a grin, which meant that she wanted to be the one to tell him herself.

"But I bet he already knows." She looked disappointed.

She continued, "You may find this hard to accept, but these things matter far more to you than they ever did to my generation. It is often the case that Koreans living abroad become more Korean, more traditional, than their counterparts living in Korea. Being uprooted made a zealot of you."

"Oh, *I* became a zealot? Is that why Father forbade me to become a professional pianist, deeming it an unfit career for an aristocrat?"

"Forbade you? No one forbade you. It just fell away. You had no talent."

"What?!" So I wasn't delusional after all; I really was raised amid cruelty.

"I shouldn't have said that, probably," back-pedaled my mother. "What I meant was, don't you remember? We took you to that piano competition. One judge said, 'Your reach exceeds your grasp,' and another said, 'You do not possess the emotional depth for this piece.' You became angry with us, accusing us of forcing you to play a piece that was too difficult for you. You gave up piano of your own accord."

Uh-oh. Now that I thought about it, her version of events seemed accurate. How very disruptive is the truth, how violent. But there was more to the story, and I was remembering it now. I said indignantly, "You heaped insults on me for days. And you co-opted the phrase 'Your reach exceeds your grasp' and relished saying it to me for years thereafter."

My mother shrugged slightly and said, "You needed toughening. The world your father thinks he grew up in was gone before he had a chance to grow up in it. Or maybe it never was. His parents did him a disservice by shielding him from this fact, and your father passed on this disservice to you. But that doesn't mean you should blame him. You had other choices besides the ones he gave you. You never paid any attention to what *I* wanted for you."

"What did you ever want for me, other than for me to have an incorrigible sense of self-loathing?"

My mother was silent, and even paler than usual. "Just because I couldn't be the sort of mother you wanted doesn't mean that I had nothing to teach you. I got a Ph.D. in the hard sciences in the sixties; women didn't do that in those days, Korean or otherwise. It didn't do any good, apparently. I hoped you would be strong, ambitious, hopeful. Instead you took after your father's side, and became so weary while you were still a child. I imagine that it's my fault. Why would any child listen to the colder of the two parents. But my responsibility was to protect you first. I bribed your teachers. You didn't know about that, did you? I don't badger people into expressing gratitude the way your father does."

I was perplexed. "Bribed them how? How was that supposed to protect me?"

"When you were attending school here in Seoul. You came home crying every day because they used corporal punishment. Sometimes you came home with welts on your shins; sometimes you trembled just from witnessing someone else getting thrashed. I paid off your

teachers every month not to hit you. Didn't you notice that the pad-
dling dropped off after the first few months?"

Actually, I'd always wondered about that.

I never cried before my mother if I could possibly help it, because
she would always respond by literally looking the other way. But I
was finding it difficult to hold back. I was moved by the act she had
kept secret, and also sorry for her that this was really the best she
could do.

I said as flatly as I could manage, "Our family does everything
through bribes, it seems. So be it. But tell me one thing: why are you
so cold?"

"If you must know . . . " said my mother, bearing the sincere but
worried expression of a tone-deaf person who has been asked to sing.

34

DEAD PETS

I ALWAYS KNEW that my mother had a bizarre phobia of forming attachments with things. Not just with people, but even with the most trivial of inanimate objects. When I visited my parents in Seoul during school holidays, I used to bring several pounds of my favorite gourmet coffee, which was impossible to find in Korea. My mother asked me to stop bringing her coffee, explaining, "When I run out of this nice coffee I won't be able to adjust back to the horrid coffee they have here. I'm quite serious. No more nice coffee."

Along similar lines, she would never allow me any mammalian pets. She would say, "When they die, you will be very, very sad." I had always cited this as an example of her heartlessness.

I was, however, allowed lower-order animals. I got my first pets when I was four. They were a pair of hermit crabs, which my father spontaneously brought home after work along with a small book with color photographs called *Caring for Your Hermit Crab*. The crabs smelled like rotting fish and made an unnerving scratching noise all night long. My father didn't understand why I was so averse to them; he would take them out of their bowl and try to force me to play with them. I awoke one morning to discover that one of the crabs had exited his shell, fully exposing its pink fleshy skin. Apparently none of us had read *Caring for Your Hermit Crab*, or we would have realized that the creature was looking for a bigger shell to occupy. Not knowing what else to do, my father threw both crabs in the trash, while they were still alive. I have found shellfish revolting ever since. The rabbi would have made some kind of wisecrack about that, if he had known.

Several years passed. By this time we had moved to Seoul. While shopping in the Namdaemum outdoor bazaar in downtown Seoul, I spotted a peddler selling tiny turtles. I bought a pair for less than a dollar. But it was almost impossible to tell whether they were dead or alive. I noticed one morning that the pair looked unusually slow, but since I couldn't really be sure, I kept them for another week. At that point, the shells had softened considerably and I took this to mean they were dead. I buried them in one of my mother's potted plants. Months later, our maid tipped over the potted plant and broke the pot, and the two blackened turtle carcasses spilled out onto our veranda. Even then, they continued to look very much as they had while they were alive.

Then there was the praying mantis. It wasn't a pet, really; just something my father caught for me and put in a jar. I fed it some drag-onflies I had caught in my butterfly net, and watched it pick up the dragonflies in its hands and eat them, looking eerily like a well-mannered human eating a chicken drumstick. When I was sufficiently disgusted, I threw out the jar, living mantis, mauled dragonflies, and all.

None of these pets was ever given a name. I don't recall ever touching any of them.

And now, here is the story my mother told me.

"When I was little," she said, "we had a dog called Betty, named after the blond girl in the Archie comics. She was very smart and I loved her a lot, a lot. Then one day we called her name and she didn't come to us. We couldn't find her anywhere. Later we found out from our neighbors that their dogs were gone, too. In Korea in those days this meant that the dogs had been kidnapped in the night to be sold for their meat. It was just after the war and people were really poor. Now you know why I wouldn't let you get a dog. I'm so sorry."

My first feeling was one of repulsion. All throughout university, during those overly frank late-night common-room chats, I fought off the claim that Koreans were dog eaters. Only the lower classes ate dog, I would argue lamely, and certainly no one I knew engaged in this foul practice. I posited that anyone who claimed otherwise was a racist. Now, hearing the story of my family's close encounter with dog eaters brought out my classist indignation.

I remained stoic before my mother, but in my room that night I cried for my mother, for her dog, for my mother's heartache that was so profound that she would not let such sorrow be visited on me.

I FELT BRAVE. There is nothing more fortifying than learning that your mother doesn't hate you. I could work off my debt to Madame in some other way; I could even bare all to my mother and beg her to arrange a payment plan.

But as it turned out, I wouldn't have to, for my dear auntie Jung asked to meet with me, and she bore tidings of great joy.

I met up with Jung in a bar near the Yonsei University campus, a student hangout with black decor and high chairs. George Michael's greatest hits blasted over the stereo, while Eric Clapton played on the video screen, also at full volume.

Jung was heavily maquillaged, which, against her pallor of mourning, gave her the appearance of Evita Perón's embalmed corpse. She wore a kerchief around her head.

"You look good," I said.

"Who cares." She sounded hoarse. "I asked you here to tell you something. Jude, I took care of your debt. Well, not me personally."

I gasped—could it be? "Was it Yevgeny?"

"Don't be daft. I've been conferring with Heike, who had a nice chat with her gay husband, Boswell. He and some guy named Chester raised the money for you somehow at that lounge where you were working; what's it called, Tom Jones?"

"Maurice Hall," I corrected.

"Whatever. Look, I can't really stay too long, because my mother has to make some arrangements, but trust me; you're out of danger now."

"Don't leave just yet," I said. "How long are you staying in Korea? When are you going back to New York? Why don't we fly back together?"

"I have to take care of some things here," said Jung. "But I'll join you in New York in a few weeks."

"Oh, more postfuneral . . . stuff?"

Jung laughed nervously, then forbade herself to be jovial. "Sorry. No. It's something else entirely. I know I should be really sad about Key, and of course I am. But I'm also sick with excitement. Emerson is coming to Seoul in a few weeks, and our families are going to meet. Well, the Lee side won't be involved, of course. Most likely we will be planning a wedding. Our families know of one another somewhat, since his background is similar to ours."

I certainly hope it's not similar to ours, I thought.

"You'll be the very best of wives," I said.

"Don't tell anyone yet," she said, using her usual refrain. "The engagement's not official. You know what the holdup is? When the groom's family found out I was illegitimate, they said they wanted to hire one of those ancestor detectives to determine that we're really both aristocrats. What a bunch of snobs."

With my blood curdling, I said, "I don't think that's a good idea at all." This was a fairly new and common practice among good families, precisely because of the preponderance of forgeries such as the one I had discovered. Not only might this jeopardize Jung's chances of marriage, but it would only multiply her suffering if she knew that her brother had coerced her into incest with the false premise of our nobility.

Jung frenetically mashed the cream into her Vienna coffee, which she hadn't sipped at all. Her eyes turned upward to me and she said, "I was thinking the same thing. I'm sick of lying. I'm going to tell my family the truth, and then they'll see the services of a detective are superfluous."

"What do you mean, 'tell them the truth'?" I said, shocked out of my mind. Had she known about the wet nurse this whole time?

"Emerson can't have babies of our own at all, so the authenticity of our bloodline doesn't matter. Emerson is sterile, remember? From childhood chicken pox. I told you at the beginning; that's why you were so surprised to find the condom wrapper on my bed."

"Let's not talk about that," I said.

"That means Emerson's family line is over, too, since he's the only male scion. Funny, isn't it, how our class self-selects for extinction?"

Just as I have maintained. Like the gods setting Valhalla on fire when they saw that their era had passed. I am almost always right.

I saw that her eyes were filling with tears. She said, "What's wrong with our family, Jude?"

I put my hand over hers on the table. She bent her head over our clasped hands and began weeping loudly and viscerally. She said, "Is it all right for me to be happy now?"

For only the third time in my life—the first being when I greeted her at the airport, the second at her brother's funeral—I embraced her.

WHEN I GOT HOME, I rang Heike on her mobile phone.

"It's true, Judith," she said. "Boswell and Chester made a plea to the boys at Maurice Hall, and they raised the funds."

"Did they pass around a hat?"

"What hat? Oh, I see, no, he said they had one of their normal wagers and they agreed that the loser would pay off your debt."

I remembered Meno and Pazzi's fifty-thousand-dollar bet over the number of angel species.

"What manner of wager was it?"

"I think it was an all-night game of Botticelli, that role-playing parlor game. Your debt was cleared by someone named Mr. Robberbaron. It's all been arranged. But, uh, you're not off the hook completely. You're to be an indentured servant at Maurice Hall."

"Meaning?"

"For the purposes of keeping up appearances, Mr. Robberbaron didn't issue you the loan directly. He issued it to Maurice Hall, and Maurice Hall paid Madame Tartakov. So technically you're indebted to Maurice Hall. They'll still pay you and all that, but your wages will be garnished to pay off Mr. Robberbaron. And you're no longer *salonnière:* you're to be their accountant instead, which is a much more pressing need. It will take five years to make yourself whole with them. But I assure you, Maurice Hall is a much more benign creditor than this Mr. Robberbaron."

"Why, what does this Robberbaron do?" I asked.

"Boswell describes him as a corporate pirate," said Heike. "Very ruthless, and famous even in my country. He brought down a corrupt organization there. They were called . . . Rumpelstiltskin? No, it was Struwwelpeter GmbH. Judith, why are you screaming?"

Sometime after, I learned how my release from bondage came about. After helping me with the translation of the Struwwelpeter memo, Joshua had reported its contents in an anonymous letter to someone at the Securities and Exchange Commission. So much for my belief that Americans can keep secrets.

Robberbaron, a high-ranking member of the SEC, looked into the matter and learned that Struwwelpeter was run by an archenemy of his who many years ago had chased Robberbaron out of Europe by reporting some corporate malfeasance for which Robberbaron may or may not have been responsible.

The paper trail led Robberbaron to the house on East Sixty-second Street, where the girls were interrogated by a private investigator. This inquiry then led to me personally, and Robberbaron incorrectly credited me with having provided the leak that would crush his enemy. Robberbaron exacted revenge against the latter in his own way, rather than going through the proper SEC channels, which turned out very unhappily for the Struwwelpeter fellow.

In covering my debt, Robberbaron was rewarding the wrong person. Still, better to be in his debt than in that of—what did Joshua call her—that modern-day Fagin, Madame Tartakov.

But that is beyond the scope of this tale. At the moment that Heike made this revelation to me, I was simply stunned.

"Say something, Judith," said Heike. "Are you happy, sad, what?"

"I'm going to be an *accountant*?" I said.

I heard some muffled conversation in the background; then Heike said, "Oh, Madame Tartakov is here. She wants a word with you."

Before I could protest, Madame Tartakov was sending high-pitched shock waves through the receiver; her voice didn't digitize well and it spiked over Heike's mobile phone. She said, "JUDITH! I MISS YOU SO MUCH! You are free to go, my darling." She had the exuberance of someone who had just received an envelope groaning with cash.

I said, "Why is Heike still at the Anthology of Pros—I mean, still living with you? Couldn't she live with Boswell? Are you holding her against her will?"

"Heike is very happy here; she likes it, but this life is not for everyone. You be happy, too, dear. That Yevgeny is a cheap no-good. And speaking of violin, your funny boy Joshua is like violin with too-tight strings, but he is very much courage. I meet him only once, but I know men; I am never wrong about these things."

"What? When did you ever meet him?" All my worlds were colliding now—Madame Tartakov, Joshua, Maurice Hall.

"He come by the house looking for you some weeks ago looking very sad. He beg me not tell you. Okay, I am lying; he didn't say not tell you. I just didn't to mention. You know, he looks exactly like chess player from my country, Garry Kasparov."

"I hadn't noticed," I said.

"And Judith, one more thing. You listen?"

"You have my undivided attention," I said. Maybe Stockholm Syndrome was afoot, but suddenly her voice seemed sweet and motherly to me.

She said, "Take care to no more get in debt, Judith. You read *David Copperfield*? In there is much advice. Here, I read to you." She cleared her voice, then began: " 'Annual income twenty pounds, annual expenditure nineteen nineteen and six, result happiness. Annual income twenty pounds, annual expenditure twenty pounds ought and six, result misery.' "

35

A Cigarette, a Prayer, a Valediction

A WEEK TO THE DAY after Joshua had arrived in Seoul, my father's driver took my father, Joshua, and me to the airport.

My father curtly thanked Joshua for coming to Seoul with me. The ride was otherwise silent.

Outside the gate, my father blindsided me by saying, "Judith, have a cigarette with me."

"I don't smoke," I sputtered. It was a falsehood more than thirteen years in the making. But one reflexively denies such things to one's parents, I suppose.

"I'll get in the line for check-in," said Joshua. "Good-bye, Dr. Lee." He bowed, Korean-style, to my father before disappearing behind the revolving door. My father grunted.

My father held out a pack of Mild Sevens. It was *my* cigarette brand, not his. How long had the old bastard known? Someone so quick on the uptake surely could not be in ignorance of the forgery surrounding his lineage. But I would conceal from him that I knew what I knew.

Reading my mind, my father said, "Not all who conceal are liars."

I took a cigarette from the pack and my father lit it for me. We smoked in silence, dragging out the cigarettes for as long as they would last. I had never noticed before that my father smokes just as I do, flicking the filter with his thumbnail to loosen the ash off the burning tip. When the cigarettes had been smoked to the filter, we dropped the butts on the ground simultaneously. My father shook my hand silently, and left.

On the plane ride from Seoul to New York, Joshua said, "I hope you're not too upset about having to be an accountant for Maurice Hall now. One form of slavery just supplants another; it's no different from the rest of us. But now you're going to be exactly what you hate—bourgeois. Can you stomach it?"

I used my teeth to open the wrapping from a deck of airline cards and said, "Can you?"

Joshua looked contemplative for a moment and said, "Are you serious about this conversion to Judaism thing?"

"I don't know yet. I want to be in full command of the facts before embarking on any new endeavors."

"I suppose I should try to be more supportive. I don't think I was being very fair when I said your own people needed you more. You wouldn't stand out that much, at any rate. You could pass in any synagogue as a Kazakh Jew, if there is such a thing, if that's what you want."

"Ugh, please do not link me to any republic of central Asia," I said.

Joshua shook his head. "You are unchanged, Judith. You're still the same little snot you were before you made this discovery in the archives. I find this strangely comforting."

We then hit a worrisome spot of turbulence, and as the plane lurched, Joshua turned pale and held tightly the armrests. He then squeezed his eyes shut while muttering something under his breath.

"Are you speaking in tongues?" I asked.

He looked sheepish. "It's a Hebrew prayer for travelers, to ensure safe passage. My grandmother, father's side, taught it to me when I was little. It's the only prayer I remember in full. I habitually recite it on planes."

I said, mockingly, "Since when are you Jewish? Is this my influence?"

He clasped my hand and said, "You, Judith, would move anyone to want to find religion. And I mean that in the worst possible way."

"So owing to me, you're now a *lapsed* lapsed Jew? I'm so flattered."

"Actually, you've helped me with something far greater than that. I've decided definitively on a dissertation topic at last. Inspired by you—or, as you and your snot set would say, *grâce à toi*. Do you know what the Kantian Sublime is?"

"Only that you've been studying it this whole time. I think we might have learned it at school but I probably wasn't paying attention. I imagine it is meant to be something good?"

"Yes and no. The Sublime shows you that everything you know is wrong; on the other hand, it makes you a better person, you might say, capable of living a life of unforeseen richness. In aesthetic philosophy, the Sublime refers to a thing or an experience so astonishing that you can't even recognize it. You don't have the capacity to comprehend it with your normal faculties. You must completely recalibrate your faculties of understanding to take in the experience."

"So in what way did I help you arrive at this dissertation topic?"

"Because the Sublime is the triumph of life over philosophy. Which I learned from you."

"So you're saying that I am the Sublime?" I asked.

"No, at least not now that you're going to be an accountant."

I play-thwacked him, but it came out a good deal more violently than I had intended; so much so that the flight attendant approached us. "She's my girlfriend," Joshua told him.

"Oh, that's all right, then," said the flight attendant, returning languidly to his jump seat.

The lights in the cabin turned off. "The movie's starting," I said.

"How about chess?" he said, producing a travel-size board from his carry-on bag.

We returned to New York. Never mind the details. As the Brothers Grimm say, "If we are not dead, then we are living there still."

Acknowledgments

Kept exists because, and only because, of the unflagging encouragement of my editors Kerri Kolen and Tara Parsons, and my literary agents: Lizzy Kremer in London, and Byrd Leavell in New York.

I need also mention Robert Thomson of *The Times* of London and Peter Beinart of *The New Republic*, two mentors who conduct their lives and careers with inimitable grace. They gave me my start in journalism and have helped me on innumerable occasions, knowing that I might never be in a position to return the favor.

Avec mes compliments.

—Valetta, Malta, December 30, 2005